the tales of true adventure

Silverlance
BOOK I

Peter Thomas Crowell

PTC

PETER T. CROWELL
PUBLICATIONS

San Francisco

Peter T. Crowell Publications
San Francisco, California
www.petertcrowell.com

Interior design by Sara Patton Book Production Services
Series logo by Tim Collins
Map by Peter Thomas Crowell
Printed in USA by Data Reproductions Corporation

Standard Address Number: 255 - 2892
Library of Congress Catalog Number: 2003092939

Publisher's Cataloging-in-Publication
(Provided by Quality Books, Inc.)

Crowell, Peter Thomas.
   Silverlance / Peter Thomas Crowell. — San Francisco,
Calif. : Peter T. Crowell Publications, 2003.
   p. cm.
   ISBN 0974029092

   1. Satyrs (Greek mythology)—Fiction.   2. Adventure
stories.   I. Title.

PS3603.R685S55 2003   813'.6
                             QBI33-1261

All persons, places, characters and events portrayed in this story are fictitious. Any perceived similarity between persons, places, characters or events portrayed in this story and actual persons, places, characters or events, is silly. Give up the idea.

Contents

To the star I follow . . .
In all its many forms.

Chapter 1

Little Lord Misrule

yron Thorn stepped in from the cold and stomped the snow from his hooves. He shouldered the door closed against the wind and dark and leaned on it with a sigh.

Byron was small for a satyr of twelve and still had faint white spots in the fur of his two goatish legs. Ice beads rattled in the long hair of his fetlocks. Byron stomped his hooves again and blew hot breath into the hollow of his hands.

At the inner door he cleared a swath on the foggy glass and looked through into the cottage. A fire blazed in the parlor fireplace. Byron stared into the reaching flames. All the cries and cheers of Toboggan Hill echoed in his mind and in the dancing orange glow, Byron saw again the deeds of his day . . .

At the west end of the Lore Pavilion, a single huge door with great iron straps stood closed against the morning dark. A smaller door was cut into it. Byron took a key from his breast pocket, went in through the hatchway and a few moments later the great door swung open with a groan.

When he closed it to leave, a trail of snow and sticks and dried pine needles led across the stone floor of the pavilion, through the wooden pillars. It followed the long sloping aisle down among the tiered bench seats to the final steps into the Story Well. At the end of the trail five snowmen stood in a circle around the stone brazier, where the fire of the Midwinter Telling stood ready to light.

Only five, that's true, but oh, they were big ones . . .

As Arden, the king's poet, entered the pavilion with the festival committee, Byron was climbing under the fence into Grubber Dillfarm's paddock. An hour later he was passing out fistfuls of oats to Dillfarm's mule team as a reward for hauling the hay sledge to the top of Toboggan Hill.

And it was easy for them to move the outhouse, too, even with a portly royal chamberlain trapped inside. It lurched and toppled when the mules pulled forward and they left it on the Moondance Lawn, sticking out of the snow at an angle.

Inside the jail, Byron heard the bailiff in the kitchen finishing his afternoon snack. Byron set the mead jug up onto the desk and went out to steal the pie from Matron Farlow's windowsill for a late lunch of his own.

A well-placed rock was all it took to stop the mill wheel at Birch Bow Tavern. When the afternoon crowd was gathered at the back windows, watching the miller and his wife get the wheel free, Byron led the mules in through the front, dumped the oats on the long wooden table and wedged the door shut on his way out.

As evening came, Byron went back to the jail. On the bench inside the lockup he found the bailiff, stretched out and snoring with the mead jug on the floor beside him. Byron pulled the door shut and the lock fell to with a clack. Then he took the keys from the peg on the wall, hid them in the desk drawer and headed for Toboggan Hill.

A grin lit his eyes. Cheers and cries came up from the bottom of the hill and he shot a glance toward the sound. The last race of the day was about to begin. He looked at the hay sledge, still poised where he had left it, fluffed, dried, heaping, leaning toward the hillside, held fast by a taut length of rope.

Now for the signature. The Misrule's Day of Byron Thorn.

"This is it," Byron said out loud. "This is the big one."

He glanced up at the gathering clouds and tossed the match into the hay.

A few straws curled red and a flame sprang up. Byron took the burning clump and went around the sledge, touching off the hay. Then he threw the clump high onto the top and ran to the edge of the trees.

Thirty yards below, at the bottom of a steep drop from the birch grove, was the starting line of the toboggan races. The teams were gathered there, lining up their snowgoing barks, settling into position.

Byron looked back. The flames were bigger and the white trunks of the birch trees nearest the sledge were flickering with orange and shadow.

Two torches flanked the finish line in the near darkness at the bottom of the hill. The banner above it and the tape across it were visible but hard to discern. Fifteen toboggans sat ready.

All along the course the crowd stood waiting. The winners of the day were about to engage. Only one team would leave victorious after the thrill of the championship run. The flames on Byron's hay sledge grew tall.

A rocket went up trailing a thick red shower of sparks. A moment of silence followed its apex and then it popped, loud and sharp. The crowd erupted. The toboggans were away. Byron ran back into the trees, cut the rope with his paring knife and set his flaming monster loose upon the Midwinter Races.

It reached the lip at the edge of the trees and fell for a moment from his sight. Byron ran after it, shouting and shrieking. He stopped at the tree line to watch. The slick runners of the sledge carried it fast and it outstripped the racers halfway down the hill. The stunned crowd watched it come. Silence took them until someone screamed. The racers threw themselves from the toboggans, rolling and diving as the sledge hurtled roaring among them, throwing light on the fleeing crowd and into the trees that lined the track.

At the bottom of the hill the hay sledge broke the tape. As it passed beneath the banner, the words *Midwinter Races* flickered into view and then caught fire. The banner itself fell in two flaming strips against the poles that held it and the sledge was dashed upon the hay bales at the far end of the finish circle in a burst of flames and sparks and smoke.

Fire took the bales at once. The sledge lay in burning ruin, smashed to embers on the snow and great tongues of flame climbed into the darkness. Byron watched his festival of fire. The flames flickered in his grinning eyes, but the grin faded even as the snow began to fall.

Far off, the last shrill cry of the fleeing crowd died away. Byron sighed and his shoulders dropped. A frown puckered his brow. The wind beat his face with snowflakes. He drew up his hood, wrapped his cape tight about him, turned and set out for home . . .

▨　▨　▨

He stared into the fire. Great shadows wagged and bobbed against the back of the room. Outside, the storm beat against the windows and howled across the roof. The little house creaked and groaned. Byron unclasped his cape and stepped out of it as it fell to the floor. He smoothed the hair out of his eyes and tucked it behind one of his horns. Then he shook the melting snow off his legs and tail and went inside.

Pots clanged in the kitchen and a cupboard door slammed shut. The house smelled of a cake baking and cider warming. Byron held out his hands to the fire for a moment. Then he flopped down into the smaller of two armchairs that faced the hearth.

Through the kitchen door came Darius Thorn, an old satyr with shaggy fetlocks and a pair of half glasses on the end of his nose. He carried a white tablecloth and four silver candlesticks, which he set down on a table by the window. He noticed Byron slouching in the chair and smiled, looking at his grandson over the tops of his glasses.

"Why it's Lord Misrule himself," Darius said. "Home from the war?"

Byron glanced at the stone of the chimney above the mantelpiece. A small wooden shield hung there, well beaten. There was a red unicorn painted on it, rampant on a field of darkest black.

"Long day at it?" Darius said.

Byron shrugged. Wind howled across the rooftop, pulling at the fire through the chimney. Rafters creaked and the whole house swayed beneath the storm.

Darius frowned and sat down in the larger armchair. "Anything wrong, Byro?"

"No," Byron said.

"Well, I might've expected more excitement and storytelling," Darius said. "This being your Misrule's Day and all. Care to tell me how it's gone so far?"

Byron sat forward and recounted his day.

Darius nodded and laughed as he listened, shaking his head and smiling. "The hay sledge may've been a bit over the top, Byro, but that sounds like a mighty day indeed."

"I guess so," Byron said. "But it was supposed to be the best ever."

"And it isn't?"

"It's been good," Byron said sitting back in his chair. "But it was supposed to be great: the Misrule's Day of Byron Thorn. After all, when's the last time a satyr was born on Midwinter's Eve? Imagine it Gradda: a Misrule Midwinter's Eve."

Byron sighed. "And now it's over."

"Over?" Darius said. "I'd say it's just beginning."

"You would?"

"That's right. I'd say you're all warmed up."

"Warmed up for what?"

"Well, there's still the Midwinter Fire tonight. Anything can happen on Midwinter's Eve."

"If the snow lets up."

"Oh, it'll clear, don't you worry. Misrule magic, Midwinter's magic . . . this is no ordinary day."

Darius rose to fetch his pipe. He stuffed it with leaf and lit it with a flaming stick from the fire. He stood a moment, thinking and puffing as a fragrant cloud of smoke gathered about him in the firelight. He pointed at Byron with the stem of his pipe.

"There's a magic in the air I've never felt or heard tell of . . . and a full moon to boot. Yes, indeed, Byron, this day of yours is far from over."

Outside, the storm raged. Within the wind was another sound that froze Byron's blood. He sat up straight, clutching the arms of his chair. His eyes were wide. "Gradda did you hear that?"

"I did, youngster," Darius whispered. He raised a hand as he took his seat. "Hush now . . . and listen."

Through the wail of the storm it came again, the distant howl of a wolf.

Darius nodded his head. "I'll wager the wolves can feel it, too."

"Gradda . . ."

"Steady, Byro," Darius said. He gripped his grandson's arm. "On a night like tonight you can expect the wolves to howl. I'd be more concerned if they were silent."

"It sounded close," Byron said, looking at the window.

"High up on a hill somewhere, carried by the wind."

"Will they come inside the Fencewood?" Byron said, sitting forward in his chair.

Darius looked at his grandson and smiled. "I should say not, Byron. The wolves have no desire to fight with the Woodland King. They prefer the peace, same as we do. Why, there was a time we satyrs were more than friendly with the wolves; we used to ride on them like horses."

"We did?"

"We did," Darius said, patting Byron's wrist. "Those were magic times, times like tonight. Keep your mind on the magic, Byron. Don't let it get away. Now, let's see about supper, shall we? I've got a nice apple cobbler baking and, as this is your Misrule's Day, you're entitled to carve the meat."

Gradda left his seat and went into the kitchen. Byron sat for a moment, listening to the wind. He glanced at the window. In the dancing firelight, through the frosted glass he saw a great grinning wolf with one blue eye looking in at him. Byron gasped and ducked behind the wing of the chair, unable to cry out. When he looked again there was only the icy fog and snow crystals edging the window. Byron blinked. He rubbed his eyes and looked again. Still there was no wolf. Pots clanged in the kitchen. The wind bore down on the little house, but the wolves didn't call again.

◈   ◈   ◈

A tall fire burned on the snowy hilltop. The storm moved away and loomed like a wall of thick gray in the east. Above the clouds the full moon rose, dimming the stars that shone at the top of the sky and in the west. Fiddle music filled the night air, woven with pipes and drums. All the people of Hiding Wood were gathered, dancing in a ring around the fire. Satyrs pranced and centaurs bucked, men and women leaped and twirled. The children screamed and laughed. Great shadows bobbed and fled into the leafless trees that surrounded the hillcrest.

A huge grizzleback bear lurched and lumbered with his mate, bumbling along with the revelers. A beautiful doe and a great antlered buck leaped high, while the old barred owl, the raven and a great many birds flew through the air above the heads of the dancing crowd. Badgers, porcupines, foxes, raccoons, all the smaller animals waddled and bounced and shuffled along with the music.

Through the dancing throng moved the Woodland King. On his head was a wreath of holly and around his neck hung a silver medallion, glittering in the firelight, stamped with the likeness of a rampant unicorn. He was a tall, broad man with a quick step and a merry face. He laughed and clapped his hands and stomped the ground with heavy, fur-shod feet. He danced with every maid and the children gathered around him, reaching to be lifted and turned.

Byron left the dancing to join his friends. They stood by the cider kegs, catching their breath and drinking. Jolik Burrow, a satyr with red fetlocks and polished horns, slapped Byron on the back and handed him a steaming mug.

"Lord Misrule himself," Jolik said.

Byron nodded and sipped. On the other side of the hill was a band of centaurs, gathered around one large, weathered centaur of great age. He had long gray hair and strange figures painted on his horse-like flanks. Beside him stood a younger centaur, larger than the rest, with a net slung across his shoulder and a long spear in his fist. The old one saw Byron and scowled until Byron turned away.

"My father says all the knights are on their guard," said Shegwin Reed, a tall human boy. "After that flaming hay sledge…" He lobbed a snowball over the edge of the circling crowd. It struck a pine branch and shook down snow over another group of woodlings.

"Byron Thorn's day of Misrule," Jolik said. "Even the king is watching. What are you up to, Byro?"

"Nothing," Byron said. He glanced at the old, painted centaur again. "How can they stand there bare-chested like that in this cold?"

"Ah," Jolik said with a laugh, "secrecy. The backbone of every caper."

"Like last year," said Shegwin, "when you threw flash powder into the paper lamps at Midsummer."

"Or the year before when you trapped the bailiff in his own pillory," Jolik said. "I've never seen anything like it."

"I don't see him anywhere," Shegwin said. "I wonder if he's still in the lockup."

Jolik laughed. "Nobody hates you as much as he does, Byron."

Shegwin tossed a snowball high and it disappeared across the fire. "How about when he redirected Gladwater Sluice onto the Fiddling Green?"

"During the Vernal Frolics," Jolik said.

"Always suspected," Shegwin began.

"Never caught," Jolik finished.

Byron shook his head and looked at the moon. "All the animals have broken their sleep," he said. "Haven't you noticed? Even the old grizzlebacks."

"Huh?" Shegwin said.

"Is that some kind of clue, Byron?" Jolik said with a frown.

"Something *is* strange tonight," Byron said.

Shegwin and Jolik looked at each other and shrugged.

"Planning your next glorious feat, Lord Misrule?" said a voice. "You're not supposed to have help, you know." A pair of woodlings drew near, still brushing off the snow that Shegwin's snowball had brought down on them.

"Byron doesn't need help," Shegwin said.

"Hello, Gretchen," Jolik said to the satyress in the approaching pair. "Come to take notes on how a Misrule's Day should look?"

"I saw you throw that snowball, Jolik," said Ulwyn Garnet, a slender human boy who sucked in his cheeks when he wasn't talking.

"No you didn't," Jolik said.

"Well, you did," Ulwyn insisted.

"No I didn't, Sheg did."

"You should be more careful," Ulwyn warned. "Byron's the only one here with Misrule privileges. I might just tell on you."

"Surprise, surprise," Shegwin laughed.

"I know you tied me in the outhouse today, Byron," Ulwyn said. "And I'll get you for it." He sucked in his cheeks.

Byron looked up at the moon. "Strange magic," he said. Ulwyn frowned and looked at the moon also.

"Great job, Byro," Shegwin said, nudging Byron with his elbow.

"How can you side with such nonsense, Shegwin?" Ulwyn demanded. "Your father is a Woodland Knight."

"And yours isn't," Shegwin replied. "I hope that's not the only difference between us."

"Misrule's Day is all nonsense, anyway," Gretchen declared.

"But you're a satyr!" Jolik said.

"There are plenty of us who feel the same," Gretchen said.

Jolik shrugged. "Just because you let *your* Misrule's come and go."

A tall young centress approached the group wearing a thick red cape that draped down along her horse's body. It was Dindra Thundershod. She looked out at them from the shadows of her hood.

"Hello, Dindra," Gretchen said.

Dindra ignored her. "Which one of you threw that snowball?"

Ulwyn folded his arms. "They won't admit it. It shook snow down all over us."

"Shut up, Ulwyn," Dindra said. "I'm talking about the one that hit Matron Farlow in the face."

"It had to be one of these three," Gretchen said. "Probably Byron. He's keeping awfully quiet."

Byron looked back at the fire and sighed.

Dindra swished her tail and frowned at him. "What are you up to, Byron Thorn?"

"Nothing," Byron said.

Dindra's frown narrowed to a glare. "You're never up to nothing."

"This time I am."

Dindra shook her head. "Byron, why can't you just behave yourself?"

"It's for the good of the people," Jolik said. He stood tall and stomped his goatish hoof.

"My father watches out for the good of the people, thank you," Dindra said.

"You're welcome," Shegwin said with a snort.

Dindra raised an eyebrow. "He's out patrolling the western fence for wolves right now and you can't even keep from causing trouble in the wood. Save all that cleverness for something useful, Byron Thorn."

Byron shrugged and looked at the moon.

There was a tremendous, rumbling horn blast. Three centaurs with shaggy beards were blowing into the mouthpieces of the Kettle Horn. The sound shook snow from the trees and filled every nook and knothole in the wood. The dance around the fire stopped. Everyone went quiet, waiting for the king to speak. A nervous murmur went through the crowd, for as the horn blast faded, from far away in the night came the howling of many wolves.

The king stepped onto a platform and all the creatures gathered around him. He put up his hands and the murmuring stopped. He smiled and waited as the last of the stragglers gathered at the back.

"Don't be afraid," the king said. "The wolves are safely far away. They always howl at the sound of the horn. Palter Thundershod is on the watch and the deepest dark of the year is approaching, the time when the sun is farthest away. In a few hours the sun will rise and the new year will be born!"

A great cheer arose from the crowd.

"Today," said the king, "the moon is full at Midwinter for the first time in a hundred years."

Another cheer followed.

"And let's not forget the Lord of Misrule, Byron Thorn, who ... eh ... celebrates, his Misrule's Day today."

A kind of growl mixed with scattered cheers swept through the crowd and heads turned in every direction, searching for Byron. Jolik and Shegwin whooped and hollered. Shegwin took the opportunity to fill Gretchen's hood with snow.

"Where is Byron?" the king said, craning his neck. "Ah, there you are. We're all eager to see what you've got in store for us tonight, but you'd better hurry, it's little more than an hour to Deepest Dark."

Byron looked left and right and at the ground. Jolik slapped him on the back. "And I'm sorry to say," the king continued, "this will be the last Misrule's Day in Hiding Wood, indeed in all of Woody Deep. After careful consideration ..."

An angry shout from the crowd cut the king short. He lifted an eyebrow and held up his hand.

"After careful consideration I've decided to end the practice of Misrule's Day altogether, with Byron Thorn as the last."

Byron and Jolik gaped at each other. More angry shouts drowned out the last of the king's words. Snowballs flew at him from scattered points in the crowd. Satyrs were hissing and calling out. The king folded his arms and waited for quiet.

"The practice has gotten out of hand in recent years," the king said as he ducked a whistling snowball. "Property has been damaged, reputations tarnished and bodily injury has occurred more than once. What's more, it's the common feeling in the wood that it's all gone on long enough. It's a fitting end, I think, that Byron should be the last ... especially after the excitement at the toboggan races today ... not that anyone knows who did it. And so," the king went on, but he stopped and stared beyond the crowd, into the eastern sky.

Byron turned to look. The snowstorm was moving off and the top of the cloudbank was filled with light.

As the clouds receded, the light grew ever brighter and lit the eastern sky with brilliant fire, white and clear. Long, slender rays shot upward from a single spot amid the glow and a gleaming sphere appeared. Byron watched. As the pulsing point of light emerged from the passing clouds it cast a maze of tree shadows across the hilltop. The storm moved on, unveiling against the cold, ancient blackness a small, brilliant sun with a tail like a sword.

"A new star!" someone hissed. "A new star has risen!"

A jostling shove went through the crowd. "What does it mean?" someone called.

Woodren heaved and pushed. A child cried out. The king dispersed his knights to calm the people and waded in to the rescue of the tiny satyrling girl before she was trampled. Panic rose, then Byron stepped forward.

"We should follow it!" he cried.

And the crowd went still.

Everyone looked at Byron as though a second head was growing from his neck. Silence fell. The king set the satyr child down and she ran to her mother. He walked up to Byron and looked down at him. A circle formed close around them.

"What did you say, Byron?" the king demanded.

"I'm going to follow it!" Byron said with wide eyes. "Aren't you?"

"Of course not!" shouted a voice. "And neither are you! Put the idea out of your head!" The crowd parted and the old, weathered centaur approached. Byron glanced at the strange markings on the centaur's flanks and his stomach trembled. The centaur grinned at him.

"Ravinath," said the king. "You are not needed here."

"This satyrish madness has gone too far," said the centaur. "Do not permit this imp to go his way!"

"With respect, Sire," said a voice. "There's nothing anyone can do to stop 'im." Another murmur passed. Darius Thorn stepped from the crowd, smoking a well-stuffed pipe. "He's the Lord of Misrule for another hour," he said. "And if I'm not mistaken, you said Byron was to have his day."

"He must not!" Ravinath said. He shook his fists and a vein popped out on the side of his head.

"And why not?" Darius said.

Ravinath glared at Darius. He turned his stare on the king, then on Byron, then on the silent, gaping crowd. He nodded. In a loud, low voice, he began to sing.

"Galéthmathud nochrásh mathess
Dona nud gothmôck naress
Drücha thrond paled ôlcharek
Nomágagat do shónanek."

Ravinath sang the verse three times and then stood there, quiet, eyes closed, fists clenched beside him. Everyone was silent. The fire roared and lapped the stars, rippling the night air with heat. At last the king folded his arms. "What does it mean?" he said.

Ravinath sneered at the king and shook his head. "I will translate for you Sire, since your knowledge fails you:

"When new light on the night sky breaks
forgotten darkness stirs and wakes
venture not upon the land
lest shadow coals to flames be fanned.

"That star is a willow o' the wisp. It will lure the witless to their deaths and so bring ours upon us."

"Ravinath," said the king. "You don't really believe some old rhyme of doom and darkness, do you? And you expect me to as well?"

"Perhaps you are right, Sire," Ravinath said. "And yet there is the star itself. If this fool goes his way he'll wake some sleeping thing, no doubt. Why, even the wolves are uneasy. Is that not reason enough?"

"Well now, Ravinath," Darius said, "you might be right. Something terrible may well come of all this, that's true. But there's a rhyme even older than the one you chose, isn't there?"

Ravinath folded his arms and looked into the fire.

Darius took several long pulls at his pipe. He squinted at Ravinath through the smoke. "Well," he said, "I remember it, even if you don't. And I'll spare everyone the fright of a language they don't understand."

Darius cleared his throat and wet his whistle with a sip of cider. Then, in a voice calm and rich, he sang:

> "At winter's deep when long is night
> the stars and full-the-moon will dance
> around a single shining light,
> the clarion call of Silverlance."

A loud murmur took the crowd. The name of Silverlance was whispered and passed around. Some of the older woodren removed their hats and hoods.

"Silverlance?" Byron said. "Who's that?"

"A fairytale!" Ravinath said. "There is no Silverlance."

"Not a fairytale, Ravinath," said the king. "I remember my

lessons well enough to know that. But a legend, surely, born of things that happened long ago."

Darius nodded. "Yes," he said. "Silverlance lived long ago. He was the king of us all. There was a war, a legendary war that covered the world. Silverlance went away, but he promised to return. He said we'd know him by his clarion: a white light in the sky. It was Silverlance who gave we satyrs our Misrule's Day, Sire, the day you took away from us a moment ago. Seems you've forgotten the promise you made when you took the throne: to preserve the trust of Silverlance?"

The king clutched his medallion and looked at the ground.

"That was probably the last time any of us heard or spoke that name," Darius said.

"This is nonsense!" Ravinath shouted. He swished his tail and clenched his fists.

"Goodness leaps for joy at the call of Silverlance," Darius said. "If that star is his clarion it means he's set to come back. And I say anyone who doesn't like it is up to no good."

The crowd was hushed. All eyes were on Ravinath. He straightened and stepped back a pace. The king stared down at the palms of his hands. He looked up at the star and then at Byron.

There was a great hammering of hooves in the snow and a dozen spear-toting centaurs came charging onto the hilltop. One of them, a very large, muscular fellow, galloped straight up to the king and saluted him. It was Palter Thundershod.

"Sire," he said. "The wolves have crossed through the Fencewood, maybe a hundred of them, silent. We've lost track of a small pack already. Something has them scared, they're wild with fear."

The crowd began to disperse. The king shouted them back and calmed them.

"We are well prepared for this, as you know," he said. "Gather your families together. When that is done send one person to find the knight in charge of your steading. Make yourself known to him so that he may command you. There are many centaurs in Palter's command still at large, we are quite safe for the moment. Remain calm and face the danger. These are wolves and we have fought them before. Go!"

Fathers and mothers gathered their children. A great din arose as order was struck and a well-laid plan was carried out. When the king was satisfied with the progress, he fixed his eyes on Byron.

"Ravinath," the king said, still looking down at the Lord of Misrule. "You and Darius stay with me please. You are both old wolf fighters. I have questions. But first, Darius, what does Byron have to do with Silverlance's return?"

"Legend has it that Silverlance can't come to us straight away," Darius said. "We have to go to him. Or someone does."

King Belden held Byron with his gaze. "Are you saying that star leads to Silverlance?" he said.

Darius shook his head. "No, Sire. I'm just saying there's a white light in the sky and a youngster with a mind to follow it."

The king looked up at the star and sighed. He frowned at Byron. "Very well," he said, "Byron may go and let no one hinder him."

"This is madness!" Ravinath shouted.

"I will not be bound by fear, Ravinath," the king said. "At least the tale of Silverlance is one of hope."

"But Sire . . ." Ravinath began.

The king put up his hand. "I'm true to my word. Even when it's slung about me like a rope. Byron is the Lord of Misrule and may do as he pleases. Good luck to you, fellow," he said to Byron, "if you won't be turned from folly. I have wolves to think about now. Darius, Ravinath, to me."

Ravinath followed the king, but turned a heavy brow on Byron. His group of centaurs gathered around the big net-wielding fellow and they glared at Byron also. Darius took Byron by the arm.

"You've got to go now, Byro," he said. "Ravinath'll be after you when the hour is up, if not before. Get to Gladwater Ravine. Get across and cut the bridge. That could buy you half a day. I can't help you much but take these …" Darius handed Byron a large knife in a leather scabbard, together with a felt pouch on a long string, which he slung over Byron's neck.

"What's this?" Byron said.

"Darius!" the king shouted.

"Never mind that now," Darius said. "It was supposed to be for your birthday. Just get to the bridge and don't stop for any-one. Good luck Byron, come back if you can!"

"Darius!"

Byron tried to speak but Darius turned and ran off. The milling crowd pushed past Byron on every side. He turned and set off walking, but soon he was running with all his strength toward the star, toward Gladwater Ravine.

chapter 2

Gladwater Ravine

ew snow fell and the moon was far west. The star filled the eastern clouds with light. Dim strips of shadow fell across the white forest floor. Byron struggled through the deep snow. At Old Fellow Rock he stopped to catch his breath.

"Should've taken the road," he said, panting. "It's too deep out here."

He stood for a while eating snow, looking east above the trees.

"Keep going," he said. He turned to set off again and as he did he heard a voice.

"Byron!" it said in a loud whisper. "Byron, is that you?"

"Sheg?" Byron whispered back. "What are you doing here?"

Footfalls crunched in the snow from the other side of the rock. Byron waited, peering into the dark, listening. Two figures approached, keeping to the shadows: a tall human form, Shegwin Reed, followed by the much smaller shape of a satyr, Jolik Burrow. Byron smiled. He threw open his arms.

"You're coming with me!" he cried.

"Not so loud!" Shegwin whispered.

Byron frowned. "Aren't you?"

"You must be out of your tree, Byron!" Jolik said. "Do you know what you're doing?"

"Sure I do! It's the Misrule Magic!"

"This is crazy," Jolik said with a glance toward the star. "Ravinath will never let you go."

"And Baruwan," Shegwin added, "with that awful net."

"They say Ravinath coaxed him in from the wild," Jolik said. "No even knows where he came from."

Shegwin shook his head. "Byron, you'll never get away from him."

Byron looked at the star through the clouds.

"That's what we came to tell you, Byron," Shegwin continued. "Ravinath sent Baruwan to cut the bridge. He's supposed to catch you and take you to Ravinath's cave."

"How do you know that?" Byron said.

"Gradda told us. He overheard Ravinath talking to Baruwan as they left Winter Hill. Ravinath is mixing a special hexmask to help him. They're serious, Byron. Gradda wanted you to know. We volunteered."

Byron pursed his lips. "Well, thanks for that, I guess. But I'm going. I'm following the star." He looked at Jolik and Shegwin. "With or without you."

"Forget it, Byron," Shegwin said. "No way."

"Me too, By," Jolik said. He took a step back. "Whatcha think you'll find out there, anyway?"

"Something," Byron said. "Something I won't find by staying here with you."

There were hoofbeats in the snow.

"A horse?" Jolik whispered.

"A centaur!" Shegwin hissed.

"Scatter!" Byron said. But it was too late. From the other side of Old Fellow Rock came the tall, dark shape of a centaur.

Byron stood trembling, eyes fixed wide on the figure. When he noticed that the centaur was tall, but not fully grown, Byron's shoulders sagged and he let go his breath.

"Is that you, Byron?" said the centaur.

"Dindra," Byron said. "Yeah, it's me."

"Are you still planning to follow the star?"

"What's it to you?" Jolik said. "Are you gonna go with him?"

"That's the general idea," Dindra said.

"Huh?" Jolik said with an astonished glance at Shegwin.

Dindra crouched down to the ground and threw back her cape. "Climb on, Byron," she said. "We have to hurry."

Byron stared at her.

"Byron, I can run like the wind," Dindra said, "even in this deep snow. If you climb on now, we've got a chance. You'll never beat Baruwan to the bridge alone."

Byron looked at Shegwin and Jolik, then again at Dindra. He bounced in place for a moment, looking up at the glow of the star. Then he leaped forward and sprang onto Dindra's back.

"Good!" Dindra said. "Put your arms around my waist and stay small!" She threw her cape over him and stood. "Not so tight!"

"Sorry," Byron whispered.

"Stay against my back and no one will know you're there," Dindra said. "You two can shut your mouths now."

Shegwin and Jolik stood slack-jawed, staring.

"And keep them shut until morning, right?" Dindra said, pointing at them. Then she shook her head. "Byron finally gets an idea worth doing and you just stand there gawking. Well, wish us luck at least. Goodbye."

Dindra wheeled and bolted into the darkness.

Byron squirmed a little in the stuffy heat beneath Dindra's cape. At the Fathom Oak he pushed the front of it open to let the air in and have a look around.

"Nearly there," he said when he saw the tree.

Moonlight shone through a break in the thickening clouds. The Fathom Oak stood tall in the center of the field, washed in the bright glow, casting an enormous claw of a shadow on the snow. Dindra quickened her pace. Byron pushed his head through her cape and looked back in time to see the last of the cottage lights vanish into the trees. Snow fell again. Another storm came down from the north, eating the stars in its path as it advanced on the full moon. Blue lightning flickered in the clouds, striking the snowflakes black.

Soon they entered the Pine Belt, a strip of evergreen forest that ran north to south along the river Gladwater. The mat of needles muffled Dindra's hooves. Weird shadows leaped around them, cast by the flickering blue light.

"I never saw lightning in the snow before," Byron said.

"Me neither," Dindra said.

They went on without speaking. At the big rock Dindra went north and broke into a trot. Byron nestled down beneath her cape and hid. "See you when we cross the bridge," he said.

Soon the snowy woodland floor was beneath them. Strong wind blew, but the snow was light. The strange lightning blinked.

"Should be at the bridge," Byron said to himself. He relaxed and closed his eyes. Dindra opened her pace to a full gallop, but a moment later she halted. "Why've we stopped?" Byron whispered.

"There's a fire burning," Dindra said. "It looks like centaurs . . . guarding the bridge . . ."

"Turn around!" Byron said.

Dindra started forward.

"Stop!" Byron hissed. "What are you doing?"

"They've seen me," Dindra said.

"Run!" Byron whispered and he started to squirm free of the cape. Dindra pulled it tight and he was pinned against her back. "Dindra!" Byron growled.

"Shut up, Byron!" Dindra said. "And don't move!" She drew the cape tighter to herself until the side of Byron's face was pressed against her tunic, between her shoulder blades. "I have an idea," she said and she broke into a trot.

Byron gaped into the darkness of the cape. Soon he heard voices and the crack of a fire. Dindra stopped.

"A dark night to be abroad," said a voice.

"And late," said another.

"Yes," Dindra said in a stern voice.

"Who is it?" Byron whispered. Dindra replied with a jerk of the cape.

"What brings you all the way out here?" said the first voice.

"I am taking news to my father, across the Ravine," Dindra said.

"Strange they don't send a hunter."

"It's a personal matter, regarding my family."

"Strange your mother sent you. Why not one of your brothers?"

"My brothers are all occupied with the wolves. If you will excuse me, Baruwan . . ."

Byron gasped. He tensed against Dindra and held still, listening.

"What is this message you bring, girl? What's so important?"

"My mother has taken sick."

"How sad."

Dindra shifted her weight. Byron felt her muscles tense. He

didn't like the tone in Baruwan's voice and could tell that Dindra didn't either.

"M . . . my father would want to hear of it," Dindra said, but the certainty had left her voice.

"Indeed," Baruwan said. The snow crunched as he strode forward.

"At once," Dindra said.

"Of course," Baruwan replied. He had drawn near. "What can you tell me of Byron Thorn?" he said.

"I . . . nothing, Baruwan," Dindra said. She shifted her weight again. "He's a festering little boil, if that's what you mean."

Byron scowled. The certainty was back in Dindra's voice.

"Yes," Baruwan said. "That is precisely what I mean: Little Lord Misrule. But, I wonder if there are others who share his . . . interest . . . in the star."

Dindra shifted heavily. "Others?"

"Others who don't enjoy Misrule privileges, perhaps?"

"I suppose . . ." Dindra stammered, "there might be . . . that is . . ."

"What is your father doing east of the Ravine when the wolf threat is from the west?"

"I don't question my father's movements Baruwan. Neither should you. For that matter, what are you doing out here? You should be helping with the wolves. I've told you my business, now stand aside."

"Very well, very well, don't be angry," Baruwan said with a laugh. "After all, the daughter of the Chief at Arms needn't explain herself to a rabble like us. I'll tell you my business, since you ask. I'm waiting for Byron Thorn to show his face. When he does I mean to cut the bridge before his eyes and watch him scurry upstream to the fords as the minutes bleed from the final hour of his Misrule's Day. Then I'm going to take him and pitch him into the Ravine. Since you have business beyond the river, I shall step aside and let you cross."

Dindra took a step and stopped.

"Your father is waiting, Dindra," Baruwan said.

"Go, Dindra!" Byron whispered. "He's gonna figure it out!"

Dindra jerked her cape again and started forward. She'd gone ten paces when Baruwan flung her cape aside, dragging Byron to the ground. Byron saw the blue lightning flash in the snow. A fire was burning near and there were angry voices all around.

"Throw them in!" Baruwan shouted. "Both of them!"

Byron looked up at Baruwan as the huge centaur slid the net from his shoulder. There were strange, terrible markings painted all over the centaur's face. Baruwan spun the net around and it whistled as it spread out in the air above him.

"Run, Byron!" Dindra cried.

Byron ducked as she leaped over him, crashing into Baruwan with her shoulder. The painted centaur lost control of the net. With one hand he grabbed her by the hair. Dindra screamed. Byron snarled. He leaped up and bit Baruwan's arm. Baruwan howled and released Dindra, but struck Byron with his other hand, sending him to the ground. Dindra sidled away.

Byron groaned with his face in the snow, but managed to roll out from under Dindra's stomping hooves. Then a cry sounded in the distance. Byron looked up to see Baruwan peering north into the darkness on the edge of the ravine. The lightning blinked, blue in the black snow. A crowd of dark shapes was bounding toward the fire. The wind was full of whining growls and hushed footfalls.

"Wolves!" someone shouted.

A huge gray wolf bounded through the firelight, into the shadows beyond. Through the sparking flames Byron saw two eyes, glowing green on the other side of the fire.

As the centaurs turned to fight, Byron and Dindra fled into the shadows across the fire. They watched in horror. Spears rose and fell, teeth and claws snapped and tore. A din of growls and whines and shouts arose. Baruwan trampled one wolf with his hooves and flung another howling into the ravine. Near the fire a centaur fell to a throng of wolves and screamed his last beneath them. Baruwan cried out, charging in to avenge him.

Lightning flashed. When it was gone, a pale white glow remained. It lit the falling snow and set shadows all around. Everyone stopped, locked in struggle and looked up. The star was shining through a hole in the clouds. Byron caught his breath. He took three steps toward the star before he heard Dindra calling him.

"Byron!" she cried, pointing to the shadows.

Byron gasped. Ten paces away the gray wolf emerged from the darkness. It stood for a moment, panting, with its tongue dangling from the side of its mouth. The wolf was enormous and had one blue eye. It looked at Byron and Dindra, then up at the star, then back again. The sound of hoofbeats came from the north.

"Look!" Byron yelled.

A swarm of torches was coming fast.

Dindra crouched to the ground and he climbed onto her back. She set off for the bridge at a trot. Byron looked back to see Baruwan fighting his way toward them. He looked for the wolf but it was gone.

"Hurry!" he shouted and kicked Dindra with his hooves.

"It's so narrow!" Dindra shouted back as she approached the bridge.

It swayed in the wind and snow piled on the tight planks. Dindra stepped out and screamed as she slid down the length of the bridge to the bottom of the curve. Byron's breath stuck in his chest as he gaped into the darkness that swallowed them. When they stopped, Dindra's front legs had buckled to the knees and she was slung on the ropes to one side of the bridge.

"Look!" Byron shouted.

At the top of the bridge, against the fire, stood the silhouette of a centaur. It slung something over its shoulder, then disappeared toward them into the darkness. Dindra felt the bridge shift beneath her.

"Baruwan," she said.

"You get us to the top," Byron said. "I'll take care of Baruwan."

Dindra struggled on and leaped onto the snowy ground across the bridge. Byron dropped from her back and slid Gradda's knife from its case. The star was still shining and the wind carried shouts from across the ravine. The torches had reached the fire.

"Father!" Dindra cried.

Byron looked up to see Palter Thundershod and King Belden himself, arrayed for battle. With them was a band of knights and centaurs and armed woodren. The bridge swayed. Byron looked into the darkness where the bridge vanished from view and heard the ropes creaking. He set to work with Gradda's knife.

"These are wolf tracks," Dindra said, looking around by the light of the star. "Some of them got across."

Byron kept cutting. The last of the ropes came apart and the bridge slipped away into the darkness. Byron and Dindra watched and listened. The wind and the faint sound of the firelit battle were all they could hear. They stood for a moment looking at the star. Dindra crouched down and Byron climbed onto her back. The snow came harder. Clouds had covered the star. Dindra lifted a hoof to set out and stopped.

"Listen!" she whispered. They both leaned forward to hear the sound of hushed footfalls bounding away into the dark.

"Let's go!" Byron said.

"We'll get lost without a reference," Dindra said. "Let's head south, along the river, until the weather breaks."

▨   ▨   ▨

For six days the storm raged on. Strange blue lightning flickered in the dense clouds. The wind bore strange sounds like voices. Byron and Dindra slept huddled together under pine trees and ate from the stores Dindra had taken from the hunting cellar in the compound of the Thundershods. It was late in the afternoon on the sixth day when Byron broke another of the long silences that passed between them as Dindra followed the banks of Gladwater.

"Is it time to stop?" he said.

"A little longer," Dindra said. "Just a while."

"I'm hungry," Byron said.

"We've only got one meal left," Dindra said. "And it won't be the biggest one yet." Then she stopped. "What was that?"

"What was what?" Byron said, rousing himself. The wind covered the sounds of the wood. Then, in the distance, wolves howled. Byron snapped his head around. The howling came again.

"Behind us!" Byron said.

"But the storm's covered our tracks!"

"Wolves don't need tracks to follow!"

A large bird swooped into Byron's face and beat him about

the cheeks with its wings. Byron cried out. It flapped around
front and did the same to Dindra. Then it swooped into a nearby
branch and cawed.

"A raven," Byron said.

Howling filled the air again, closer by. The raven dropped
from his perch, bounced off both their heads and back into the
tree. Then it flew away south into the woods.

"He wants us to follow," Byron said.

Dindra nodded and set off.

Cawing and flapping from branch to branch, the raven led
them on. The lightning blinked, showing a stone bridge arching
across Gladwater with the raven winging above it. Beyond the
bridge they came into a grove of fat beech trees. There the raven
came to rest on the broken wall of a ruined stone tower.

A tall tree grew up through the open top. Inside, the corners
of the tower were deep with drifted snow, but most of the floor
was only dusted. Fallen branches littered the place. Byron dropped
to the ground.

"Gather the wood!" he cried. "We need fire!"

"Fire?" Dindra said.

"To fight the wolves! Look for wood!"

"We can't fight a pack of wolves! We need to block the doorway!"

Byron straightened up with a bundle of sticks under his arm.
He looked at Dindra, then at the fallen branches scattered around.
"We'll never keep them out for long," he said. "First the door,
then the fire!"

❖ ❖ ❖

Three stout branches reached across the doorway, bolstered
with stones. Two more branches lay near as replacements. Byron

tended the small fire he'd started with the last of his matches. Dindra chose out a bunch of branches and set them aside.

"Give me your knife," she said.

"What for?" Byron said without looking up.

"We'll have to defend this fence, you know. I'm making spears."

Byron looked at the bundle of branches in her hand. "We can burn those."

"And have nothing to fight with? Fire won't save us, Byron. Give me the knife."

Byron sighed. "All right," he said. "But save the shavings for me will you?"

They worked until they could think of nothing more to do. The dark before morning drew in and there was no sign of the wolves. Byron sat with his back against the tree trunk. Dindra stood by the door. Firelight danced orange inside the tower and cast shadows into the branches of the tree.

"Where's the raven?" Dindra said.

"Flew off somewhere."

Dindra lifted a hoof and let it drop. "Maybe they won't come. Maybe they kept going south."

"Ya' think?" Byron said.

"No."

Dindra hugged herself and pulled her cape tight around her. The lightning flashed again. The snow had stopped. Inside the tower they could hear the wind, but it was quieter.

"The storm is passing," Byron said. "I'm hungry."

Dindra turned to face the doorway. "Me, too. I don't like this quiet. Why don't they howl or something?"

"Gradda says we satyrs used to ride on wolves like horses. I wonder what happened."

"My grandfather thought they were under a spell," Dindra said.

"A spell?" Byron said.

"Mm-hm. He kept a journal. Some of the entries mention a pair of old gray females he saw during the war. Witches he called them. They'd stand apart from the battlepacks, silent, watching. He wrote about one wolf that threw himself in front of a centaur charge so the witches could get away. The entry swears they made the wolf do it. What did he write? 'If I'm to believe my own eyes . . . the witchwolves commanded . . . and he obeyed. Others would have followed, had there been a need.'"

Byron's eyes were wide. "I didn't know the wolves had witches."

"Mm-hm," Dindra said.

And then she screamed.

Through the barricade of branches blocking the doorway, Byron saw the eyes glowing with firelight, the bared fangs and the dangling tongue. The wolf was glaring up at Dindra. It ceased its panting long enough to give a low growl. It was huge and stood so close that Dindra could have reached out and touched it.

It started snapping and tearing at the branches. Byron took a stick from the fire and threw it. Sparks flew. The wolf yelped and when the air cleared it was gone. A howl went up, echoed by another, then another and still a third. The howls lingered and rose together for a moment, then faded. From the darkness outside the door came the sound of many quiet feet bounding through the snow. There were muffled growls and whines. A pair of firelit eyes appeared between the branches and disappeared. Then all was still.

Dindra clutched a pointed stick and stood back from the

door. Byron stayed close to the fire. Both of them watched and listened. Silence. And then the wolves, three of them, biting and tearing at the barricade. Byron lifted a branch and charged the door. Dindra stepped up and thrust her stake through the tree limbs. Sparks exploded, wolves yelped and barked and there was silence again, except for the sound of Byron and Dindra breathing hard. They looked at each other, wide-eyed, breath like smoke in the cold.

"We can't keep this up," Dindra said.

Byron gaped into the fire. He shook his head.

The wolves came again. Two terrible snouts poked through gaps between the branches, snapping and barking. They tore at the wood and the whole barrier shifted.

Dindra gasped and lunged forward. "No!"

She jabbed her stake into the snapping jaws and one wolf withdrew. But another took its place. Byron struck with fire once more and again the wolves backed off. Again they came on, hurling themselves against the barrier. It shifted again, scraping against the stone of the tower and a wolf head poked through the side. Dindra wielded her stake and the wolf scrabbled back. There was a pause.

"Oh, how many are there?" Dindra panted.

Blue lightning flashed. They came again. The barrier lurched and bounced away from the wall. Two wolves tried squirming through and a third attacked the side. Byron raised his flaming branch and then something caught his eye. The dirt floor beneath the barrier fell away and two paws worked to widen the gap. A snout appeared for a moment, sniffing. Then the paws returned.

"They're digging!" Byron cried. He leaped forward jabbing and swinging with his flaming branches. "They've been digging!"

Dindra screamed and jabbed her stake again and again.

Byron echoed her cry and raced from wolf to wolf, brandishing fire. The barrier shifted and a huge gap opened above Byron's head. A wolf appeared. It glared down, snapping and growling. Byron stared up at it, clutching two smoking stumps in his hands.

The wolf's eyes went wide. It yelped and cried and tried to turn its head around. Then it flew back from the barrier altogether, scratching and clawing for a hold. The night was filled with growling and yelping. The wolves were frenzied, berserk in the darkness outside the door. Dindra and Byron listened, gaping at each other. The sounds moved all around, into the distance then close at hand. Byron peered through the branches.

"Byron, get back!" Dindra said, moving to the far side of the fire. Byron kept looking. Dindra frowned. "What do you see?"

"Darkness. Nothing but darkness."

A loud fit of growling broke the silence very close to the door. The barrier lurched with the weight of a wolf thrown against it. Byron staggered backward, reaching for balance. Dindra caught him and lifted him over the fire. The mayhem of the wolves stopped. Dindra and Byron listened. Quiet paws in the snow faded and were gone. For a while, the only sound was the fire popping until, in the tree above them, the raven cawed. Nothing stirred again in the darkness. Lightning flickered in the south. The storm had moved on. Byron and Dindra stayed awake all night, listening. They did not speak, they only sat, huddled together looking about with wide eyes, keeping the fire high.

chapter 3

Shilo

our dead wolves lay twisted in the red snow. A jumble of tracks circled the tower, wandering about the beech ring that surrounded the place. Dindra crouched down to let Byron on and together they scouted the area. The wolves had approached from many different directions. Nine sets of tracks came in from the forest and five led away, one trailing blood.

"What could've done this?" Dindra said. "And not leave any tracks?"

"Maybe some giant bird," Byron said. "Or, something . . . from the sky."

"A bird?"

"Gradda told me once about a tribe of huge owls. Maybe they live around here somewhere."

Dindra shook her head. "But why didn't they take the bodies? And why did they leave us alone?"

"Let's just be glad for it and hope they've gone to sleep for the day."

"Maybe it was a ghost," Dindra said, gripping her chin.

"A ghost?"

"This is an old beech grove, have you noticed? Somebody planted these trees in circle on purpose, probably for magic. This

is just the sort of place you'd find a ghost living in. Maybe . . .
maybe the shade of some wizard or priestess, or . . . or the restless
spirit of some hapless sacrificial victim."

Byron frowned and thought for a moment. "No, I think it
was owls."

"Suit yourself," Dindra said. "Whatever it was, it's gone."

The raven perched in one of the mighty trees. He shifted
back and forth from one foot to the other and cawed at them. A
cardinal was perched beside him. As Byron and Dindra came
near the cardinal sang out and shot away, bright red against the
gray and white of the forest. The raven dropped out of the tree
and bounced from Dindra's head to Byron's, then flapped away
with whistling wings after the cardinal. Dindra looked back at
Byron with her eyebrows up.

Byron shrugged. "He got us out of one fix."

"But they're going the wrong way," Dindra said. "That's
southwest."

"Seems like he knows what he's doing."

Dindra shrugged. Byron settled in on her back and they set
off after the birds.

All the wood sparkled with a mild thaw. The sun was bright
in the blue sky. The raven was nowhere in sight. Winging from
branch to branch the cardinal guided them along. Sometimes he
flew off into the woods and brought back a tiny pine cone or a
seed, which he dropped on somebody's head. The sun was low
in the west when the cardinal flew in and dropped something
from his beak into Dindra's hair.

"This is chestnut meat," Dindra said, tasting the morsel.

"Chestnut meat?"

"Mm-hm," Dindra said. "And it's warm."

Byron sniffed the air. "Do you smell that?"

"A wood fire," Dindra said.

Byron rubbed his belly. "And spiced apples."

As evening deepened, they spotted a cottage light away in the trees. The cardinal called again and led them into the small clearing where the cottage stood. The star hung above the house, bathing the snow-covered roof with light.

Smoke billowed from the chimney and the smell of apples baking was strong on the cold air. An old man made his way along a well-trod path in the snow. He carried an axe in one hand and a bundle of logs under his arm.

"Ah," he said as he reached the porch. "There you are. Supper's almost ready. There's a tubful of water hot for washing up."

They peered at the man but couldn't see his face for the shadows on the porch.

"Well, come along, come along," he said, laughing.

Dindra didn't move.

"No wolves to fear here," the man said.

Dindra remained still.

"See you inside, then," the man said with a shrug. "Don't bother about knocking."

He set the axe by the door and went in. A warm glow splashed onto the porch as the door opened. The cardinal sang from the roof peak.

"I guess we're here," Byron said.

"Where?"

"Wherever it was we were going."

"He's a wizard of some sort," Dindra said.

"Why do you say that?"

"How'd he know about the wolves?"

"Hmm," Byron said with a nod. "Maybe it was him who drove them off."

"Do you think?"

"I don't know."

Dindra sighed. The snow came on very strong and clouds covered the star. "Well, we're pointed in the right direction anyway," she said, pulling up her hood. "Let's get out of this, at least." They both snugged their capes tight and set off toward the house.

Inside, a tall fire burned. The bundle of wood the man had been carrying was there on the hearth. A table, lit with candles, stood set for five, with a whole side arranged for a centaur's use. A door swung open and in walked a woman carrying a covered platter.

"There you are," she said as she set the platter on the table. "Decided to come in from the night, I see. Shilo!"

Through the same door came a yellow-haired girl of about twelve. She stopped and stared at Dindra and Byron and nearly dropped the bowl she was carrying.

"Come, come, girl," the woman said. "This is no surprise, we've been waiting all day for them. Take their capes and offer them cider."

Shilo set the bowl on the table. She approached Byron with wonder in her face and lifted her gaze to Dindra. She looked over her shoulder as her mother went into the kitchen.

"You're following the star," Shilo whispered.

Byron and Dindra looked at each other.

"How did you know that?" Dindra said.

"The cardinal told me."

They looked at each other again.

"My ma and grappa don't know. I didn't tell them. I only said the cardinal was bringing you this way."

"Shilo!" the woman called from behind the kitchen door. "Will they have something hot to drink?"

"Give me your capes," Shilo said. "Go and warm yourselves at the fire. Don't mention it," she whispered, "it isn't safe!"

Above the mantelpiece hung a black shield with a red unicorn rampant. It was well beaten and scratched with clear claw marks. Byron stared up at it. The old man came in from a shadowy hallway, wearing a housecoat and a pair of heavy slippers. A large pipe stuck from his teeth. He smiled at his guests, looking them over through a pair of thick glasses.

"Milo Prinder is my name. The two of you are most welcome."

"Thank you, sir," Dindra said.

"It's a long time since we had visitors from Hiding Wood," Milo Prinder continued. "Not since before the Wolfen War. You're the first findrels little Shilo has ever seen."

"Findrels?" Byron said.

"That's the old name for you centaurs and satyrs. Used to be common as nightfall to have a centaur drinking cider by this fireplace. Not anymore. Long time."

Milo Prinder shook his head and glanced at the shield above the fire.

"My gradda has one just like it," Byron said.

"Does he now?" Milo Prinder replied. "A scout was he? For Queen Belma? You satyrs were great ones for scouting."

"Yes, sir," Byron said.

"And what's your gradda's name?"

"Darius Thorn, sir," Byron said.

Milo Prinder blinked at Byron. He caught his pipe in one hand and set the other on his hip. "You don't say, Darius Thorn?"

"Yes, sir. I'm Byron."

"Pleased to meet you, Byron. Darius Thorn ... Well, that's a name I've not heard ... He went away after the war ... didn't come back until ..." Milo Prinder stopped and set a soft gaze on Byron. "Ah, yes," he said. "I remember now. He came back to care for his grandson."

"Yes, sir," Byron said, looking into the fire.

"Well," Milo said. "How is the old fox, eh?"

"Just fine, sir," Byron said.

The old man shook his head and tapped his pipe out on the hearth. "It's been too long." Then he reached into his housecoat pocket for a satchel of leaf and stuffed his pipe again. "Too long. Well, life takes over after all."

"Yes, sir," Byron said.

"Darius was my good friend long ago. What about you, miss?" Milo Prinder said to Dindra. "What's your name?"

The kitchen door swung open and Shilo came in carrying two steaming mugs. "Dindra, sir," Dindra said. "Dindra Thundershod."

"Thundershod?" Milo Prinder said. "Does that make Palter Thundershod your father?"

"Yes, sir," Dindra said.

"And that makes Madican Thundershod your grandfather, I suppose."

"Yes, sir."

"Madican was mighty centaur," Milo Prinder said. "A great warrior. I was there that day in the birch grove when the wolves finally took him. I saw him die."

"I never met him," Dindra said.

"No," the old man said. "I suppose not. Though your father is as like him as any could be, so I hear."

"Yes, sir," Dindra replied.

Shilo stepped up and handed the visitors their mugs. Milo smiled at her. "Shilo told us to expect you," he said. "She speaks with animals, you know. A wonder. Who knows what all they tell her."

Shilo glanced at Byron and Dindra. "Supper's ready," she said.

◈　◈　◈

Milo and Fidelia Prinder nodded and frowned as Byron and Dindra told the story of the ruined tower.

"A mystery," the old man said. "Sounds like a story from the Ghostwood."

"Ghostwood?" Byron said through a bite of dumpling. He nodded to Shilo as she filled his cup with steaming cider.

"East of here, nearer the mountains," Fidelia said. "Some say the woods there are haunted."

"East?" Dindra said. "That's where we're headed."

As soon as she said it she winced. Byron's glance ricocheted off Dindra, hit each of the Prinders and landed back on Dindra. Shilo froze with the cider pitcher hovering over Byron's cup. She stared at his hand.

Milo Prinder raised an eyebrow. "You don't say."

"Anyone for pie?" Shilo said and she ran off into the kitchen.

Milo Prinder sat back in his chair and looked at Dindra. "What might you be headed east for, youngster?"

"I . . ." Dindra said. A pot clanged in the pantry.

"Oh, just tell them," Byron said. "They've guessed it already. We're following the star."

Fidelia Prinder sat up stiff. Several pots clamored to the kitchen floor.

"And with King Belden's permission," Byron said.

"The king?" Milo Prinder said. "Is that so?"

"Well," Dindra said, "Byron has permission. It's his Misrule's privilege."

"Ah," Milo said with a nod.

Fidelia pursed her lips and frowned. "That silly tradition," she said.

"And you decided to go along with him, is that it?" Milo said.

"Well, you see sir, Byron needed help and . . . well . . ."

Byron and Dindra told the whole story from the beginning. When it was over, Milo lit his pipe.

"Ravinath," he growled.

Fidelia shook her head. "Shilo," she called. "Won't you come in, instead of listening by the door?"

Shilo came in, smiling, carrying a plate of pie wedges. "Here you are," she said without looking at anyone. She put the plate on the table, turned on her heel and headed for the kitchen again.

"Just a moment, young lady," her mother said.

Shilo stopped.

Fidelia Prinder locked eyes with her daughter. "You knew," she said.

"Knew what, mamma?" Shilo said. She smiled, but her eyes were wide and cautious.

"Don't hand me a ration of feathers," Fidelia Prinder said. "You knew what these two were up to. Tell me I'm wrong."

"You're wrong," Shilo said and bolted for the kitchen again.

"Shilo, come back here," Fidelia Prinder said.

Shilo stopped and turned. Her eyes were rimmed with tears and she wrung her hands.

"Shilo, why didn't you tell us?" her mother said. "You know the danger around here . . . and with your father gone to the king. These two might have ended up at any house in the village."

"No they wouldn't," Shilo said. "Not with the cardinal guiding them."

Fidelia let her shoulders sag. "Shilo, if we'd known we could have been more secret. We could have hid them, or at least warned them away. Why would you keep something like that from us?"

"Because ... because I want to go with them!"

Fidelia Prinder gasped. "Shilo, no!" she whispered, putting a hand to her mouth.

"I thought you'd try to stop them ... us ..." Shilo said.

"Shilo! Oh, not my Shilo!" Fidelia said. "Say something, Milo! The villagers!"

Milo looked into the candle flame.

"How did some cardinal know what we were doing, anyway?" Byron whispered to Dindra.

"Byron, hush," Dindra said, looking around at the Prinders.

Byron shrugged. "Well, how'd he know?"

"Shadetree told him," Shilo said, "the raven who led you to the tower."

"Oh," Byron said. "Well, where is he now?"

"Gone back to Manakar, I suppose," Shilo said.

"Manakar?" Byron and Dindra said together.

"The old grizzleback bear," Shilo said. "And Lucia, his mate."

"From Hiding Wood?" Dindra said. "What about them?"

"They're following the star, they and some others: Shadetree, Onya the doe, Bard the Owl, Milly and Brace, the badger and the raccoon. A flying squirrel has joined them also but he won't tell anyone his name."

"Stop this at once," Fidelia cried, "all of you! I'll not have it, not in my house! Milo will you *say* something!"

Milo sighed.

"But we have to go, ma'am," Byron said. "It's the call of Silverlance."

Milo caught his pipe from his mouth. "Silverlance is it? Who says so?"

"My gradda," Byron said.

"So," Milo Prinder said, "that's why young Belden gave his leave."

"Milo," Fidelia pleaded. She clutched the old man's wrist.

Milo patted her hand and stood from the table. At the fireplace he reached up and lifted the shield from its hook. "Darius Thorn bid his own grandson go, Fidelia. He stood hoof to hoof with Ravinath himself. What if he's right?"

"Could it be, Milo?" Fidelia said. "Silverlance is just a legend after all."

"A legend indeed," Milo said. "But what if Silverlance really did come back and no one went out to meet him?"

Fidelia clutched her apron and looked at Shilo. "I wish your father were here."

"Well he isn't," the old man said. "He's gone to the king to seek an answer to this very question. Seems it snuck in behind his back. I'm afraid it's for you to say, Fidelia, whether Shilo goes or stays. Whatever else, we've got to help these two any way we can."

❧   ❧   ❧

Byron lay awake in his room. He remembered the pouch Gradda had given him and fetched it from the chair in the corner. He took it back to the bed with him and nestled in to examine it.

"His monocle," Byron said as he emptied the pouch into his hand. "He never even let me touch it before. There's a note."

Byron unrolled the small paper and read the greeting.

To Lord Misrule,

Greetings on your big day, Byro. It's time you had this. It's served me well, but it's yours now. I won't tell you how it works, you'll have to find that out on your own. Here's a clue: Don't look at the light.

Happy Birthday, Byron.

Gradda.

Byron frowned. "Don't look at the light," he said. Then he put the monocle in his eye and looked straight into the lamp.

Everything went white and a cruel pain jabbed through his head. Byron dropped the monocle, jammed the heel of his hand into his eye and buried his face in the pillows. When the pain stopped Byron opened his eye. The light from the lamp was still very bright and it was some time before the eye could adjust. He peered down at the monocle in the folds of the bedcovers.

It was a ring of brass with raised marks all around it. There was smoke swirling around in the glass. Byron turned his back to the light and put the monocle in. It didn't stab his eye with pain, but the light was irritating and itchy. He hung the monocle around his neck by its leather strap, blew out the lamp and put the monocle back in his eye.

He saw the room as clear as day. Byron opened wide the eye without the monocle and everything went black. He closed the eye again and the room returned, clear and bright through the monocle.

"Wow, Gradda!" Byron said, waving his hand in front of his face. "This is . . . this is . . . wow!" He dropped to the floor and went out for a prowl.

He crept down the hall to Dindra's room and listened. Nothing stirred. The next door was Shilo's. Byron could hear her moving around, opening and closing drawers, muttering. Two doors further on and across the hall, he had to cover his eye. Lamplight streamed out at the bottom of the door. Inside Fidelia and Milo Prinder were talking quietly. Fidelia was weeping and Milo was hushing her.

Byron moved on, making for the kitchen and the last piece of pie left from supper. Standing there on a chair next to the counter, Byron set to eating. Then there was a knock at the front door of the cottage. He jumped down from his pie and peered out through the swinging door.

Lamplight appeared from the hallway. Milo Prinder emerged wearing his housecoat and a flat cap on his head. He carried a lamp before him. Byron snatched the monocle out of his eye before the light could hurt it.

"I'm coming, I'm coming," Milo Prinder shouted. "What can you possibly want?" He opened the door and lifted the lamp. "Tarn Greeley, is that you? What can the matter be at this hour? And with the snow falling?"

"Nothing, I hope," said a voice. "May I come in?"

"I think not. What do you want?"

"Very well. There is some concern among the villagers regarding the business of your visitors."

"They're only youngsters. What business of theirs could concern the village? And since when is it *your* business to begin with?"

"You're aware of the recent precautions taken by the council to ensure the peace ..."

"I got the letter," Milo said. "Curfews and house calls after dark. Nonsense. All over some silly tale of shadows and death."

"The council has considered the matter very seriously."

"And sicced Tharnis Micktern on Jaspin Fairbriar for going hunting after Midwinter? Same as he's done for thirty years?"

"Fairbriar was expressly warned . . ."

"And where is he now?"

"Really, Milo . . ."

"Here's your answer, Tarn Greely. These children have come for the Twelve Days of Midwinter. When I take them to the village square tomorrow to show them around I hope the people of Branchbrook will put on a bit more polish than you're showing tonight. These youngsters are from the king, after all."

"The king . . ."

"Good night to you, Tarn Greeley," Milo said and he slammed the door.

He turned and headed for the hallway where the bedrooms were, lifting the lamp toward the kitchen door as he went. "You might as well come along, Byron," he said. "I'll wake the others, meet me in Fidelia's chamber. You can bring your pie if you want to."

◈　◈　◈

Byron sat chewing as Milo told Fidelia of the encounter with Tarn Greeley. Dindra was rubbing the sleep from her eyes and Shilo had a wide cautious look on her face.

"You shouldn't have been so cross with him, Milo," Fidelia said. "You'll make them angry."

"Cross was called for," Milo said. "Besides, cowing would have made them suspicious."

Fidelia clutched her nightgown. "We're lucky they didn't burst right in! Oh, I wish my Filo were here."

"It hasn't come to that, yet, surely?" Milo said.

"It will, Milo," Fidelia said. "They're afraid of the stories."

"What stories?" Byron said.

"An old cycle of tales," Milo said. "About the Weg."

"What's that?" Dindra said.

Shilo cleared her throat and spoke:

> *"The voice that hides*
> *in the creaking of the cemetery gate*
> *it creeps among the tombstones*
> *where it lurks and broods and waits.*
> *It watches you and hates you from the corner of your eye,*
> *When ghostlight climbs the Weg will come*
> *and get you by and by."*

Milo Prinder frowned and nodded. "A rhyme to frighten children," he said. "But the Weg was real, whatever it was, long ago. And that bit about the ghostlight . . . well, that's what all the panic is about."

"Jaspin Fairbriar is only the beginning," Fidelia said.

"I'd say you're right," Milo Prinder said with a sigh. "Well, you two will have to leave tonight, right now and no stopping."

"Who are they?" Dindra asked.

"The villagers," Milo said. "The townsfolk. That star has them scared to the bones."

"The whole village?" Byron said.

"No," Milo said, "not everyone, but a good many and some not to be dallied with. They've made no end of commotion over what that star could mean." The old man sighed. He looked at his daughter-in-law and fell still.

Fidelia held Shilo in a teary gaze. "Shilo," she said. Shilo ran into her mother's arms. "Be careful, child."

"I will, Mamma," Shilo said and she buried her face in Fidelia's breast.

Milo clutched his nightcap in his hands and his lip quivered. "Are you sure, Fidelia?"

With a single firm nod, Fidelia released her daughter and stood up. "The child speaks to animals, after all. So, we must be very brave. There's work to do. Byron, Dindra, follow me. You mustn't go off as empty-handed as you arrived. Shilo, go and get that bag you've been packing and meet us out front."

Shilo looked at her mother with her mouth open.

"Did you think you had me fooled?" Fidelia said. "Hurry on now, no time to lose."

Milo Prinder sighed. "It'll be hard going for a while, but if you move quickly for a few days you should get there ahead of anyone who might follow."

"Get where?" Byron said.

"Why, the only place between here and the mountains where the villagers won't have the nerve to look. Ghostwood. It's your only chance."

Snow and darkness swallowed the house. Dindra clutched the stout hickory staff Fidelia had given her. Byron sat on her back wrapped tight against the cold. Toward dawn the sky cleared to fading stars. The one star blazed in the east. In the afternoon they passed the ruined tower. A blanket of snow covered every sign of struggle. As the sun set, they reached the stone bridge and crossed Gladwater together.

"Here we part," Milo Prinder said. "March all night. I know you need a rest, but you can't risk it yet. Eat as you go and keep on until the sun goes down. Don't make a fire unless you're desperate."

"What's going to happen to you?" Shilo said.

"It's not safe in Branchbrook Village," Milo Prinder said. "There's some mind poison at work there, I'm sure of it ... people not acting right. We'll keep the river between us and them and make for the king. That's where your father is and it's the safest place for us now. You watch for those centaurs, you hear?"

"We will," Dindra said.

"Don't worry, Shilo," Fidelia said. "We'll get there safe. Look to yourself and your friends."

"I will, Mamma," Shilo said. "Tell Dadda I love him."

"I will," Fidelia said. "Too cold for tears, now."

She clutched Shilo to herself. Shilo hugged her grandfather and the Prinders turned away, heading north up Gladwater. Shilo, Dindra and Byron watched them until they blended with the dusk and were gone.

Twenty paces on, hidden at first by the trees and darkness, the snow was broken with the tracks of many hooves. A wide swath had been cut, moving from west to east.

"Centaurs," Dindra said. "Six or more. They must've tracked us to the stone bridge."

"These tracks were left in falling snow," Byron said. "They're partly filled in."

"They missed us in the storm," Dindra said. "They're ahead of us."

Byron looked back. "It's lucky we went back across the river or they'd have had us."

"Let's get going," Shilo said. "I never thought I'd say it, but I'd like to get to Ghostwood as quickly as we can."

Byron settled in on Dindra's back and the three companions set off again, marching east, more easily in the trail broken by the centaurs.

Chapter 4

Rufus and Rafter

hree nights out they built a fire. Byron dreamed. Shadows lurked in the trees and wolves howled. A terrified child called his name. Byron called out also. "Dadda!"

He woke with a jump and looked around. Shilo and Dindra were fast asleep. Byron turned over and looked at the star. In the morning they woke to find they had camped on the edge of a vast snowbound grove of ancient oaks.

Stout gray trunks stood in line from north to south as far as anyone could see. Facing the mighty trees was a row of posts stuck into the ground, each as tall as a man, thick as a spear shaft, with an animal skull fixed to the top. Just below each skull was a crosspiece adorned with feathers and furs. On the forehead of each skull was painted a strange mark. Morning grew in the forest. Daylight recovered the enormous trees and the strange fence from the shadows.

Byron peered at the mark on one of the skulls. It made his stomach tremble to look at it. "I've seen that mark before," he said.

"Tharnis Micktern," Shilo said. "He made this fence."

"Who's Tharnis Micktern?" Dindra said.

"He's the chief hunter in Branchbrook Village. I remember

51

hearing of this fence, now that I see it. All the young men who want to become hunters have to spend a season out here maintaining it. It marks the edge of his hunting grounds. It's an initiation, and sometimes a punishment."

"What's so hard about tending a fence?" Byron asked.

"Well, because of what's beyond ..." Shilo said. "In the oaks."

"Why, what's ...?" Byron began. Then he blinked and looked into the trees. "Ghostwood," he whispered.

"Ghostwood," Shilo said with a nod.

"Ghostwood," Dindra agreed.

They all peered into the depths of the ancient grove. The morning grew bright, but it didn't chase out the silence of the oaks.

"Where've you seen that mark, Byron?" Dindra said.

"Ravinath," Byron said, still peering into the oaken deeps.

Dindra frowned. "Ravinath?"

"Uh-huh," Byron said. "He wears it painted on his flanks."

Dindra stepped up and took a closer look at the skull. "You're right," she said. "I think Baruwan had it too, at the bridge, remember?"

"I remember he had paint on his face," Byron said with a shrug. "I couldn't really see."

"I don't like it here," Shilo said. She looked up and down the length of the strange fence. "Let's get moving. We shouldn't waste the daylight if we're going ... in there."

"He had that mark," Dindra said. "I'm sure of it."

"Just look at all those oaks," Byron said. "Gradda says oaks are the last stage in a forest. They take over slowly and change the soil so nothing else can grow."

"It sure is quiet," Dindra said. She squinted a little. "The trees seem ... watchful."

"Watchful?" Byron whispered. He looked about sidelong, wide-eyed.

"This is silly, scaring ourselves," Shilo with a laugh. "Come on you two, let's pack up and ..."

There was a singing sound above their heads and a loud thud as an arrow struck the bole of an oak tree, the shaft of it quivered.

Everyone jumped and looked around.

"You can't escape!" shouted a voice. "Stay where you are!"

In the woods behind them was a band of horsemen, spread out in a line, trotting forward as one. The deep snow muffled the sound of the hooves to a whisper. The men held spears and drawn bows. Horse and rider wore white pelts and blended with the snowy woods. One very tall man came in before the rest and leaped from his horse. He marched straight up to the little fire and kicked snow over the embers. He put his hands on his hips and glared at the companions.

A semicircle of riders formed around the camp, closed against the boundary fence. Byron noticed the fellows closest to Ghostwood fidgeting and eyeing the oaks with caution.

"Mr. Micktern," Shilo said.

"My fence menders saw your fire, Miss Prinder," Micktern said. "Friends of yours, I think." He motioned to four young men near to Shilo in age. They smiled at her and sat taller in their saddles.

"Very foolish," Micktern continued. "Winter isn't the time for escaping in secret. You should have waited for summer. You'd have had less need of warmth and your tracks would have taken some skill to follow."

"The star didn't rise in summer," Byron said.

"The star," Micktern said and he spat on the snow-covered

campfire. "As it is, I have saved you from yourselves. No one passes through Ghostwood without dying or losing his mind. Bind them."

Five men dismounted and took coils of rope from their saddles. Tharnis Micktern headed for his horse. Dindra trotted forward a few steps and called out to him. "Are you taking us to Ravinath?"

Micktern stopped. He lifted his hand and the advancing rope men halted.

"What can you mean by that, girl?" Micktern said.

"When you see him," Byron said, "tell him I'm sorry about Baruwan."

"Baruwan is alive and well," Micktern said with a laugh. "The fool galloped into Ghostwood two days ago, well ahead of you, blind as a bat with no trail to follow. He's as thick brained as his master is arrogant."

Micktern sneered at Dindra. "Yes," he said. "Ravinath wants you. But I don't take orders from anything on four legs. So, watch what you say. There are no bridges to cut here."

"We'll tell Silverlance about you when we see him," Dindra said. "You and all your friends."

Micktern's face darkened and he started toward her. As he came he drew a long hideous knife and raised it. "That moment will never come," he said. "Forget the ropes. We'll finish this here!"

Byron stepped back. Shilo screamed. The knife flashed in the sun. Dindra whirled and shot her rear hooves backward. Micktern let out a kind of shout muffled by all the wind that emptied from his lungs as Dindra's kick landed on his chest. Byron winced at the sound of it. Micktern flew backward and landed flat in the snow.

Dindra crouched low. "Get on!"

Shilo caught hold of Byron and pulled him up behind her just as Dindra sprang forward and bolted into Ghostwood.

"Get after them!" someone shouted. There was a jam up around Micktern. He didn't move. Horses were neighing and rearing. Several riders gave chase for a few paces, but halted at the skull fence.

"After them, I said!" shouted one rider as he broke free from the knot. He galloped past one of the young fence menders and struck the boy across the head with an open hand. The boy lurched forward and rolled out of the saddle. "Fool of a squib!" the rider shouted and he charged into the oaks.

Looking back, Byron saw the young hunter standing by his horse, red-faced, staring at the ground, striving to keep the tears from his eyes. Byron almost fell as Dindra made a sudden turn. He clutched Shilo's cape with all his might and pressed his face into her back.

Dindra hurtled breakneck among the trees, swerving and darting. The forest shot by. Shilo screamed as Dindra leaped over a ruined stonewall without slowing. They came to a long straight stretch through the trees and Dindra galloped as fast as she could. She tore clear through the snow to the dark soil beneath. It wasn't long, with the weight of two riders on her back, before she began to tire. Dindra veered right and took to the trees again.

"Where are you going?" Byron cried.

"Away from *them!*" Dindra shouted back.

Shilo looked back. "They're coming up beside us!"

In the trees to the right, two riders gained pace with Dindra. To the left, still charging along the lane she had abandoned, were three others. The shouts of several more came from behind.

"Just stay on!" Dindra cried and there was fear in her voice. Byron and Shilo clung tight.

A dry streambed cut across their path. Dindra turned to the left and headed up the winding course of the stream. She passed under an arched stone bridge just as the pursuing riders on the open lane thundered across it.

It was rough and uneven beneath the snow. The river turned and wound and the banks were steep. Dindra struggled over hidden rocks, ducked fallen braches. The banks grew higher until they deepened into a narrow gully.

"Are they back there?" Dindra called.

"I don't see them," Shilo answered.

"They're back there all right," Byron said.

A lakebed opened before them. The banks were even higher, though not so steep. Ahead of the group stood an enormous mound of branches and twigs, covered with snow.

"A beaver dam!" Shilo cried.

"We're trapped!" Byron answered.

Dindra charged ahead and stopped at the foot of the dam. She stood there, swishing her tail, panting with smoky breath. They all turned at the sound of hooves thundering into the gully behind them.

"I'm sorry," Dindra croaked and her shoulders heaved a little as her fear and exhaustion gave way to tears.

Byron watched as the hunters arrived and took their posts. Silence filled the place, broken by the snorts and jingling tack of the horses. The lead hunter ordered the others to string their arrows and bend their bows.

"Well run, centaur," the leader said. "A chase worthy of your father's daughter. A pity he will never hear of it. And now, as we have already come deeper into this wood than I like, you die. On my command," he said to his hunters and he lifted his arm.

Wood and strings creaked as the hunters tensed their bows.

Another sound followed, a small whirring followed by a thud. The lead hunter swayed in the saddle. He pulled the reins with one hand and clutched his neck with the other. His horse reared beneath him and the man fell to the snow.

Another hunter jolted back and shot his arrow wild into the beaver dam, then another fell and then a fourth. The other hunters turned their arrows on the woods, searching for the source of the attack. There was laughter from the trees on every side.

One by one the hunters fell, clutching neck or thigh or shoulder. Three tried to escape up the banks and fell backward off their horses. One sped away down the mouth of the stream and his horse returned riderless. Soon the lakebed was strewn with white-clad hunters, lying still.

"Look!" Byron whispered. He blinked and rubbed his eyes and looked again.

It seemed that they stepped right out of the trunks of the trees. They came in great number, five or six to every fallen hunter. They were nearly as tall as men, and from a distance seemed to be men. But there was something strange about them.

First they collected the darts they had used to fell the hunters. Then each of the hunters was gathered up by four of the strangers and borne away into the oaks. A group of the strangers took the reins of the horses and led them away. Shilo, Byron and Dindra watched in silent wonder.

"Have no fear for the horses," said a voice. A group of the strangers approached, led by one bright-eyed fellow. "Or their riders for that matter. The horses we will keep and their lives will be much improved. Tribute for trespass, call it. And your pursuers? What shall we do with them? Hmm?"

Like his companions, the stranger had dark skin and deep, silvery eyes. There were tiny, leafy vines, dried and gray with winter, mingled in his hair. A single vine came out from under his sleeve, wrapped around his wrist and disappeared into the flesh at the base of his thumb. He had a long bow as tall as himself, which he leaned on as he gazed down at Byron.

"You are a wondrous pair," the stranger said with a glance at Dindra. "Jomalla din thad na Findrelene!"

His remark was answered with laughter and more comments in the same strange language. Byron looked at Dindra. Dindra shrugged.

"Wondrous indeed," the stranger said. "They are only sleeping, your pursuers, not killed. They will wake up outside that fence of theirs with a tale of ghosts to tell. And you? What shall we do with you? You are trespassers also."

"You should let us go," Shilo said with a firm nod.

The remaining strangers had gathered round and gave a mighty laugh.

"Very reasonable, Rifkin," one fellow said. "Wouldn't you say?"

"And shall we freshen your stores as well?" said another.

Rifkin smiled. "Why were they hunting you?" he said.

No one spoke.

"What can you tell me of the centaur band that passed through this wood two days ago?"

"You let them go?" Byron said, smacking his own forehead.

"One shouldn't tangle with such as they without great need. Might it be that they too were hunting you, but lost you in the storm and snows of late?"

No one spoke.

"Well," Rifkin said, "there are ways of gaining the cooperation of the unwilling. In this case I think we shall try the fabled torments of rest and food. Come, you are the prisoner guests of the dryad folk. You owe us your lives already, a bit of comfort and provision won't tip the scales too greatly in your favor."

⬙   ⬙   ⬙

At dusk they reached the guard fires. Sentinels greeted them from platforms in the trees and waved them in. Rifkin led the companions up onto the hanging walkways and a pair of young dryads approached.

"Rifkin!" they called together.

"Well," Rifkin said. "Rufus and Raefer! Look what the woods have given us today!"

"Welcome back, Rifkin," said the younger fellow.

"Hello," said the older boy. He held out his hand to each of the companions. "I'm Rufus. You're very welcome."

"Raefer," said the younger one. He greeted Shilo, but never took his eyes off Byron and Dindra.

"I will leave it to you both to see our prisoners tended," Rifkin said. "I must go and report. We needn't bother about a guard. Escape would do you more harm than good, I think. Farewell," Rifkin said and he left them.

Rufus and Raefer looked very much alike. They wore the same cloaks and tunics and britches all in wintry colors. Each carried a long knife and a sharpened twig stuck in his belt. They both had the same fine, leafy vines, gray with winter, mingled in their hair. Rufus had one around his neck and Raefer had one under the corner of his jaw, behind his ear. Their eyes were silvery and their skin dark and clear.

"Rifkin is our brother," Raefer said. "He's a scout captain. Rufus is training to be a scout. I start next year. It takes a long time but I'll make it."

"It's lucky he found you," Rufus said. "There were wolves spotted south of here a little while ago."

"How many?" Byron said.

"Eight," Rufus said. "And the centaurs didn't just pass through as we'd hoped. They spent some time at the eastern fence of the grove hunting around. They split up into two bands and went north and south."

"Gosh," Shilo said. "That *is* lucky."

"That's not all," Rufus continued. "The southern band met up with the wolves and had some sort of meeting."

"What?" Dindra said.

"The centaurs hate the wolves more than anyone," Byron said.

Raefer shrugged. "These centaurs were strange for lots of reasons. They were all painted with odd markings and symbols, even on their faces."

"Did the wolves and centaurs leave the grove together?" Dindra said.

"No," Rufus said. "The centaurs regrouped to the north and the wolves continued east."

"So," Dindra said, "nobody has any idea where we are."

"That Tharnis what's his name does," Byron answered.

"But the hunters are afraid of this place," Shilo said. "As far as they know we've been murdered by ghosts."

"Is that what happened?" Rufus said with a laugh. "Well, we'd better get you to your houses. Even ghosts need what's left of the daylight to get their chores done."

"I'll show Byron the way and settle him in, Ruf," Raefer said. "Dindra and Shilo are in your direction anyway."

"All right, then," Rufus said. "Follow me you two. You've got beds and supper waiting."

Raefer lit the lamps inside Byron's hut. There was a bucket full of steaming water, a basin, a cot with fat pillows and a pile of thick, soft blankets. The floor was covered with heavy mats. A deep bowl of hot stew, a plate of bread and a small crock of butter waited on the table. A fire burned in a small brazier in the middle of the floor and everything was warm and dry. Byron dropped his pack and sighed.

"Well, thanks, Raefer," he said. "I'm really tired, so . . ."

"You're following the star!" Raefer cried.

"Shhhh!" Byron hissed. "Not so loud!"

Raefer winced and made a fist. He looked behind him at the closed door. "Sorry!" he whispered. Then he smiled. "So it's true!"

Byron frowned and narrowed his eyes. "Maybe."

"Of course you are. You're a findrel, that's how I knew. I won't tell anyone, I swear. I mean, that would be bad for both of us."

"Both of us?"

"Well sure, I'm going with you. Me and Rufus, only he doesn't know it yet."

"You and . . . hey, hold on Raefer," Byron said.

"I can't stay," Raefer said, holding up his hands. "I've got fire duty. This is gonna be great! Don't tell anyone, right? We'll find a way to have a meeting. Gotta go!"

Before Byron could speak, Raefer was gone into the full fallen darkness. Byron sighed and shrugged and sat down at the table. When the bowl was clean and the bread was gone, Byron threw himself on the bed and didn't bother about the covers until hours later when the fire was down and the cold of night came and found him.

CHAPTER 5

Rafter Leads the Way

yron woke to snow falling. The sky was dark. From the window by his bed he watched the dryads going about their morning business. Smoke from the chimneys told him that most of them were snug at home, enjoying the deep hush of the oak grove in heavy snow.

Just after lunch a sharp knock sounded on his door. Byron rolled over, snuggled down and yawned.

"Come in," he called.

Rifkin Nimbletwig walked in and took off his cloak. "You mustn't let your fire die," he said, placing a chunk of wood in the brazier. "That's a cold day out there."

"Mm," Byron said.

Rifkin smiled. "You need rest more than you know. You're wise to take it so seriously."

"Mm."

"I've been out watching the woods. I've never seen so much traffic. Centaurs and wolves."

Byron sat up and wrapped the blanket around him.

Rifkin nodded. "So, you've set out to follow this new star of ours."

Byron was silent.

"Fair enough," Rifkin said. "Keep your secret. But there are some who want to stop you, these strange centaurs for instance. And you have led them to my home."

"We didn't mean to," Byron said.

"Can you tell me what they want with you?"

"I guess they don't want Silverlance to come back. At least that's what my gradda said."

"And you? Do you want Silverlance to return?"

"Of course."

"Really? What can you tell me about him?"

Byron frowned and looked out the window.

"Yet you set off to find him without a moment's hesitation."

"Well, I wanted to go before I even heard of him."

"To follow a star? Why?"

"It felt like . . . like the only thing to do."

Rifkin nodded. "Little is remembered about Silverlance except his name. But we dryads still tell what stories remain. His lance could bestow the Silver Wound. It was feared by his enemies."

"Enemies?" Byron said.

"Indeed, powerful enemies. Long ago they waged war on Silverlance. One story tells that his return will bring a time of darkness and danger and that war will erupt again."

Byron looked at Rifkin with wide eyes.

"You have become involved in something very old," Rifkin said, "something that began long, long ago. The days ahead may require things of you that you are not prepared to give. This is where the star has led you."

Byron looked into the fire.

"Perhaps you're beginning to understand, Byron, why the name of Silverlance might be a fearful thing? But you're not alone. Much will be required of us all. If that star is what it seems to be, even good people will have cause to be afraid."

Sparks rose up in a small cloud as the fire collapsed in the brazier. The wind sighed against the window next to Byron's bed. Rifkin rose.

"No one will hinder you when you decide to continue. As my companion said at our meeting, Shilo's request was reasonable, though it needed testing. And we will fill your skins and top your packs. In the meantime, rest and eat well. Stay no longer than you think wise, but don't go without saying goodbye, if it can be helped."

Rifkin went out. Byron leaned back on his elbow and gazed into the gray day. A moment later there was a knock. Byron opened his mouth to respond as Raefer walked in.

"What did he ask you?" Raefer said without pulling back his hood.

"Who?" Byron said.

"Who? Who've you been talking to in the last hour?"

"Well, he asked me what I was up to . . . and he said a lot of things I don't really understand. But he seemed right, I guess."

"Never mind that, did he say anything about me going with you when you leave?"

"No."

Raefer took a deep breath. "Good," he said and he sat down in the chair. "I had kind of a close call. Well, listen, come with me. The others are waiting in Shilo's house. We've got some things to talk over."

"Like what?" Byron said.

"Like the Griffin Stair, for instance."

"What's that?"

"Come with me and I'll tell ya." Raefer said. He stood and handed Byron the cape that hung beside the door. Byron put it on and they went outside into the snowy gray of morning.

"There's an old rhyme about you satyrs," Raefer said as they walked along the wooden platform, "and how Silverlance was so fond of you. It goes like this:

"Moila Nene tognethen wain nafald
Dun preshen alma burn
Wethel prene gobalan culkenald
Mignifin durmalantha jenma thurn."

Raefer gazed into the wood with a faraway look on his face. Byron looked at him with his eyebrows up. "Well?" he said.

Raefer blinked. "Hmm? Well, what?"

"What does it mean?"

"Oh! Right! Sorry. Well, let's see . . . Silverlance loved his . . . loved the satyrs . . . for the way they danced under the moon . . . for the way they loved the stars and . . . came to him however far they had to walk . . . something like that."

"That's a poem?" Byron said.

"I guess it loses something in the translation."

"I *guess.*"

Smoke was rising from Shilo's chimney. Reafer led the way up to door. Inside they heard laughter and talking. "First the star and now a real live satyr," he said. "That's more proof than I need. When I heard you'd been found I was sure it was the star of Silverlance."

"You got all that from some old rhyme?"

"Well, yeah," Raefer said with a shrug. He gave a scouting glance around and knocked twice on the door. Inside, they found Shilo, Dindra and Rufus gathered around Shilo's fire, sipping cider and eating some sort of cake.

"Good," Raefer said. "You're all here."

Byron took off his cape and hung it on a peg. Shilo handed him a steaming cup as he sat down satyr fashion beside her. Raefer remained standing with a wide smile on his face.

"Well, I can't stay long," Rufus said. "I've got fire duty."

Raefer lifted an eyebrow and smirked. "Fire duty? Did you say fire duty? Rufus, my dear fellow, I've asked you here today to talk about adventure."

"Oh, all right," Rufus said, rolling his eyes. "Half an hour."

"So what about this Griffin Stair?" Byron said.

"The Griffin Stair?" Rufus said. "Is that part of your plan, Raef?"

"How else do we get across the mountains?" Raefer said.

"That's just it," Rufus said. "You don't. Those mountains can't be crossed. Everyone knows that."

"Except by the Griffin stair," Raefer said.

"If it even exists," Rufus said.

"Sure it does," Raefer said. Then he turned to Byron. "It winds up through the Crestfalls somewhere near the Old Mountain. They say there's never any snow on the stair, or very little, because of the wind. We just have to find it."

"How do we do that?" Dindra said.

Raefer smiled. "That's where Shilo comes in. I figure she can ask the cardinal to scout around."

"Oh, right," Rufus said with a laugh.

"What's funny about that?" Shilo said.

"Nothing," Rufus said, still laughing.

"Have you got a better idea?" Dindra said.

"Yeah," Rufus said. "How 'bout not going?"

"Oh, come on Ruf," Raefer pleaded. "You said you were in. All we have to do is reach the platform and wait."

"I *can* talk to animals," Shilo said.

"Of course you can," Rufus said.

"Wait for what?" Byron said.

Raefer shrugged. "Well, the griffins, I guess."

"Griffins?" Shilo said. "Do you really think there are any?"

"Why not?" Raefer said. "They're in lots of stories aren't they?"

Shilo shrugged. "Well, yes."

"And all we need to do is find the stair," Rufus said. He shook his head.

"That's the best we can do, Ruf," Raefer said. "If we want to find Silverlance."

Rufus leaned back on his elbow. "And how do we get away from camp without Rifkin finding out?"

"Good question," Raefer said. "Now, the moon will be dark in three days. That'll be the best time to go. Shilo, Byron and Dindra announce they'll be leaving. When the time comes they head out south. Using that as a distraction, you and I will go out to the north where the guard is lightest. Then we all head east and meet up at the broken road."

"Why is the north end guarded so lightly?" Shilo said.

"Because of the marsh," Raefer answered.

"It's very hard to cross and there's really only one way through," Rufus said. "The most we need up there is a watcher and a messenger to send word if anyone approaches."

"Won't that make it difficult for you to get out?" Dindra said.

"Mm-hm," Raefer said. "But it's our best chance of any. Hopefully you leaving to the south will keep everyone busy."

"What about the horses?" Shilo said.

"Well, that's the hard part," Raefer said. "Rufus and I would never get through leading horses. We'll have to come up with a reason for you to need two extras."

"Why do we need two?" Dindra said.

"Yeah," Shilo agreed. "We can take a pack horse and a horse for me to ride. Then when we meet up, you and Rufus can ride together while Dindra and I handle the supplies. That is, if that's alright with her."

"Sure it is," Dindra said. "Byron, you'll just have to get comfortable back there with the rest of the baggage."

"Just wake me when we get there," Byron said.

"Oh, will you stop it?" Rufus said. "Raefer this is crazy. You want to sneak out past a dryad sentinel, cross the northern bog in the middle of winter, then march all the way to the Old Mountain to find some passage you heard about in a campfire story? And you want to put all your hopes of finding it on a girl who claims she can talk to animals? What is it about that plan that *doesn't* seem crazy?"

"Nothing," Raefer said. "But not trying would be even crazier."

"Raefer," Rufus said with a sigh. "I mean . . . What sort of person is this Silverlance, I'd like to know. Seems to me he's asking an awful lot."

"Well," Raefer said, "are you coming or not?"

"Alright, alright," Rufus said. "But only because you're my brother. I can take Silverlance or leave him, if he exists at all."

Three days passed. In the dark of the moon Shilo, Dindra and Byron gathered at the stables to meet Rifkin and pack the horses. New snow was falling.

"Where are those brothers of mine?" Rifkin said as he placed a saddle on the wooden rail. He smoothed the blanket on the horse's back and lifted the saddle into place.

R

"They'll be here," Shilo said with a glance at Byron. "They promised."

"Well," Rifkin said, patting the horse's neck. "This is Old Weatherby. The pack horse is called Melody. They're both warmed and ready, though a bit uneasy. I can't say I blame them. Dark of the moon is an ill-chosen time for setting off. I wish you'd reconsider."

"Well," Dindra said. "We want as much cover as we can get."

"I suppose that's wise," Rifkin said with a nod. "And the choice is yours to make. Still, my heart stands against it."

"Thank you for all your help," Shilo said. "And for the horses."

"I'm sorry we couldn't give you a more fitting farewell," Rifkin said. "The comings and goings of late have us occupied and watchful."

"Have the wolves been seen again?" Byron said.

"No," Rifkin said. "And neither the centaurs. What that may mean I can't say."

"One never knows what a wolf'll do," Byron said, looking out the stable door into the darkness. "Least my gradda says so."

"So does my father," Dindra said.

Rifkin raised an eyebrow. "If blood runs true it speaks well of your kin that daughter and grandson should undertake the quest you've chosen. And you Shilo, courage must flow in your veins from of old."

Shilo shrugged.

Rifkin smiled. "It must be so. Great hearts are handed down. Into the saddle with you and I'll adjust Old Weatherby's stirrups."

Rifkin slid the stirrups into place and Shilo nodded when they were set to her liking. A dryad woman ran in from the darkness carrying a torch.

"Rifkin!" she said. "The wolves have returned. They entered the northern marsh headed south. Two runners just reported!"

"Wolves on the marsh," Rifkin said. "And centaurs?"

"Not by the last report," she said. "But runners are moving as we speak."

"The northern marsh ..." Shilo said.

"Rufus and Raefer ..." Byron said.

Rifkin's face flashed in alarm. "What about them?"

Byron looked at Dindra.

"Come, come, what about them?" Rifkin demanded.

"They're headed for the marsh," Dindra said.

"What?" Rifkin said. The messenger gasped and her eyes went wide.

"They were coming with us," Byron said.

Rifkin blinked. "They were ..." He paused to think and then turned to the messenger. "Jevén," he said. "Yandara nell si nofathan ... Dona Resh ... fineliden fin." The messenger nodded and turned to go. "Jevén," Rifkin said and she looked back. "Fineliden fin ..." The woman's face calmed and she nodded, then she turned again and was gone.

"We're sorry, Rifkin," Shilo said.

"You can't have known about the wolves and my brothers have chosen for themselves. You are not to blame. It seems courage flows out of my past also. Well, I can do no more for you. Good luck. Blast you Rufus and Raefer! You little brigands!"

Rifkin wheeled and ran out into the night. Shilo, Dindra and Byron stood there in the stable, gaping at each other.

"What're we gonna do?" Byron said.

Shilo shook her head. "We have to help them."

"How?" Byron said, throwing up his hands.

"By sticking to the plan," said Dindra. "That's what they'll do, if they can."

"What if the wolves get 'em?" Byron said.

"We can't help them better than Rifkin can," Dindra said. "And we can't help them at all unless we know where to look for them, which we don't."

Shilo nodded. "Jevén said the wolves had entered the marsh. It might take some time before they're close enough to catch Rufus and Raefer ... maybe enough time."

"Maybe not," Byron said.

"We just have to hope they make it through," Dindra said. "But let's get to the broken road as fast as we can. We may be able to help them yet. Come on."

☒　　☒　　☒

A wide swath of white cut through the trees from north to south. Dindra halted at the roadside holding Melody's reins. Byron sat upright and alert on Dindra's back. Shilo came up behind, riding Old Weatherby. No one spoke. The horses stood still and quiet. Then in the distance to the north, they heard the sound: shrill and numerous, the howling of many wolves.

"Have they reached the camp?" Dindra said.

"Rufus and Raefer still might've got out," Shilo said.

"Where are we supposed to meet them?" Byron said.

"We figured on running into them," Shilo said, "headed toward us."

"We still may," Dindra said.

She set off north along the road. The snow was unbroken. Byron trained his eyes left and right into the forest and on the road ahead. Without warning Dindra broke Melody into a gallop.

Shilo snapped Old Weatherby's reins and followed. Byron leaned out and looked ahead. Two shapes were standing in the middle of the road.

"They made it!" he whispered, clutching Dindra's arm.

A moment later they drew up beside the figures. Byron dropped to the snow and waded over to them.

"Byron, wait ..." Dindra said, lifting a hand.

"I knew you'd get through," Byron said. He slapped one of the figures on the arm and the cape gave way like a window curtain on the breeze. Byron frowned. "Rufus ... Raefer?" He drew back one of the capes and saw that it was draped on a gibbet made of tree branches tied together.

Then Shilo gasped.

Byron turned to see an enormous dark shape standing among the trees. It was a centaur and it swished its tail as it stepped out onto the road.

"You must try not to blame your friends," the centaur said. "They would have warned you if they were not bound and gagged."

Seven more centaurs, all holding long spears, moved in from the trees and stood in a circle around the companions. Rufus and Raefer were tied and slung over one fellow's back like a pair of saddlebags.

"Baruwan has commanded you be brought to him alive," the first centaur said. "I would sooner kill you now and not be bothered with tending you on a day's southward journey. Only Baruwan's orders have saved you. Bind them. Leave the horses for the wolves."

Raefer started to squirm. His muffled voice cried out in protest. The centaur who bore him reached back and slapped him on the head. Then Rufus started to squirm and shout through his gag. The centaur reached back and slapped him also. He turned

at the waist, slapping the brothers one then the other, laughing
with the other centaurs.

There was a singing sound.

The centaur leader jerked his head back and gave a choked
grunt. He coughed once, clutching at his throat, then buckled to
the ground with an arrow through his neck. A moment later a
dozen dryad fighters came running in from the east side of the
road.

Three dryads went straight for the centaur that carried Rufus
and Raefer. He spun his spear into a jabbing grip and countered
them as his companions moved to his aid. They reared and
gored with their hooves, thrust and slashed with their spears and
flailed with their great fists and the dryads darted among them,
slashing and stabbing. An archer stood off to the side taking aim,
unable to loose the arrow she'd notched for fear of hitting one of
her own.

"To me, Shilo!" she called.

"Jevén!" Shilo said, prodding Old Weatherby toward the
archer. A centaur moved to stop her and was felled by the
dryad's arrow. When Shilo looked Jevén had notched another
and was already taking aim.

"Dindra!" Byron said, tugging her cape and pointing to the
centaur who bore Rufus and Raefer. "Get along side 'im!"

Dindra started forward. A pair of dryads fighting another
centaur stepped in front of her. Clutching her cape, Byron
choked her as he pulled himself to his hooves. He jumped from
Dindra's back onto the back of the centaur who blocked them.
The fellow turned when he felt the prick of Byron's hooves. As
he did, the dryads moved on him and brought him down. Byron
drew his knife and leaped again, landing between the brothers
on the back of their captor.

At once he attacked the ropes, hacking and slashing. He cut the flesh of the centaur's back. The centaur cried out and wheeled, rearing high. Byron caught hold of the ropes and kept cutting. The dryads on the ground came at the centaur with their swords raised and he turned to face them. The ropes came loose. Rufus and Raefer dropped into the snow. Dindra and Jevén dragged them to safety as Byron waded out behind them.

"Who is it, Jevén?" Rufus said as she pulled the gag from his mouth. "Is it Resh?"

"Resh and ten of his fellows," Jevén said, cutting away the ropes. "Rifkin sent me for him. No time now, get going!"

"You're letting us go?" Raefer said, rubbing his wrists.

"No questions," Jevén said.

"What about Resh?" Rufus said.

Jevén sheathed her knife. "Resh doesn't need your help."

"When we get back I'll marry you, Jevén," Raefer said. "I promise."

Jevén smiled and kissed Raefer on the top of the head. Then she stood and notched an arrow. "I'll guard your backs," she said. "Get moving!"

"Byron and Raefer, climb on!" Dindra said. "Rufus, ride with Shilo. We'll rearrange the horses when we're clear of here."

They mounted up and set off east. Byron peered into the woods to the south. A shadow was moving among the trees. He put in his monocle and saw a huge wolf stop and look at the group. Byron watched it turn and bound away south into the deep of the forest. As Dindra moved out, a stand of shadowy oaks blocked Byron's view. He craned his neck to see around or between and when at last they came clear of the trees, the wolf was gone.

Chapter 6

The High Road

ays passed. The mountains drew near with the star bright above them. Rufus and Raefer took turns scouting ahead and behind, going on foot to search for signs of their pursuers. The way was clear and no one was following. The group marched on beneath sunny skies by day and camped beneath vast, brilliant stars by night.

"Are you sure we're not being followed?" Dindra said as they broke camp one morning. "I have a funny feeling."

"Sure I'm sure," Rufus said, taking a sip of water. "I'm a dryad scout aren't I?"

"No," Raefer said, kicking snow over the fire.

"We're not being followed," Rufus said. "I did a full sweep before you sluggards were even awake. There's nothing back there."

Several days passed in quiet, steady marching. Shilo sat on her horse, laughing on occasion at the chirpings of the cardinal. Byron rode on Dindra's back and watched the forest go by. He spent long hours staring up at the star. Rufus and Raefer kept up their rounds of scouting and one day, as Raefer came back from a foray ahead, Dindra gave him a long, searching gaze.

Raefer frowned. "What?" he said, glancing at her sidelong. He walked along on foot, stepping high in the knee-deep snow.

"I just remembered something," Dindra said. She glanced at Rufus riding along beside her.

Raefer shrugged. "Well?"

"Something I read."

Raefer raised his eyebrows. "And?"

Dindra squinted at the brothers again. "Dryads are supposed to be ghosts."

"Ghosts?" Byron said.

"Sure," Dindra said. "You know, spirits."

"We used to be," Rufus said.

Byron gaped. "You did?"

"Well, sort of," Rufus answered. "I mean, Raefer and I never were. It was a long time ago."

Byron frowned. "What happened?"

"Well," Rufus said, "we had a queen named Parnassa. She warned the Judges when the Shadowbreather came to kill them. They escaped, or most of them did. Anyway, they rewarded her by granting her one wish. She wished that she could have a body with blood and bones."

"What's a Shadowbreather?" Byron said.

"A dragon," Raefer said. "The stories say he breathed shadows instead of flames."

Byron blinked. "Gosh."

"Why'd she wish for that?" Shilo said. "For a body, I mean."

"Because it's better having a body," Rufus said.

"You can throw snowballs," Raefer said and he pelted his brother in the back of the head.

Rufus leaped from his horse and wrestled Raefer to the ground. Everyone stopped to watch as Raefer's head disappeared into the snow. Rufus held him there until Raefer put out his hands in surrender. Rufus let him up. When Raefer stood, his face was red and wet and he was laughing.

"There are poems about her," he said, breathing hard and wiping his face. "One says she loved the trees and the birds and the mountains so much that she wanted to walk among them. Another says she was in love with a human king and wanted to marry him, so she became like him. How does that one go ... *Parnassa alata nun infarnene* ... something, something, *demneth tor belfarene* ..."

"What does it mean?" Byron asked.

"It means 'brave Parnassa ... went out to meet him in the flesh where he lived' ... something like that."

"What does *that* mean?" Byron said with a frown.

Raefer shrugged. "I don't know, but we dryads have had bodies ever since."

"Who were the Judges?" Shilo said.

"They ruled everything, long ago," Rufus said, clearing a bit of snow from the back of his neck.

Dindra pushed a branch out of her way. "What happened to them?"

"The Shadowbreather got them," Rufus said. "One by one."

Shilo frowned. "So ... who ruled after that?"

"He did," Rufus said, "the Shadowbreather. Or he tried to at least. That was the beginning of the Years of Fire."

Raefer climbed onto the horse with Rufus and the little company set off again.

"Do you know anything about the griffins?" Shilo said.

"No," Raefer said.

Rufus shook his head. "You?"

"Not much," Shilo said.

Dindra shrugged. "I've seen them in books."

Byron raised his eyebrows. "You have?"

"Of course I have," Dindra said. "You should try looking at a book now and then."

"The stories say they're horrible," Shilo said.

"Horrible how?" Byron asked.

"They can eat you with one bite," Shilo said. "They have awful claws and great, jagged beaks. And they don't like to be disturbed."

"Well," Raefer said, "the Griffin Stair is the only way over the mountains . . . unless you can fly."

"So, where's this cardinal of yours?" Rufus said.

"Looking for food," Shilo said. "He'll catch up."

"Oh, he said that did he?" Rufus said.

A frown puckered Shilo's brow. "Yes."

"Right," Rufus said with a laugh.

Shilo straightened in the saddle and put her hands on her hips. "He *did*. Here he comes now, you see?"

The cardinal swooped in and landed in a snowy pine tree. The group stopped for a rest and everyone reached for their water skins. The horses put their noses down and nibbled at the snow.

Rufus shrugged. "Ask him a question."

"No," Shilo said.

"There, you see, Raef? She can't talk to animals."

"I can too." Shilo said.

"Then do it," Rufus said. "Ask him something."

Shilo glared at Rufus. She pursed her lips and hopped down from Old Weatherby.

Rufus leaned on the pommel of his saddle. "Where are you going?"

"Just wait," Shilo said without looking at anyone. She tied Old Weatherby's reins to a tree.

"Where are you going?" Rufus demanded.

"I'm not letting you watch," Shilo said and she started off into the trees.

"But you could just make something up," Rufus said. "That doesn't prove anything."

"Give her a question to ask him," Dindra said.

"How do we find the Griffin Stair?" Raefer said.

"Good one, Raef," Rufus said with a laugh. "Go on, ask 'im!"

Shilo plodded off into the trees with the cardinal following. After a few minutes, Shilo returned. "He hasn't seen anything that looks like a stair. He said he'll have to ask a local."

"A local?" Rufus said.

Shilo nodded. "He's gone to find someone."

"This is even better than I imagined," Reafer said to Dindra. "Of course he's asking a local."

"Raefer, stop believing her," Rufus said.

Raefer shrugged. "Well, who would you ask?"

The cardinal returned and chirped at them from the snowy pine. Then he flew off. Shilo started after him. "He's found a squirrel," she said over her shoulder. "I'll be right back." A few minutes later Shilo returned. "The squirrel says he knows where the stair is, but he wants payment. Do we have any nuts?"

"I do," Dindra said, rummaging in her cloak pockets. "Here."

"Thanks," Shilo said, taking the nut. "One more thing. He won't tell me his name. He says if we get caught using his information, he never saw us before and if the word 'squirrel' even gets mentioned to anyone, he'll get even. He says squirrels have ways of getting even. Agreed?"

Everyone nodded. Rufus sat with his mouth open.

A few minutes later Shilo returned with the cardinal on her shoulder. "By the way, Rufus," she said, "you dropped your spare mittens two hours back. So much for not leaving a trail."

Rufus turned and groped in his saddlebag. "How do you know that?"

Shilo smiled at Dindra. "It's one of the things the cardinal couldn't tell me because I can't talk to animals."

"What's the cardinal's name?" Raefer said with a smile.

"It's untranslatable," Shilo said. "Any other questions?"

No one spoke.

"All right," Shilo said. "The stair isn't far. Let's go."

▣   ▣   ▣

Rocks as tall as trees littered the woods. The squirrel led them on, jumping from branch to branch following a dry streambed. The mountains drew near and the star went out of sight behind the snowy peaks. Just before sundown the streambed went to the right and disappeared into the rocks. A trail split off to the left and climbed up between two tall, pointed stones.

"This is it," Shilo said. "The squirrel has to stay the night here, Dindra. Could I give him another nut?"

"Sure," Dindra said. "Give 'im a bunch."

"Thanks. I'll be right back." Shilo disappeared behind the rocks. When they returned, the cardinal was chirping and Shilo was laughing. When Shilo saw Rufus she bit her lip to stifle a laugh, but it got out through her nose. Rufus put his hands on his hips and frowned.

"Well, now what?" Raefer said.

"We keep going," Byron said.

"It'll be dark soon," Dindra said. "Is anybody hungry?"

"It's gonna get pretty cold once the sun goes down," Raefer said.

"Well," Byron said, "we can't have a fire here in the open. Let's go on until we're out of sight of the forest."

Tall peaks surrounded them. As the companions climbed higher, cold wind fell upon them from above, blowing sand and snow before it. The great forest of the world west of the mountains disappeared and the Griffin Stair began.

The first steps were simple flat places where the trail had been terraced. Further up, they were chipped from the rock and well leveled, but rough. Still higher the steps were cleaner and sharper. The wind gathered force. To the left of the stair a sheer cliff rose up to form a wall. To the right, a deepening valley formed around the streambed, now hidden in the shadows of evening. The group labored on, heads bowed before the frigid blast.

Their faces were red and chapped with wind and the sting of icy sand as they stepped onto a balcony paved with wide, flat stones. The wind stopped. The companions dropped their packs.

"There's plenty of wood here," Dindra said, leading the horses to the shelter of the wall. "Shall we camp?"

Rufus nodded. "Let's get a fire going, Raef."

A rumble shook the ground. Everyone stopped.

"Thunder?" Byron said.

"It came from inside the mountain," Dindra said, steadying Melody and Old Weatherby.

"Will ya quit it?" Raefer said to Rufus as they crouched over the tinderbox.

"You always use too much," Rufus said.

"Just lemme do it!" Raefer said.

Soon there was smoke and flame. Before long, a tall fire was burning.

"Look at *that!*" Byron said, pointing at the wall.

"What *is* it?" Raefer said.

"A carving," Dindra said.

Byron took a branch from the fire and held it up to the wall. A great carving began where the stair stepped onto the balcony and continued on around to where the stair resumed, leading up and into darkness out of sight.

A rampant unicorn reared high and two parades of creatures marched toward it from the left and right, all dancing and leaping. There were satyrs and centaurs, humans and dryads, short, stout little human-like creatures and enormous ones as tall as trees. There were fabulous winged creatures with heads like eagles and bodies like lions. Water folk bobbed along in pools and streams, waving their arms. In the sky above the unicorn was carved a single star.

No one moved for a long time. They lingered, viewing the carving with wide eyes and open mouths. One by one they went back to the fire, until only Byron remained, holding the torch. He stayed until the light went out and then joined the others who had gathered around the fire to eat their supper, watch the stars and fall asleep.

A rumbling woke him. Byron sat up on the shaking ground. The sun was up. It threw light on the far side of the ravine but left the balcony in shadow. The fire was out. Byron shivered. The rumbling came again and another sound with it. It was a sound he knew, like crow feathers when they fly low, but much louder and . . .

What else . . . bigger?

Byron turned and before he could move or scream or even feel afraid, a pair of enormous talons plucked him off the balcony and lifted him into the air.

He looked down on the snowy world. The talons were strong as tree roots and he could not move. He saw feathers and the tips of vast beating wings. The air was terribly cold and his eyes watered.

High, snowy peaks were beneath him. The world beyond the mountains opened and he saw the star, so close he tried to reach out and touch it. His insides leaped for joy at the nearness of it. Hills and valleys rolled on and on, with forests and rivers and lakes all locked in winter's grip. A loud noise, like thunder, came from the west face of one of the mountains. A blast of dust and rock, like steam from a kettle, shot sideways into the air.

Byron's captor let out a call like a roar and a shriek both at once. The great wings shifted and the creature banked away south. The view of the spewing mountainside was replaced by a sky filled with huge winged creatures. Two were close at hand, like lions with the heads and wings and front talons of eagles. Each of them held one of his companions in its grasp. Byron saw Shilo's yellow hair and the gray-white cape of one of the brothers. The call was echoed from the cave entrances in the peaks that drew near.

"Griffins!" Byron said.

"Yes!" said his captor.

They headed for the dark opening. The griffin began a dive and fell faster and faster from the great height. The sudden swoop as they entered the darkness threatened Byron's stomach and his breath left him as he was snatched back in a sudden stop and set down upon his hooves. Byron fell to a seat on the ground, gulping for air.

As the shaking left his legs, he saw Dindra and Rufus standing together between a pair of the magnificent creatures. Byron looked up. Two enormous, beautiful eyes looked down on him. The griffin had brown feathers and a jagged, silver beak. Byron would have been afraid, but there was humor and kindness in the griffin's gaze.

Dindra galloped across the floor of the wide cave. "Byron!"

"What's going on?" Byron said.

"You have come to the aeries of Gulthenna, the Griffin Queen," said the griffin. "I for one am glad. I've always wanted to meet one of the findrel folk. Now I have not one but two! I am Cryolar and until my queen decides otherwise, you are welcome."

"Why have you brought us here, Cryolar?" Byron said.

"No one may pass the stair of the griffins without leave from the queen. You have nothing to fear, so long as you show respect and your reason for using the pass is sound. If it is, you will be allowed to continue. If not, well, the law will determine your fate. Come, I will lead you to the queen."

◈   ◈   ◈

Arched openings to the sky filled the halls with light. The passages were wide and paved with smooth white stone. Frigid wind howled through the arches. The companions bundled themselves against the awful cold, but Cryolar fanned his wings and put his face to it.

"The heights are breezy this time of year," he said.

"Breezy?" Raefer said with chattering teeth. He pulled the side of his hood down over his face and ducked his head. "Did he say breezy?"

Byron nodded. "That's what he said."

"Who built this place?" Dindra said.

"The dwarves," Cryolar said. "Long ago, for Weln Six Pinion."

"Who?" Rufus said.

"The great six-winged griffin, the mother of our race. She lived long ago. The dwarves are masters of stone and metal and were like kin to the griffins in ages passed." A rumble echoed up from far below as another blast quaked the mountains. Cryolar sighed and shook his head. "In ages *long* passed," he said.

He led them through a tall, wide passage into a vast chamber with arched portals open to the air all the way around. Sunlight and blue sky filled the place. At the far side of the chamber, a single griffin sat on a raised platform, glaring down at a young griffin who had dappled brown feathers and wings not fully strong. As Cryolar reached the place where he stopped to wait, the queen finished with the griffling who made her way toward the companions. Another griffin waited ahead of Cryolar and turned to greet him as he came up.

"Hello, Cryolar," she said. "Ah, the trespassers!"

"Passage seekers, Irolene," Cryolar said.

"We'll see," Irolene said. "Hello, Princess Quill."

"Hello, Princess Quill," Cryolar said.

Quill said nothing. She was staring with wide eyes at the visitors. Her pace slowed as she passed. She turned her head until she had to walk half sideways to look back.

"Irolene?" the queen said. "Ah, Cryolar. Why don't you both approach together, we can finish things more quickly. I need to get out and stretch my wings."

The queen eased herself down until she was lying on her side. She was enormous. Her wings, beak and talons were all golden, her fur was deep brown and her eyes were old and clear.

"Now then, Irolene," the queen said. "I hear for myself that the dwarves are still blasting. You have not persuaded them to stop, as I asked you to do. Have you at least found out why they are doing it?"

"Yes, Your Highness," Irolene said. "They are opening holes for light in the west faces of the mountains and sealing off the east-facing portals. It's an effort to gain 'relief,' as King Thrudnelf puts it, from the sight of the star."

"Madness," said the queen. "The star has driven everyone to madness. Even the king of the dwarves! Thrudnelf is a dull-witted fool but I've never known him to be afraid of anything."

"The move was counseled by the king's brother, Prince Dornthelf."

"Ah, yes," the queen said. "Dornthelf the schemer. Well, enough, we'll come back to this matter another time. Cryolar?"

"These are the visitors that were reported, Your Highness. They seek permission to pass the stair."

"Do they indeed?" the queen said. "How courteous! And whom do we have? A pair of shades from haunted Ghostwood." The queen looked at Rufus and Raefer closely. "And brothers, if not twins, by the look of you."

Rufus and Raefer straightened and glanced at each other sidelong.

"And you three, I think, are from the Woods of Deep," the queen said to Byron, Shilo and Dindra. "A pair of findrels and the daughter of a woodsman."

"Yes, Your Highness," Shilo said.

"Yes," said the queen. "You are the second band of creatures to pass this way in as many weeks, though the first to ask permission. A strange sight it was to see: a pair of grizzlebacks in company with a raccoon and a rabbit."

"Manakar!" Shilo said. "So they found a rabbit who wanted to go! They were hoping to!"

"Go? Go where?" the queen said.

"Why . . ." Shilo said. "After the star, of course . . ."

"What?" the queen said. She flapped her wings and pulled herself up straight.

"But that's what we're doing," Shilo said.

"Shilo!" Byron said. Raefer, Rufus and Byron all smacked their foreheads.

"What . . . ?" Shilo said. "I just . . . oh . . . sorry, everybody." Her shoulders sagged and she looked at the floor.

"So," the queen said. "This insanity has reached the western wood, has it? I might have known. You satyrs haven't changed, I see. I'd expect more from a centaur. You've got four hooves on the ground, after all. And what other mischief is afoot? Cryolar, send a scout. It's too long since I looked in on that part of the forest."

"I'll go myself, Your Highness."

"Good. Choose a flight party and take these truants with you. No doubt their grown folk are worried to death about them. It frightens me to anger when my daughter even mentions following the star. Here these five have gone off and *done* it!"

"Yes, Your Highness," Cryolar said. "I'll see they are all taken where they belong."

"Good," said the queen. "The next time you seek passage on my stair consider what reason you can give me for letting you. Consider it carefully."

"But Your Highness—" Byron began.

Gulthenna let out a shrieking roar that shook the columns. Cryolar and Irolene bowed low and covered their faces with their wings. The companions froze and cast down their eyes. Byron forgot to breathe.

"Not another word," the queen said. She stepped down off the platform, spread her wings and took flight out one of the arches. The wind bore her up and she was gone.

chapter 7

The Low Road

ryolar and his griffins watched with stern gazes while the companions picked up after themselves. Rufus and Racfer got snow from the rocks along the stair and cleaned the fire scar from the great paving stone. Shilo was still crying to herself as she packed her rucksack, sniffling and wiping her eyes.

"No sense crying about it now," Byron said, wiping his own tears. He frowned as he rolled up his blanket. "It's over and done with."

"I'm sorry, Byron ..." Shilo said. Her tears came stronger, but she kept working.

"You can wish me luck getting away from Ravinath again," Byron said, sniffling and shaking his head. "First the centaurs try to throw me in the ravine, then the wolves try to eat me, people from your own village hunt me down ..."

Shilo stopped packing and folded her arms. She bowed her head and began to shake from concealing her sobs.

"I should've known ..." Byron said. "I'll never get there now ..."

"All right, Byron, that's enough," Dindra said, slapping her side bag shut. She turned to face him. "This isn't Shilo's fault and you know it."

"She just blurted it out!" Byron said.

"And what were *you* going to do?" Dindra said. "Lie?"

Byron wiped his eyes and glanced at Cryolar. The griffin captain was looking at him; all the griffins were.

"Did you think you could lie to *her*?" Dindra said. She shook her head and sighed. "Look, Byron, I know how badly you want to follow the star—"

"You don't know anything," Byron said.

Raefer shrugged. "We'd never have found the stair at all if not for Shilo."

Byron glanced at Shilo. He sat down on his pack and folded his arms. "Yeah."

"I'm sorry, Byron," Shilo said. She walked over and sat down beside him.

"You didn't do anything," Byron said. He looked at the star and wiped his eyes again. Shilo put her arm around his shoulders.

"Come on, Byron," Rufus said with a laugh. "We're not finished yet. Raefer and *I* aren't stopping, are we Raef? They can take us home if they want to, but we'll get away somehow."

"That's right," Raefer said. "We'll dig a tunnel through these mountains if we have to."

"An interesting idea," Cryolar said. "But it won't be necessary."

The companions looked at him.

"The job's been done," Cryolar said.

The companions exchanged glances and frowns.

"A tunnel," Cryolar said. "I'm talking about a tunnel."

The group frown deepened.

"Under the mountains?" Cryolar pressed. "You *do* still want to *go*, don't you?"

"But you're taking us home ..." Shilo said.

"No. I'm not."

Dindra shook her head. "But we heard you tell the queen—"

"That you would all be taken where you belong," Cryolar said. "And so you shall. My friends here won't tattle. Neither will I if you won't."

"There's a tunnel under the mountain?" Byron said.

"Yes," Cryolar said.

"Where?" Dindra said.

"I'll show you."

The companions looked around at each other with bright, wide faces.

"How long will it take?" Byron said.

"Three hours of flying," Cryolar said, "and three more on the march."

"Wait," Raefer said. "What about the horses?"

"We can't take them under the mountains," Rufus said. "They'd be too scared."

"Well, we can't leave them to the wolves," Raefer said.

"You might leave them with us," Cryolar said. "As payment."

"Payment ..." Raefer said. "You mean ... to eat? No way! You're not eating our horses!"

"Well you can't take them with you," Cryolar said. "You said so yourself."

"After all," said one of the other griffins, "we *are* sticking our necks out."

"That seems fair, Raef," Byron said.

"Byron!" Raefer shouted. "That's Melody and Old Weatherby, remember? They got us here! No way. The answer is no. You take these horses somewhere safe!"

Cryolar looked around at his companions.

"Promise!" Raefer said.

"Oh, very well," Cryolar growled.

The other griffins grumbled amongst themselves.

"All right, then," Raefer said. "That's your word on it, right?"

Cryolar sighed. "Yes."

"All right then," Raefer said. "Sorry if I got a little cross there. You understand."

◈　◈　◈

They took what supplies they could from the horses and filled their own packs to brimming. The griffins took flight, circled around and swooped down on the companions one by one, bearing them up into the cold blue sky. The company soared high above the mountains. The wintry world looked very small. The woods of the west stretched on to the horizon.

"There is your home!" Cryolar called out to Byron. "The realm of the Woodland King. See your Hiding Wood and the Hidden Hills."

"I can't make it out!" Byron called. "It's very far away!"

"Not as the griffin flies!" Cryolar called.

"I wish I could fly!" Byron called.

Cryolar gave a great laugh. "You *are* flying!"

At last the whole company banked away to the west and began to descend. Soon the tops of the tallest trees were close enough to touch. Cryolar set Byron down beside the shell of an old stone house.

"You'll have to walk from here," the griffin captain said. "I still have orders to fly west today. It's another two or three hours, no more. When you reach the pine grove, keep to the left and follow the wall. You'll come to a clearing. At the back of the clearing, in the wall of the hollow, you'll find the entrance. You must beware of the tunnel. Local rumor speaks of a sentinel living there."

"What kind of sentinel?" Raefer said.

"I've never known," Cryolar said. "Good luck to you. I hope to see you again."

"Thank you, Cryolar," the companions said together.

When the griffins were gone the companions set off. A snowy trail led up into the rocks. The pine grove stood in a sort of bowl with steep sides. Keeping to the left as Cryolar had told them, they followed the curve of the bowl until they came to the clearing.

Huge rocks were scattered around. The companions crept in, ducking from tree to boulder, until they could see the tunnel. It was a tall, carved arch as black as ink.

"That's the Old Peak," Raefer whispered, pointing to a tall mountain in the distance above the tunnel. "We can see that from home."

Byron nodded. "So can we."

"Hush you two!" Rufus said with a frown.

"Who's gonna check it out?" Shilo said.

"I will," Byron said. He stepped out from behind the rock.

"Wait a second!" Rufus said. He grabbed Byron's wrist and pulled him back. "Just hold on!"

"We should all go," Dindra said. "At least as far as the entrance. We should stay together."

"Wolf tracks!" Raefer said, pointing. "They head straight inside."

Rufus gripped his chin. "We'll go around the boulder field and come at the entrance from the right. Everybody ready? Let's go!"

They followed the wolf tracks around the clearing. Nothing stirred. At the valley wall they began picking their way among the snow-bound boulders. A blast rumbled in the distance; everyone stopped and ducked for cover. For a long time no one moved. Rufus stood and watched the cave mouth.

"All clear," he said.

They pressed on.

Inside the cave mouth, they stood looking into the dark, to let their eyes adjust. Rufus squinted and peered ahead.

"I think . . ." he said. "I think there's a fire burning."

"You're right," Byron said.

Deep inside the cave, around a bend, a faint light bobbed on the rocks. Strange, faint sounds could be heard inside. Rufus took a deep breath. "All right," he said. "Here we go."

The sounds grew louder. The firelight grew brighter and danced on the roof. Soon, huge shadows stretched out behind the companions and everyone stopped at the long, hideous, unmistakable sound of a belch.

It echoed on the rock of the cave. It was so horrible and what followed was so repulsive that for years after Raefer could not bear to hear anyone belch and would leave the table irretrievably if they did. The smell in the cave had a similar effect on Dindra. In fact, no one in the group escaped that cave with their idea of manners and courtesy intact. What they saw when they rounded the bend churned their stomachs and froze their hearts.

Bones covered the cave floor and a fire burned in the middle. A young tree, torn from the ground by the roots, leaned against the cave wall. Its branches were stripped and it was chipped and battered and bloodstained. Behind it was a high, barred gate set in a passage carved from the rock. The orange light from the fire filled the chamber with dancing shadows. Seated on the ground beside the broken tree was the master of the cave.

It was like a huge man, knotted with muscle, sitting cross-legged on the ground. No clothes covered its filthy, hairy body and it had two heads. One frowned and laughed, smiling as it chewed. The other pouted and grumbled, equally intent on its meal. The pouting head leaned over and snatched a bite from the hand that fed the grinning head. It caught the fingers of the hand in its teeth and cried out from the pain of it. The grinning head cried out too, snapping and snarling at the pouting head. Then they both continued their meal. It was an uncooked, hideous mess. Several minutes passed before any of the companions realized that the brute was feasting on a hapless wolf.

Byron covered his mouth. Turning away he spotted the barred gate on the far side of the chamber. He pointed it out to Rufus, who signalled the others to slip back up the passage.

As she turned, Dindra kicked a stone. The sound of it filled the chamber. They all stopped in their tracks and looked back at the monster. It was staring right at them with both heads.

The pouting head glared at them. The grinning head looked toward them, but its eyes wandered all about, each in its own direction. The giant screamed a horrid scream with two voices and leaped to its feet.

It took up the broken tree, swinging it like a hickory switch. One head frowned and grinned. It opened its eyes wide and cackled with laughter. The other winced and turned red and began to cry. It let out a wail and fell into an angry tantrum. Both faces were still covered with the meal the brute had been devouring. It ran toward them with thundering feet.

Rufus, Byron and Dindra ran back up the tunnel. They turned expecting to see the giant close behind. The cries of the raging heads filled the darkness, but nothing came. They could hear Shilo screaming Raefer's name. Rufus looked at Byron and Dindra. His eyes were wide. He dashed back inside the cave and vanished into the darkness. Byron and Dindra followed.

Inside the cave they found Shilo huddled near the barred gate and Raefer harrying the monster with stones and bits of bone.

He kept the brute running around the fire. The giant was insane with fury and the deafening sound of its cries filled the chamber. The heads turned on one another in their frustration, biting and spitting.

Rufus joined Raefer at the fire. Together they kept the monster busy while Shilo crept from her hiding place. The monster turned and saw her. Shilo screamed.

Byron ran for the gate. The monster wheeled around and looked straight at him. It wailed with both heads and sprang forward, slashing the air with its club. Byron froze in his tracks.

Dindra galloped across the cave to Shilo. Shilo leaped onto her back and they fled. Rufus caught the monster's attention with a piece of charred bone to the wailing face and Byron had a chance to run. The giant was confused for a moment, looking at Byron and the brothers as they scurried around. They all ran up the passage behind Dindra and Shilo. Rufus and Raefer hurried out into the sunshine of the clearing. Byron stopped and looked back.

"Byron!" Raefer shouted from the clearing. "Come on!"

Byron didn't move. Shilo and Dindra shouted to him from the rocks. Everyone watched. The cries of the monster rang from the tunnel and a thick shadow appeared in the darkness. The monster emerged. Byron took a deep breath and bolted forward, running between the filthy, hairy legs into the darkness of the tunnel.

The giant looked down and all around with both heads, lifting its feet and twisting backward as it screamed and growled with a howling that filled the valley. The heads bit and spit at each other as it turned and charged back down the tunnel.

Byron ran across the bone-strewn cave. He reached the gate and gripped it with shaking hands. Light from the fire danced on the floor of the tunnel beyond and shadows from the bars stretched away into the dark.

A blaring, two-voiced cry filled the chamber. Byron wheeled around and pressed his back to the bars. The monster charged across the cave, leaping the fire with a stride, lifting its club high. The ground shook as it came. Byron's whole body quivered. He stood paralyzed, watching the monster draw near. It appeared from the lapping flames like a nightmare.

Byron stared at the two horrid faces, one mad with cruel anger, the other wild with sinister glee. The gnarled, bloodied club rose high in the air as the brute prepared to strike. Byron turned and grabbed the bars, screaming with all the breath he had. When he could scream no more he stopped and there was silence. Byron blinked and turned around.

It was standing still with a strange look on both its faces. Its eyes went dull and the heads wobbled. The laughing head had a half grin that twitched at the corner of its eye. The wailing head gave a kind of snort. The monster stepped back and staggered a little, letting go of the club. Beyond the fire, Byron saw his companions watching from the entrance to the chamber.

"How much did you use?" Raefer said.

"All of it," Rufus said.

It swayed. It teetered back and forth from its heels to its toes. It leaned forward and its shadow stretched across Byron, who lifted his arms to ward it away. Then it leaned back again and kept on leaning. The two-headed giant fell, straight as a plank. A great, bone-crunching thud sent dust high into the air. Rufus, Raefer, Dindra and Shilo gathered in stunned silence around it where it lay.

"Here it is," Shilo said. She bent down and picked up a curved twig about a foot long, sharpened to a point.

"Is it still good?" Raefer said.

Rufus nodded. "Think so."

"That was some shot, Rufus," Dindra said. "Way to go."

"And it had to be in the neck," Raefer said. "With a creature this size. So . . . we don't have any sleep juice left?"

"Not a drop," Rufus said.

Shilo stared at the creature. She put her hand over her nose and mouth. "Well," she said. "It was worth it."

Byron crept up and peered out from behind the safety of his friends. His eyes were wide and he was still breathing in great heaves. He looked at the club that lay near the monster's open hand. It was at least three times his own size.

"We should make more," Raefer said.

Rufus shrugged. "How? We'll never find any moratene this time of year."

"I could ask a bird or something," Shilo said.

"I know you could, Shi," Rufus said. "But it has to be fresh, just picked. Moratene only blooms in the summer."

"It almost got me," Byron said. "It almost did."

"What'd you mean running back in here like that?" Dindra said.

"I . . ." Byron began. "I dunno, Din."

"Never mind," Shilo said. "Let's get going before it wakes up."

"And don't forget the wolves," Dindra said. "There must be more around than just the one poor thing he caught."

"Poor thing?" Rufus said. "Are you forgetting your night in the woods?"

"I haven't forgotten," Dindra said folding her arms before her.

Rufus shrugged. "Well, let's see about that tunnel."

Chapter 8

A Fork In the Road

Byron shook the rusty bars. "The lousy thing is locked!"

A hollow was clawed away beneath the gate. Bloodied fur stuck to the rusted bottom rail. Shilo crouched and peered into the darkness.

"So, the wolves have gone through," she said.

"What'll we do?" Raefer said.

Dindra shrugged. "The rest of you can fit under the gate."

"But you can't," Byron said.

Rufus nodded. "We have to get it open."

Shilo frowned. "Wait a minute ..." She started snooping around the cave.

"What are you looking for?" Dindra said.

"The treasure trove."

"The what?" Rufus said.

"This thing is an ettin. My dadda told me about them. Ettins hide treasure."

Rufus and Raefer glanced at each other with their eyebrows up. "We'll help you look!"

At the end of a dead end passage was an old, rusted cauldron covered with a rotted animal skin. It was filled with all sorts of things: a broken, rusted hunting knife, a bent, twisted cartwheel, a tangle of barbed wire. There were bottles and broken pots, several horseshoes and a lot of stuff no one could recognize.

"What kind of treasure trove is *this*?" Byron said.

Shilo shook her head. "I guess ettins aren't very bright."

"There's a box over here," Rufus said from the shadows. "Bring a torch."

A small iron chest was hidden in the darkness near the wall. It was attached to a heavy chain, which was bound to a ring set in the stone floor. In the lock of the chest there was a rusted key with a ring full of other keys hanging from it. Rufus tried to turn it, but the key was stuck fast.

"I'll bet that old ettin doesn't even know it's here," Dindra said.

"He'd get it open," Raefer said. "Key or no key."

Byron nodded. "We could use him right now, to pull that gate off."

"Wait a second!" Rufus said. He lifted the keys dangling from the ring and looked around at the others. One by one their faces lit up.

"Get it out!" Dindra said.

Rufus wiggled the key side to side, up and down. He nodded to Raefer who crouched and pressed his shoulder against the front of the box. Rufus set the bottoms of his feet just below the latch and gripped the key with both hands.

Raefer pushed and Rufus pulled. They both grit their teeth, grunting and groaning. The key came loose with a loud snap. Rufus hit himself in the face with both fists and rolled over backwards. Raefer flew over the lid of the chest, toppling it as he went. It burst open and lay on its side. The brothers rolled around on the ground moaning and clutching their injured parts. Dindra, Shilo and Byron looked inside the chest.

"A map!" Shilo said, unfolding a large parchment.

Dindra lowered her torch and read. " 'The Raven's Gate Passage.' "

Rufus stood and looked over Shilo's shoulder, still rubbing his nose. Raefer appeared out of the shadows behind the box. "A map of the tunnels?" he said.

"Looks like it," Dindra said. "All sorts of passages." She peered closer and read: " 'To Durfellen's Web,' 'To the Pargan Circuit.' "

"Some go off the edge," Rufus said. "They must go to other phases of the mine."

Dindra nodded. "This map is part of a series."

"Does it go all the way through?" Rufus said.

Dindra squinted. "Seems to. It looks like we're standing in the main shaft. All these others are offshoots heading deeper down."

Shilo pointed to one of the offshoots. "I don't like the sound of this one."

" 'The Fire Warrens,' " Dindra read. "Wonder where it goes . . ."

"Let's not find out," Byron said.

Raefer stooped to look at the key ring in Rufus's hand. "It broke off in the lock."

"The key!" Shilo said, folding up the map.

Rufus jangled the ring at his friends and headed for the gate. "Come on!" he said and everyone followed.

Shilo tucked the map in her pouch. They waited at the gate while Rufus tried the first of a half dozen keys. It fit, but not quite and he spent a moment trying to make it work.

"Try another," Dindra said.

Rufus let the key fall to one side.

"Keep track," Shilo said. "They all look alike."

"I know what I'm doing," Rufus said.

Byron turned and frowned in the direction of the cave mouth. "What's wrong?" Reafer said.

"Thought I heard something," Byron said. "I'll be right back." He headed for the tunnel entrance.

"Be careful," Shilo said to Rufus.

"Don't break it off in the lock!" Raefer said.

"I know what I'm doing," Rufus said. "Dang! Which one was next?"

Byron headed up the tunnel. When he came in view of the cave mouth, he peered out into the late afternoon daylight from the concealment of the shadows. Nine centaurs were lurking by the mouth of the cave, listening and peering in. Byron turned and bolted into the chamber.

"Centaurs!" he hissed. "In the clearing!"

"No!" Shilo said.

"Keep going, Rufus!" Dindra said.

Rufus fumbled with the keys. "Help me keep track or we're done for!"

Byron ran back and forth checking on the progress. Three of the centaurs trotted into the darkness of the tunnel. Byron crept back in, quiet as he could. He waved his arms, jumping up and down. "They're coming!" he said as loud as he dared.

"Three more . . ." Rufus said in a trembling voice.

"Steady," Dindra said. "Keep working to the left . . ."

"They're coming!" Byron hissed.

"We know!" the others said together.

Rufus tried another key. It fit but didn't turn. He wiggled it and tried to get it to go.

"Move on!" Shilo said.

"I know what I'm *doing*!" Rufus said.

"Last one . . ." Dindra said.

Byron turned and hollered as loud as he could with a kind of growling howl into the tunnel. He looked back to see Rufus jump and hit his head on the bars. The cave entrance echoed with the sounds of centaurs retreating back out the passageway. "Hurry up!" Byron said. "That won't work twice."

"Get back in there!" shouted an angry voice from outside the tunnel.

"There's something down there!" came another voice.

"Never mind," the first voice growled. "I'll go myself." The sound of charging hooves filled the chamber.

"Give me the keys!" Dindra said, snatching the ring from Rufus's hand. "There!"

Byron heard the lock come free with a dull clack. There was a loud creak as the gate swung open.

"Byron, come on!" Dindra said as Rufus and Shilo went through the gate.

"Come on, Byron!" Raefer said, close on their heels.

Dindra held the gate for Raefer and stepped in after him, waving at Byron to hurry. Byron ran across the cave and followed them in, pulling the gate shut behind him.

"Byron!" Dindra whispered from the darkness ahead.

"I'm right behind you!" he said. The sound of her hooves rang in the passage as she and Raefer pressed on. Byron ran after them as fast as he dared, groping ahead with his hands, blind in the darkness before him. Then he stopped.

"The keys!" he said. He called to the others with a loud whisper. "The keys are still in the gate!"

Dindra and Raefer didn't stop. Byron looked back and forth in the darkness, then ran back to the entrance.

Centaurs prowled the cave. Byron paused. Then he took up a handful of loose, sandy dirt from the floor. Keeping to the shadows, he reached the other hand through the bars. The keys were hanging in the lock and he took hold of them, gritting his teeth in his efforts at silence.

A huge hand seized him by the arm.

The keys fell to the ground outside the gate.

From the side of the entrance stepped a tall centaur with terrible markings on his face and chest. He wore a heavy net slung over his huge shoulder and grinned down at Byron with wild eyes.

"Baruwan," Byron said, wincing from the pain of the centaur's grip. "Dindra! Raefer! Help!"

And someone answered.

"Raefer!" shouted a voice.

Byron looked into the dark of the tunnel where Raefer had gone. Baruwan turned toward the entrance of the cave.

"Raefer Nimbletwig!" shouted the voice again.

"Rifkin?" Byron said. "Rifkin!"

Baruwan turned to face Byron again. Byron took the fistful of sandy dirt and flung it into the centaur's face. Baruwan hollered and snapped his head back, covering his eyes. He let go of Byron's arm and Byron collapsed to the ground. A group of dryads came running into the cave through the entrance. The centaurs turned at once and engaged them. Rifkin dashed in with a bent bow, fired an arrow into the centaur charge and drew his sword. Then Byron's gaze fell to the ground outside the gate.

"The keys!" he said and he jumped to his hooves to reach through the rusty bars.

Baruwan stretched out his hand. Byron lunged forward and took hold of the key ring just as Baruwan reached it. They plucked it from each other's grasp and the keys fell to the ground again.

Baruwan cut his free hand on the bars as he forced it through to grab Byron. Byron dropped low for the keys. Baruwan caught hold of the monocle strap and gave a tug. Byron winced and choked as his head hit the gate. He clutched the keys and tried twice to pull them in but the ring was too big to fit through the bars. With his free hand he unsheathed Gradda's knife and cut through the leather strap that held the monocle.

Baruwan pulled the monocle through the bars and looked at it. He threw it to the ground and nearly stepped on it as he came up and put his face to the gate to stare at Byron. "Unlock this door, little one," he said through gritted teeth.

"Yaaaah!" Byron cried and threw the knife at Baruwan. It struck the bars with clang, just as Baruwan pulled his face away. The huge centaur staggered back with a growl. Byron turned and ran into the darkness, not caring to fend with his hands. Twenty paces in he dropped the keys. He came to a turn and then another, not pausing to note how he'd gone. Soon he was lost. Byron stopped and listened. All was quiet. Even the sounds of fighting died away. Byron slid himself down the tunnel wall to the cold stone of the floor. He hugged his arms around himself and sat there staring into the darkness.

◈　◈　◈

"Is it too low for you, Dindra?" Raefer said. "I heard you hit your head back there."

"I'll manage. Where are Rufus and Shilo?"

Raefer shook his head. "Did we pass any turns, so far?"

"I can't tell in this dark," Dindra said. "I didn't feel any."

"We never should've run off like this," Raefer said, crouching to spark his tinder.

"What choice did we have?" Dindra said.

Raefer lit the torch from his smoldering tinder and held it up. "Where's Byron?"

Dindra looked back up the tunnel. "I thought he was behind us."

"He was," Raefer said. "He called out to us, remember?"

"Byron!" Dindra called. Her voice echoed and died away. She called again. There was no reply. "How long will it take Baruwan to force that gate open?"

"Not very, I'd say," Raefer said. "Should we go back?"

Dindra sighed and shook her head. "Could we even find our way?"

"Maybe, as long as we don't turn anywhere."

"How do we know we didn't already?"

"Well, do we just keep going?" Raefer said.

"No, we have to go back," Dindra said. "But we have to be quiet."

Reafer held up the torch. "All right, then," he said with a nod.

They crept along quick and quiet. Raefer whispered his amazement at how silent Dindra kept her hooves on the stone of the tunnel floor. "I'm not a horse, you know," she said, shaking her head. After what seemed a very long march, they heard a rattling sound from the darkness ahead.

"That's the gate!" Raefer whispered.

"Snuff the torch!" Dindra said.

There was a loud clang and then voices. A moment later there were hooves clopping in the tunnel. Dim torchlight appeared in the distance.

"Centaurs . . ." Dindra whispered in Raefer's ear. They clasped hands, held their breath and listened.

◈   ◈   ◈

Shilo turned. "Did you hear something, Dindra? Din—? Raefer? Byron? Rufus stop!"

"What? Why?"

"They're not back there. None of them."

Rufus turned. "Were they with us at the turn?"

"I don't remember a turn. I've just been following the sound of your feet. I heard them, then you started getting ahead and . . ."

"But Raefer was right there when we left the gate."

"We have to go back."

"We sure do."

"Do you remember the way?"

"I think so," Rufus said as he knelt to spark a torch. "A little light won't hurt." He waved the torch into the tunnel where he had been headed. Then he waved it behind and sighed. "All right, then," he said. "Let's go."

Jogging along on tiptoe they made their way back up the tunnel as they had come. Shilo clutched Rufus by the arm.

"Listen!" she said.

From the darkness ahead came a faint rattling sound.

"The gate," Rufus said.

"Snuff the torch!" Shilo said.

There was a loud clang and then voices. A moment later there were hooves clopping in the tunnel. Dim torchlight appeared in the distance.

"Centaurs," Shilo whispered in Rufus's ear. They clasped hands, held their breath and listened.

"Which way now?" said a voice.

"Who knows?" another voice replied.

"We'll never track them in here. These tunnels could go on for miles."

"The little snakes have a hole to hide in," said a single, cold voice.

"We could split up."

"No. I don't like the air in here," said the cold voice. "And there is said to be a shadow under the Old Mountain. I won't go staggering about blind in this maze."

"We could go to the dwarves. They're a lean-witted brood, but they made these tunnels long ago."

"Curse the griffins. We could be waiting on the other side right now if not for their arrogant laws."

"Never mind," said the cold voice. "We'll find some other way."

Clopping hooves receded up the tunnel and the torchlight faded.

Shilo started to move but Rufus restrained her and covered her mouth. From the place where the centaurs had been came the sound of a single hoof falling to the stone. Shilo froze and took a stifled gasp.

"Go then, little snakes," said the cold voice. "I'll wait for you beyond the mountains where nothing can save you. I'll catch you in my net and drag you screaming before Ravinath. Then you'll learn what it *is* to scream."

For a moment there was silence. Then the centaur turned and clopped away toward the gate.

Rufus and Shilo held still. The faint sound of voices calling out echoed down to them from the ettin's chamber. Then it was quiet again. They crept on tiptoe back down the way they had come and kept on for a long time before they dared to light a torch, or speak, or even stop moving.

Rufus dug out his tinderbox. His hands appeared in small flashes as he began to spark his torch.

"Well, we know they got away," Shilo said.

"We'll just have to hope they make it," Rufus said. He lit the torch and held it up. "And that we do."

Shilo opened the map. "Let's see ... that was a three-way fork back there, where the centaurs were."

"Well, we took the way to the right," Rufus said.

"Are you sure?"

"Sure I'm sure. I had my hand to the wall the whole time."

"All right, then," Shilo said. "We're in the main shaft. The middle one goes ... 'To Mushroom Forest ...'"

Rufus shifted the torch. "What about the left one?"

"The left one ... Oh! The Fire Warrens, I hope nobody went down there."

Rufus pursed his lips and shook his head. "Well, let's get moving. I don't like the air in here any more than that centaur did."

Raefer started to move but Dindra grabbed him. She covered his mouth with her hand and he fought her. From the place where the centaurs had been came the sound of a single hoof falling to the stone. Raefer froze in Dindra's grip and they both held very still.

"Go then, little snakes," said the cold voice. "I'll wait for you beyond the mountains where nothing can save you. I'll catch you in my net and drag you screaming before Ravinath. Then you'll learn what it *is* to scream."

For a moment there was silence. Then the centaur turned and clopped away toward the gate. Dindra did not release her hold on Raefer. The faint sound of voices calling out echoed down to them from the ettin's chamber. Then it was quiet again.

At last Dindra relaxed and let Raefer go, but even then they stood for a long time in utter silence.

"So, they got away," Raefer said at last.

Dindra shook her head. "But what about Byron?"

Raefer said nothing.

"Come on," Dindra said and she set off toward the gate.

"Where are you going?" Raefer said. "Are you out of your mind?"

Dindra kept walking. "If I was do you think I'd know it?"

Raefer let his shoulders sag. He stood in the darkness, fidgeting. "Well, let me light a torch at least!" He spent a moment with his tinderbox, lit the torch and set off to follow.

"What's this?" Dindra said as they came in sight of the gate.

"The keys," Raefer said, stooping to pick up the ring.

"Come on," Dindra said and she continued up the passage.

The gate was shut and locked. The ettin lay still by the dying fire inside the cave. Dindra and Raefer peered through the bars.

"Byron's knife," Raefer said, stooping to the ground. "And there's his monocle. D'you think they caught him?"

"Byron doesn't get caught," Dindra said. "But I'd say he had a close call. I'll bet you anything he came back to take the keys from the lock, to keep the centaurs from following. It had to be him who dropped them back there."

Raefer gripped his chin. "So he got away, but left his things."

"He was running for it. And now he's alone, down those tunnels somewhere."

Raefer shrugged. "Maybe he found Rufus and Shilo."

"Maybe," Dindra said. She put Byron's knife and monocle into her sidebag. "We'll keep these until ... well, we'll just keep them."

In the firelight they saw the three-way fork in the tunnel. Raefer thrust the torch into each of the openings.

"Which one?" he said.

"The middle one," Dindra said.

Raefer stepped forward and raised the torch. The shadows fled before them and the two companions set off into the mountain.

CHAPTER 9
Outlaws

ufus and Shilo walked for hours. They came to a small spring running in glistening sheets down the wall of the tunnel. Rufus traded his torch for Shilo's water skin and filled it. They shared the last of his water between them and he filled his skin also. Shilo held the torch and looked at the map.

"It's very accurate," she said. "We haven't passed a single turn that wasn't marked."

Rufus wiped his mouth on his sleeve. "Is this spring on there?"

"Mm-hm, look."

"What's this next thing?" he said, peering close. "Tharrow-fend ... what does that mean?"

"We'll find out soon enough, I suppose," Shilo said, folding the map. "I wonder how long it is to the end."

Torchlight filled the chips and ridges left by the picks and chisels of the dwarves. The air was cool and damp. An hour's march brought them to an enormous face carved into the wall. It reached from the floor to the ceiling and had long hair bound by a diadem set on its heavy forehead. Thick, bushy eyebrows shadowed the large, deep eyes. A great beard and mustache spread down onto the floor.

Rufus touched the rough stone. "He doesn't look so lean-witted."

"Anything but," Shilo said. "He looks ... wise."

"Do you think this is Tharrowfend?"

"I bet so," Shilo said. "Must've been a king."

Rufus and Shilo burrowed deep into the dense maze of tunnels. The walls were carved in places; creatures, spirals, interlocking circles and grids adorned the passages. They came to a square chamber, wider and taller than the tunnel. Three other tunnels joined it and the walls were carved with intricate scenes.

A tall alcove was cut into the wall. The floor of the alcove was recessed into a deep basin. On the back wall of the alcove was cut in relief the shape of a tall, jagged mountain.

At the top of the mountain a great flame was carved. Just beneath the flame, from a crack in the rock, a heavy trickle of water seeped out and flowed down, glistening into the basin. The water came to the very top, but did not flow over. It went out through some unseen way, back into the stone of the mountain.

"I wonder what the fire means," Shilo said.

Rufus shrugged. "What makes you think it means something?"

"Any fool can see it means something," said a husky voice.

A small flame appeared in one of the adjoining tunnels and into the chamber stepped a short, broad-shouldered man with a thick beard and a frowning brow. He wore a leather apron, heavy boots and gloves and a flat leather cap with a burning candle fixed to a mirror on the front. He held a pickax across his shoulder, which he swung down to the ground to lean on.

"Well," he said, "I knew such folk as you existed in the world, but never did I think to find 'em here." His voice was friendly, but he frowned at them.

"A dwarf . . ." Shilo said.

"I can see he's a dwarf," Rufus said, nodding and smiling at the stranger.

"That's what I am," the dwarf said. "You'll want to keep your voices down. If the prince finds you here he'll fork trouble over you like bad straw."

Rufus and Shilo glanced at each other.

"Of course, the same could be said of me. I suppose that makes us friends. My name is Thrym."

Shilo smiled. "I'm Shilo."

"Rufus."

"Pleased to meet you both," Thrym said. "If you wouldn't mind, the patrols come here pretty regular for water and talk. Follow me."

Thrym went down the same way Shilo and Rufus had come. They watched him go and stood frowning after him. The light from Thrym's candle glowed on the wall of the tunnel.

"Stay if you want to," he said from around the bend, "but you'll be caught. I'm going where it's safe. You're standing where it's dangerous."

Shilo and Rufus listened to Thrym's footsteps fading. The light vanished. Shilo turned to the fountain, filled her water skin, corked it and followed the dwarf. Rufus opened his mouth and closed it again. Then he set off behind her.

"It's not my business, you being down here in the Crypt," Thrym said, taking hold of a metal ring set into the wall, "but how you got here is a matter that concerns me." He gave the ring a turn and a hidden door slid open without a sound.

Rufus and Shilo looked at each other.

"Now, now, you just suit yourselves," the dwarf said, stepping through the door, "but if I wanted to hurt you I could've done it back there at the fountain or anywhere along the way. All I'd need is these."

Thrym held up his hands. They were large and gnarled and strong as stone. Shilo nodded. She and Rufus followed Thrym into the chamber and told him everything.

"So your friends are wandering around the Crypt without a map," Thrym said, clutching his beard. "That's not good. Well, you've told me how you got here. Would you mind explaining why you came?"

Rufus put his hands behind his back and shifted his weight from one foot to the other. Shilo looked at the wall.

"Some kind of trouble?" Thrym said.

"Well ..." Rufus said.

"We should tell him," Shilo said. "He's nice enough."

A smile twinkled in the corners of Thrym's eyes.

"We're following the star," Rufus said.

Thrym nodded his head but the twinkle went away. He sighed. "I see. I might've known it. That blasted star."

"What's so bad about it?" Shilo said.

"Well, it hasn't helped me any. It's because of that star that I've been declared an outlaw."

"An outlaw?" Rufus said.

"That's right." Thrym sighed again and paced the floor. "Remember that fountain? That was the likeness of Rathrágodrak, the Old Mountain." He looked up at the ceiling. "Above us now, visible from every corner of Everándon."

"Everándon?" Shilo said.

"The lost country?" Rufus said.

"Nothing lost about it," Thrym said. "If you can see that mountain, it means you're standing on Everándish soil. And long ago, it meant you could see the Balefire."

"The Balefire," Rufus said. "The fire in the carving?"

"A magic fire," Thrym said with a nod. "It burned day and night, for everyone to see. But it was stolen away."

"Stolen away where?" Shilo said.

"That's what I'm trying to find out. Seventy years now I've been searching, excavating the trail of king Thárrowfend."

Shilo lifted the map. "The carving!"

"Thárrowfend was a great king," Thrym said. "Maybe the last. He went looking for the Balefire. He cut most of these tunnels in his search. He was lost, went down into the Fire Warrens and never came back. Since then it's been unlawful to come down here at all, never mind carrying on the search."

"What happened?" Shilo said. "To Thárrowfend, I mean."

Thrym shrugged. "Nobody ever knew. Some say he found Jargadda."

"What's Jargadda?" Shilo said.

"A vast and ancient system of tunnels, all gold and gems. The digging is hard and never-ending. It's where we go when we die, or while we're alive, if we're very lucky. Some think Tharrowfend found the Balefire and it was so beautiful he didn't want to come back. I don't believe it. He'd've come back for sure. I think trolls got him, or gnomes. Whatever happened, he was lost. The tunnels were sealed off and to go there has been forbidden ever since. They came to be known as Thárrowfend's Crypt."

"Trolls?" Shilo said.

Thrym shook his head. "I've never seen one down here. But the gnomes are real enough."

"I don't understand," Rufus said. "What's all this got to do with the star?"

"Once the star appeared, there were whispers about following it, what with the tale of Silverlance and all. Prince Dornthelf got scared, some old prophecy about doom and darkness. He convinced his brother, King Thrudnelf, to start sealing off the east-facing portals in the mountains above. Some youngsters were caught trying to make their way out through the upper tunnels of the Crypt, off to follow the star. After that Dornthelf sent patrols down inside. They found my journals and maps."

"Now you're an outlaw," Rufus said.

"They'll never catch me. I know these tunnels blindfolded."

Shilo shook her head. "Is Silverlance really real?"

Thrym nodded. "I'd say so, real as rock. It's said that when he comes, he'll claim all thrones for himself. I think that's the real reason Dornthelf is nervous. Nobody wants to give up their throne, however small it might be. Yes, indeed, that star marks the start of great and terrible days, if you believe that sort of thing."

Shilo folded her arms. "Silverlance must be very strong."

Thrym nodded. "He's still king in Everándon. Make no mistake. There are some who've never thought otherwise, some who'd be willing to fight to see he gets his crown back."

"Like you, maybe?" Rufus said.

Thrym shrugged his massive shoulders. "Let's just say I'd rather see the mountains torn down than pretend a thing isn't there that is."

"Well, nobody's fighting yet," Shilo said. "Will you show us the way out of here?"

"I will. That map shows you the long way. It'll get you there, but it would take days. I'll have you to Great Cave in ten or twelve hours."

"Thrym," Shilo said. "Will you keep an eye out for our friends?"

"I'll do that, too. And I'll spread the word."

"To whom?" Rufus said.

Thrym smiled. "There are others who share my . . . interest in these tunnels. There's a good chance we'll find your friends. That is if they didn't end up in the Fire Warrens. But let's get moving. I've got work to do."

⬧　⬧　⬧

They spoke little during the torchlit march. Thrym whispered to them of the carvings and arches they passed. There were fountains and alcoves with benches, stairs and ramps and columns hewn from the stone.

"The old mastery had faded by the time this project was begun," he told them. "After Thárrowfend was lost the pride just went out of it. His daughter, Queen Fulda, turned to other matters, started playing it safe where tunneling was concerned. The craft went into decline and never recovered. The Griffin Stair is a monument, of course, but the finest work, the very best, is said to be at Dwarvenhearth, wherever that is, made by the dwarves of yore, when Weln was queen of the griffins."

Thrym stopped at the top of a wide stair. He cocked his head and listened into the darkness that swallowed the steps. Nothing stirred. He nodded and pointed with his thumb.

"There's your way out," he said. "Down those steps and into the Great Cave. You're just in time for sunrise. Once you're out, head north. Look for Hixima. She'll help you. Keep a clear watch for giants. Good luck. I hope you don't get killed."

Thrym turned and walked back into the tunnel. Rufus and Shilo watched his light vanish around the bend. The sound of his steps faded. Thrym was gone.

At the bottom of the stair was a high ledge in the back of an enormous cave. A narrow stair led down to the floor of the cave, where huge mineral columns reached up to the ceiling. At the cave mouth, they stood and looked out. The star shone clear and below it the sun was rising on a wide, snowy valley that glittered with morning.

❖ ❖ ❖

Raefer crouched beside his tinderbox, blowing on it. "We can't put the torch out every time you think you hear something," he said as an orange glow appeared.

"I *did* hear something," Dindra said.

"I'm sure you did," Raefer said. "I didn't mean it that way. It's just I'm almost out of tinder."

"I swear I heard a pot clang."

"The echoes are funny in here," Raefer said. A small flame sprang up in the tinderbox and he reached for the torch. "I just wish we could be sure before we go snuffing ... hey!"

Dindra kicked the tinder box and the dim light vanished.

"Fmmmph!" Raefer said as Dindra clamped her hand across his mouth.

"Quiet!" she whispered. "Look!"

Torchlight flickered in the tunnel head. Dindra hauled Raefer to his feet and they backed away into a side passage. Heavy feet drew near.

A short, broad fellow stopped at the opening to the side passage where Raefer and Dindra were hidden. He wore heavy boots and gloves and a studded leather jerkin. On his head he wore a flat cap with a candle fixed to a mirror on the front. On his back he carried a pack as big as himself with pots and pans and all sorts of things dangling from it. He touched his chin with his finger and frowned.

"Dang," he said. "Which way was it?"

He turned and took three steps up the tunnel where Dindra and Raefer stood watching. They both held their breath as the light of the candle fell upon them. The young dwarf was frowning and never looked up. He put up one finger as if making a point.

"Ah, yes!" he said, still looking at the ground. He turned and went back the way he'd come.

Dindra and Raefer exhaled together. They listened for a moment. The pots clanged and rattled and the sounds faded into the tunnels.

"Follow him!" Raefer whispered. "He's getting away!"

They hurried after the dwarf as the light from his candle vanished around bend after bend. The pace quickened until at last they rounded a turn and found total darkness. They took hold of each other's forearm and pressed ahead. After twenty paces, Dindra stopped.

"This is useless," she said. "We've lost him."

"Well, now *we're* lost for sure," Raefer said. "Should we light a torch?"

"Good idea," said a voice and the passage appeared in bobbing light.

From an alcove in the wall stepped the dwarf. In one hand he held a small round shield with a spike in the middle. In the other he held a short, broad sword.

Raefer looked at the candle on the fellow's cap. "How'd you get that lit so fast?"

"Never mind that," the dwarf said. "Tell me who you are and why you're following me—a pair of law breakers, I'll wager, come here to hide. Well, you're not gonna rob *me* anytime soon."

"Rob you?" Raefer said.

"Sure, only you saw that I was too much for you and you wanted to sneak up behind. But I was too smart."

Dindra laughed. "Too much for us? You?"

"That's right. Besides, if you're not law breakers and fugitives, why are they searching for you?"

"Who?" Dindra said.

"Others, like you," the dwarf said, pointing at Dindra with his chin. "Only different. These fellows were all marked up with paint."

"Baruwan," Dindra said.

Raefer nodded. "You've seen them?"

"No," the dwarf said. "I only heard about 'em. A griffin embassy came to my father's hall and the subject came up. These friends of yours tried to cross on the Griffin Stair. The griffins turned 'em away. The ambassador said they had spears and nets."

"They're not our friends," Raefer said.

"So, you *are* running," the dwarf said.

"Anyone with half their wits would run from Baruwan," Dindra said. "Oh, all right then, you might as well know. We're following the star."

"So am I!" the dwarf shouted and the tunnels rang. His eyes brightened and he smiled wide, opening his arms. He glanced at his sword. "Oh, uh, sorry about that," he said and he sheathed it. Then he hung the buckler on the side of his pack and opened his arms again. "So you really *are* outlaws. If my father knew you were here he'd pop an eyeball. Well, I'm an outlaw, too. Or I will be when they find my note. My name is Nosh, pleased to meet you."

"Dindra."

"Raefer."

Nosh shook their hands and Raefer winced from the strength of the young dwarf's grip.

"Well, it's good to have companions," Nosh said. He slapped Raefer on the back and the dryad staggered forward. "Three is better than one or two. Plus, I know the way out of here. You're not lost anymore, right?"

Raefer winced and tried to smile. "Right."

Nosh smiled wide. "All we need to do is find Hixima."

"Hixima?" Dindra said.

"The Warra priestess … lives in a hidden dell north of the Old Mountain. She knows spells and things and reads the planets. Word is she'll protect us. Let me have those torches."

Nosh turned away from his new friends and crouched down to the ground. Raefer stepped up behind him and peered over the top of Nosh's pack. Nosh saw him and hunched down low over his work. "Quit lookin', will ya?" he said.

Raefer shrugged. "Sorry."

Shadows fled into the tunnel as Nosh lit the torches. He stood up and handed them to Dindra and Raefer.

"I sure like that hat you're wearing," Raefer said.

"I've got an extra in my pack you can have, but I'm not digging it out now."

"Who's your father, anyway?" Dindra said.

"Thrudnelf, Dwarven King," Nosh said. "All right, then. Follow me."

It was cold beneath the mountains and there was a constant dripping sound. They came to knee-deep water and Nosh just stomped through it as though he had not seen it. Dindra shrugged at Raefer and trotted through after. Raefer shook his head and sat down on the ground to take off his boots. Nosh only laughed at Raefer's loud complaints of frigid water and sharp stones.

"I could've told you that," Nosh said. "That's why I left my boots on." He turned and sloshed away into the tunnel.

There was a musty smell in the air and the tunnels were shiny with seeping water. Small patches of fungus grew on the craggy, jagged walls and ceiling. Clusters of capped mushrooms sprouted among the rocks on the floor.

First the mushrooms were small and ordinary. Soon they were ankle deep and Raefer marveled to Dindra about their size. After a time the mushrooms were knee deep, then waist deep, shoulder high and so it went until at last the group was walking beneath the caps of enormous mushrooms the size of trees. Dindra and Raefer gazed up and around, amazed at the vastness of the chamber they were walking in.

"It doesn't have a ceiling," Raefer said. "It has a sky!"

"No one knows how far the system goes," Nosh said. "There aren't any maps."

"Can you eat the mushrooms?" Dindra said.

"The big ones are too tough," Nosh said. "Can't cut 'em with a hatchet. Some of the smaller ones'll kill ya. But some you can eat. I can never remember which."

There were mushrooms of all sizes and shapes and colors. Some had tall caps and narrow stems, others were thick-stemmed with wide, flat, ruffly caps. Some had one cap with many stems, others had one stem with four or five caps. Some were glowing with green or red or blue light. Some wiggled and retracted as the torches passed by. Some made popping sounds, others whistled or hummed. High above, patches of glowing fungus blotched the walls and ceiling of the cave.

"It looks like stars," Raefer whispered.

Cave after cave full of mushrooms went by. In one, a wide stream flowed through. In another, a waterfall rushed down to a lake with patches of glowing, bulbous toadstool things floating on it.

"Keep your eyes open for boats on the lake," Nosh said. "The gnomes like to spearfish sometimes."

"Are they dangerous?" Raefer said.

"Nah, just a nuisance," Nosh said. "But this is their territory. We, uh, really should have permission to be here."

"And we don't," Raefer said.

"Heck, no. It's a big deal to get permission. You need all sorts of papers and agreements. My father would have found out for sure."

"What'll happen if they catch us?" Dindra said.

"Oh, we'd be in violation of some article of the treaty or other. The important thing is they'd tell my father. Well, we might as well save the torches."

Nosh snuffed the flame on the narrow path. He tore off a fistful of glowing fungus and held it before him. Dindra and Raefer did likewise. The light lasted for several hours before it faded. Cave after strange, glowing cave went by.

"I could do with a splash of water," Raefer said.

"Me, too," Nosh said, walking as he sipped.

"And a rest," Raefer said.

"Rest?" Nosh said. "Oh, well, if *you* have to ..."

"I wonder how the others are doing," Dindra said. She frowned and thought a moment before taking a drink.

"They'll be alright," Nosh said. "As long as the dwarf guards don't catch 'em, or the gnomes, or the trolls ... and so long as they stay well clear of the Fire Warrens. Come on, rest's over."

"What *is* that, anyway?" Dindra said, capping her water skin as she started forward. "I saw it on the map."

"The Fire Warrens is where old King Thárrowfend disappeared. It's a system of tunnels that goes *way* down, even deeper than the gnomes will go."

"What's down there?" Dindra said.

"Nobody knows. It was newly discovered when Thárrowfend vanished. It's been off limits ever since."

"Why'd he go there?" Raefer said.

"Searching for some special fire supposed to be burning deep under the mountain. A magic fire they say. My cousin Thrym knows all about it. He's mad about the whole thing. Careful there, Dindra, that mushroom'll spit needles out of those tubes on top of it. One hits you and you'll be asleep for hours. Always amazes me, all the different kinds . . ."

A deafening cry blared out at them. In a huge clay pot stood a round mushroom the size of a pumpkin, glowing bright blue. It let out such a blast that Dindra, Raefer and Nosh had to cover their ears for the pain of it as they ran away down the path.

"What was *that*?" Dindra said.

"Trumpet fungus," Nosh said.

From up ahead came the sound of running feet.

"That way!" called a voice. It was shrill and angry.

"Hide!" Nosh said. "Gnomes see better than cats in the dark!"

Into the dim glow of the luminous mushrooms came folk shorter than Nosh, wiry and nimble, carrying torches and spears and knives. They had dark skin and large eyes and blue paint on their fierce faces. The leader stopped and peered into the mushrooms on both sides of the path. Then he waved his troop forward and the gnomes ran off up the trail.

Nosh shook his head as he stepped into the open. "I should've known they'd have some kind of sentry this close to the shaft."

"So we're near the end?" Dindra said.

Nosh gave a nod, still looking up the path where the gnomes had gone.

"How far?" Raefer said.

"Half a mile, maybe," Nosh said. "They think we were headed *in* but they'll figure it out. We don't want to be here when they do."

"I thought you said they weren't dangerous," Dindra said.

"Well, they are," Nosh said. "Now let's get going before they decide to double back."

ᴄhaᴘᴛᴇʀ 10

Tʜᴇ Fɪʀᴇ Ɯaʀʀᴇnꙅ

yron stopped. A mound of jagged stone blocked the passage almost to the ceiling. He stood panting, shaking, gaping into the darkness. It was quiet behind him. He scrabbled up the pile, shoving his pack ahead of him into the gap at the top.

"Too . . . tight," he said as he squirmed through.

He twisted and got stuck.

His arm wedged beneath him, Byron grunted and strained, groping in the darkness behind him. A sharp edge dug into his back. He caught hold of a stone and pushed. The stone broke and Byron's cheek struck the rocks beneath him.

He saw a flash of light and the pain came. Blood oozed down into his ear. Byron clenched his teeth to muffle an angry shout. His eyes filled with tears and he flailed with all his might. The stones beneath him shifted. He pitched forward and fell. There was a loud rip. Byron's cape caught on the stone, snapping tight. His wrist was pinned beneath him and he dangled there, halfway down the rubble pile, choked by the clasp of his cape.

Byron rolled to shift his weight. His cape held him fast. It was torn in half from hem to hood. The free half flopped down over his face. When he reached to loose the clasp, he twisted his pinned wrist. When he shifted his weight off his wrist, he strangled himself with his cape. When he reached to push the torn strip from his face he was choked and twisted both at once.

Byron wriggled and squirmed and grunted. Then he tugged and kicked and growled. He stifled another shout. Flailing and lunging, Byron pitched forward, turning and reaching. He found a stone with his hoof and rested his weight there. The cape relaxed its chokehold and he freed his wrist. He sighed and smiled in the darkness. Then the stone gave way and his legs came out from under him.

He landed on his side stuck between two large rocks, with one arm pinned beneath him and his wind knocked out. His torn cape flopped down over his head again. As he lay there, gulping for air, Byron heard the sound of his punctured water skin draining away somewhere out of reach in the darkness. As the last cough escaped the tear in the water skin, Byron gasped a breath of air and started to cry. He lay there for a long time and didn't bother to push the torn cape from his eyes.

In the quiet he slept and dreamed.

Hoofbeats echoed in the tunnel. A horse was neighing. A fire burned on the high peak of a faraway mountain. Above the fire burned the star. There were drums and pipes and voices. The horse's neigh came again, more hoofbeats in the tunnel. Byron shook his head and opened his eyes. It was quiet and dark beneath his cape. He struggled to sit up. The image of the flame dancing on the mountain remained when he opened his eyes.

"A torch," Byron said. He shook his head. "Hello, stupid."

He pulled himself free of his bind between the stones and rummaged through his pack. In a few moments he was sparking the tinder. Shadows leaped. The passage came alight. Byron gasped and dropped the torch. The young flame flickered and nearly died, but he snatched it up in time and held it out. There was a wolf on the floor of the tunnel, back at the foot of the rubble pile.

It was huge and torn and dead and stretched across a gap in the rubble where Byron could have walked through standing. Drops of blood led from the wolf right between Byron's hooves and into the shadows of the tunnel ahead. He followed them with his eyes. No tracks were visible on the stone floor. Byron glanced back at the wolf and set off again.

He crept along. The tunnels were jagged and rough and so low in places he had to duck. Dark passages branched away to the left and right. Byron pressed on, ever downward, along a steep, sandy decline.

It was very quiet. At a two-way fork in the tunnel, Byron waved the torch down each of the passages and chose the one to the right. He frowned and squinted into the gloom. Around a sharp bend he came face to face with two enormous wolves.

The wolves looked at Byron. Byron looked at the wolves. A moment passed. Byron turned and ran as fast as he could. At the fork he paused. The way he'd come was too steep. Byron heard the growling of the wolves, their paws upon the stone. He turned to the left-hand tunnel and fled.

Left and right he turned, again and again. Passage after passage opened into the light of Byron's torch. He stopped and crawled under a low ceiling, then stood and pitched forward as the ground dipped beneath him. He dropped his torch and the weight of his pack shifted, dragging him down. He sprang to his hooves but the torn cape caught him. The eyes of the lead wolf flashed in the torchlight as it waddled under the low tunnel ceiling. Byron yanked his cape free of his hoof, snatched up his torch and bolted.

Every turn, every tunnel led downward. Byron ran too fast, always near to stumbling on the steepness. The wolves drew near, their panting, their whines, their padding feet. Byron looked back and saw them, blazing eyes and wagging tongues in the torchlight. He started crying, running, looking back.

"Dadda!" he cried and didn't see the low ceiling.

All the weight of the mountain met the crown of Byron's head. He screamed and dropped his torch, gripping his skull with both hands. Byron reeled and staggered into the darkness before him. The ground vanished and he fell.

He struck the water flat on his belly and face, swallowing a great gulp. It was warm and sweet and he coughed and gasped for breath. Byron tried to swim, but his strength was gone. Something sharp and hard took hold of his arm, pulling him. Byron let his face sag into the water and knew no more.

▨   ▨   ▨

Voices were screaming. One rose clear above them.

Run, Byron!

Byron ran. *Dadda!* he cried and his words choked him. *Mamma!*

Away in the trees was a satyr, a little older than himself, barging through the undergrowth, screaming as a great dark shape closed in from behind. Byron ran and ran and stepped into a rut in the ground. His whole body jerked and he woke.

"Garvin?" he said and his voice mingled with the sound of dripping water. It was dark and when the echo of his voice faded, it was quiet. The water dripped again. The pain in Byron's head was terrible. He took a breath and sat up.

A huge welt had risen with an oozing gash in the middle of

it. Byron winced and held his head. He touched the wound and stabs of pain shot down into his eyes. There was pain in his wrist also. The skin wasn't broken, but the bones hurt when he made a fist. Byron sighed a deep, thorough sigh. He clutched his wrist and peered into the darkness.

His cape was turned on his body so the hood was sideways.

"Seems dry enough," he said, righting it with his good hand. "How long've I been here?"

Byron stood and staggered a few steps. He dropped to a seat and his head throbbed. The ground felt like sun-baked stone. His hand brushed against his rucksack; it was open and empty. Feeling around, he located his second torch.

A long slow search led him to the edge of the pool where he found the tinderbox perched on the brink of falling in. Byron bumped it with the side of his hand. He realized what it was and snatched at it in the dark, catching it just before it hit the water. He rolled on his back and waited for the pain in his head to die away. It throbbed so hard he could hear it.

"It's like an oven in here," he said as he knocked the flints together. "Guess that's lucky."

In the light of the sparks the tinderbox and the open rucksack came and went from sight. A small flame sprang up in the well-dried tinder. Byron blew on it. Soon the torch was blazing. Byron collected his things and shouldered his pack. Then he noticed the creature.

It had the body of a lizard only much, much larger. The torso and head were like a man with dark red skin and it had a thick mane on its head and back. It lay still on the floor of the cave, dead. Byron approached it and found a bloodied spear in its grip. Then he saw the entrance to another tunnel and two dead wolves lying there. Byron turned and waved the torch around the chamber. As he did he heard a low growl and found another wolf lurking in the shadows, staring at him.

Blood stained its face and jowls. It labored to its feet and stood with its hackles bristling. The bloodied lips drew back from long, red fangs. The wolf crouched and snarled at Byron. Its eyes were wild and glowed in the light of the torch. Byron looked close at those eyes and saw that one of them was blue.

It was the biggest wolf he'd ever seen. The deep growl rumbled in its throat. Byron stepped back. Then he turned and ran for the tunnel.

He squinted through the pain in his head, forcing himself onward. He turned and turned again, hoping to shake off pursuit. He thought of the blood on the face of the wolf and hoped the brute was too injured to follow. Byron stopped to catch his breath and listen. When the throbbing in his head calmed down and the pounding of his heart left his ears, all was silent. He gaped into the shadows and found a faint glow coming from the walls of the tunnel.

Thick moss grew in a clump at the curve between the wall and ceiling. It was orange and yellow and looked like the coals of a campfire. Byron touched it and it spat a stream of sparks in his face. He cried out and fell back, burying his face in his hands. He stumbled and bumped his welt against the stone. Byron hollered again and fell to the ground. The torch landed on its top and went out.

Sparks showered down on him from the flaring moss. Byron clenched his teeth and growled and kicked his hooves, fighting back the tears. When the pain subsided he uncovered his face and found he could see by the light of the firemoss. Byron stood and leaned against the wall.

His torch lay smoking on the ground. In the tunnel ahead

were more patches of moss growing on the walls. The passage was full of orange light. Byron sighed and went on, leaving the torch behind him.

Still the tunnels led downward. Byron kept to those best lit by the moss. The walls were warm to touch. He came to a ledge that circled and looked down on the floor of a huge chamber. It was lit by masses of firemoss high up on the ceiling. The floor was like a vast cooking fire of glowing mosses and mushrooms and low-growing shrubs of brilliant red and yellow and orange.

Sparks and flames shot up everywhere. Standing in the flames with long rakes and hoes were dozens of lizard creatures. They marched about in the fire, tending the glowing crops.

In the middle of it all was a huge bank of coals. The air above it trembled with heat. Lizard creatures were busy trying to keep open flames from sprouting among the embers. Large entrances to other caverns opened in the walls of the chamber, through which dozens more of the creatures came and went. Byron crept along to the first tunnel he came to and went in.

It sloped downward and at the bottom there was a junction of three tunnels. The one to the right and the one straight ahead were well lit with firemoss. The left-hand tunnel had a locked gate across it. Byron started to go straight and saw a pair of lizard creatures headed toward him.

One of them stopped and pointed. At the same moment another pair approached from the right. Byron turned to run away up the passage he'd come down, but there were shadows approaching from above. The first four creatures cried in alarm and ran toward him with incredible speed. From the upward tunnel came a cry of response and the sounds of running feet. Byron flung himself at the gate and started wriggling through.

He slipped out of his pack and let it drop. His cape caught in the bars and the first pair of creatures to reach the chamber lunged at him. The bars were tight and scraped Byron's back and chest as he wrenched himself through. He stepped back and straightened his torn cape.

One of the creatures hissed and reached for Byron through the bars. The other picked up his pack and dumped it out. The second pair arrived. Byron turned to go on and still another creature arrived from the upward tunnel with a ring of jangling keys. Byron heard the slides of the lock fall and he broke into a run.

With a creak, the gate flew open and the lizard creatures clamored through. Byron ran on and came to a long patch of white-orange firemoss covering the floor, a long walk of fire, shimmering with heat. Here and there a small spray of sparks shot up and wisps of thick smoke streaked the air, but there were patches of open ground, like islands, scattered all through.

Byron set out hopping from one open patch to the next. Soon he found himself too far from the nearest open spot to reach it without touching moss. He stood for a moment, considering. The lizard creatures appeared and dashed right out onto the moss. The tunnel came alive with streams of bursting sparks. The dark forms of the creatures appeared amid the showering spray and came toward him fast. Byron turned and ran for it.

Moss clusters sprayed him with burning sparks and he cried out as he ran. The fur on his legs and fetlocks smouldered and smoked. He fell into a thick bunch of the stuff and landed on his palms. He was lost in the glowing rain and could not see ahead of him. He got up and ran on, wincing and crying out, waving his arms before him.

When his hooves struck stone, Byron kept running, patting out the little fires in his fur and hair. His palms and chest were blistered and his face was hot. He looked back to locate the creatures and found his cape was on fire. He popped the clasp and let it drop. The lizard creatures emerged from the firemoss and charged after him.

They closed the gap fast and Byron could hear them drawing near. A large tunnel mouth opened in front of him. He ran through without slowing and glanced backward to see the creatures, black against light of the raging firemoss. They did not advance, but stood there at the entrance of the tunnel, looking in.

Byron stopped. The creatures hissed at him and waved their spears. He frowned and looked forward into the dim light. Small patches of red firemoss lit the tunnel until it disappeared around a bend. The lizard creatures didn't follow. Byron turned and hurried on.

He walked a long time. The air was hot and the rocks were painful to touch. He came to a kind of balcony that looked down into a vast chamber. Huge swatches of firemoss lit the ground. The high roof was lost in shadow. Great glowing mushrooms sprouted up from the floor. They looked like metal heated to red. A stair wound down from the balcony, along the cavern wall to the ground hundreds of feet below.

In the middle of the chamber, among the mushrooms, Byron came to an open place where the ground was black and charred. He kicked something in the deep ashes.

It was a rod of some sort, as long as Byron was tall. It looked like a club, wider and rounded at one end, narrow and almost pointed at the other. The whole thing was caked smooth with black soot, glazed and hardened as if by fire. It was light in Byron's hands. He gripped it at the narrow end and held it like a weapon. Then, out of the corner of his eye, Byron saw something move.

A black dot raced across the red light of the mushrooms. Whatever it was it was quick; it stopped for a moment, then headed straight for Byron. Byron tensed. The thing disappeared into the shadows but he could hear feet padding through the ashes at a run. Byron crouched and held the club-thing before him. When the creature appeared, Byron stood and smiled. He let his shoulders sag and almost laughed out loud.

It was smaller than Byron, stocky and running on two legs. It had rough, bumpy skin and horns at the knees and elbows. Its tall conical head was studded with small spines and it had huge, shining black eyes. Byron was so amused he didn't mind the fact that the creature kept coming straight for him.

With astonishing strength, the little brute hit Byron full on and knocked him to the ground. Then it circled around and came again. Byron swung out with the stout end of the club. The blow fell squarely on the creature's tall head but the monster did not stop. It fell upon Byron and held him in an unbreakable grip.

It clung to Byron with all four limbs, taking his left horn in its teeth. Byron screamed so loud it hurt his throat as little teeth sank into the skin around his horn and tore it loose from his skull. Byron screamed and screamed and screamed but could not get free. The monster clutched him with its arms and tore him with its teeth and started kicking him with its feet.

Then it shrieked and twisted and let go.

There was a savage growl. Byron fell to the ground. He looked up to see the wolf with one blue eye shaking the creature in its mouth. The little brute shrieked again as the wolf tossed it aside. It landed on its feet and ran off squealing into the darkness. The wolf took a step to follow it, then turned to look at Byron. Its fur was still bloody and it limped, but the wolf licked its fangs and set off after the goblin. Byron watched the huge shape lope away into the shadows.

All was quiet.

Byron lay curled in a ball among the ashes, covering the wound where the horn had been. A small, tender root stuck out of it. It throbbed with pain and there was a lot of blood. Byron couldn't move with all the horrible aching in his body and head. The strange club lay in the ash beside him.

A sound came from somewhere in the deep reaches of the cave. It was faint. Byron didn't move, but he listened. It came again. He heard hoofbeats and a horse neighing. It echoed to the unseen roof of the chamber. Byron uncurled a little and listened again. The sound came louder and clearer. With all his strength, Byron came to an elbow and looked around.

His whole body throbbed. His stomach was sick, his head ached with dizziness and he could hardly see for the blood trickling into his eyes. Even so he stood up, leaning on the strange club for balance. The sound came again, louder and clearer. Byron glanced into the glowing mushrooms where the wolf and goblin had gone. The horse neighed again. Byron set off to follow, staggering a little over his first few steps.

He went out through the glowing mosses and mushrooms to a crack in the far wall of the cave. It was almost too narrow for him, but the hooves were clopping and the horse neighed somewhere deep inside. Byron turned sideways and scraped through, holding his breath. The burns on his hands and chest hurt him. He shimmied through for a short way and the crack opened to a wider passage leading upward. Byron could see nothing. The sound seemed far away. He let a wave of dizziness pass, then put his hand to the wall and pressed on.

Ever upward, the passage climbed. At times it was carved with steep, narrow stairs. At every dark intersection the neighing and hoofbeats sounded, leading the way. So it went. Byron climbed up and up into cool, moist air. At last he felt the chill of winter and the movement of a breeze across his face.

It stung the wound on his head. Byron winced, but further on he saw a faint light. The horse neighed again. Byron found his way to a ledge that looked out at the nighttime sky. He shivered in the cold, gazing into the dark vastness before him and his eyed filled with stinging tears.

Dark and bright, the sky was alive with stars. Huge among them, the one star burned clear and white above the land beyond the mountains. Byron's heart leaped toward it. A wave of pain shot down through his head into his eyes. His vision blurred to a fog and his strength failed him.

Byron leaned on the club-like staff, holding it with both hands. As he rested his cheek on his knuckles, his eyelids sealed themselves shut. Covered in soot and sweat and blood and tears, Byron lowered himself to the cold ground and fell sleep.

Chapter 11

Bilérica

A bird was singing. Deep, sweet smells filled the air. Soft, warm wind carried laughter through the open window and lifted the curtains. Byron woke without opening his eyes and reached far above his head in a stretch that left him coiled into a ball. He blinked and looked around him and sat up.

He was in the very middle of an enormous bed, beneath a large window in a room with great wooden beams and a polished wooden floor. A table stood against the wall beside a door, the bottom half of which was closed and the top half of which was open. Blue sky shone through it and the leafy branches of a tall tree reached down into view. The breeze came again carrying the laughter and a flying thing hissed by. Byron settled back on the pillow and sighed.

"Hello, Byron," said a voice.

Byron sat up. At the foot of the bed was a woman, seated in a wooden chair. Her hair was long and dark and hung down the front of her in a braid. Her eyes were sky blue and she was beautiful. She smiled at Byron and closed her eyes in a long, slow blink.

"Who are you?" Byron said, pulling the sheets up to his neck.

"My name is Hixima."

Byron looked around the room. "Where am I?"

"Here."

Byron frowned. "Where is here?"

"A hidden place called Bilérica. You're quite safe. And so are your friends."

"My friends are here?"

"Yes."

"All of them?"

"And two new friends as well. They're all eager to see you, when you're able."

Byron touched the wound on his head. A bandage covered him like a helmet. His left horn stuck out through a hole in the cloth. He pressed the wounded spot on the right side, but there was no pain. He looked at his hands and chest, his arms and the hair on his legs. All his hurts were mended, or close to it. Hixima laughed and smiled at him.

"Very different from when Quill found you," she said. "You were covered with ash and burns and the blood and tears of struggle. You looked like a blacksmith's imp. You nearly died. But we reached you in time."

Byron gave Hixima a puzzled look. "Who is Quill?"

"You have met her once, or nearly. She remembers you very well. Quill is the daughter of Gulthenna; Gulthenna is queen of the griffins."

"She brought me here?"

"Quill found you. Miroaster brought you in."

"Miro ... m ..."

"Miroaster is a friend. He's gone off again, somewhere into the world. Will you eat? You must be very hungry. You've had nothing but broth for eleven days now. It has sustained you, but also sharpened your appetite, I daresay."

"Did you ..." Byron said, sinking back down into the sheets. "Did you heal my horn?"

"I healed the wound. But the horn is gone. It won't grow back, unless by some miracle. Is it hurting?"

"No. I'm ... I'm not. I feel light."

Hixima smiled. "Yes." She looked out the window and sighed. "Bilérica has that effect, especially for those who are wounded. You've come to a good place. Can you tell me about the ones who hurt you?"

"I'd rather not think about it."

"I understand. And that curious staff you were holding?"

Byron sat up and threw his glance around the room. "What happened to it? Where is it?"

"Alright, alright, be easy. It's there, in the corner. No one has taken it from you and no one will. You were clinging to it for very life, even in your sleep."

Byron searched the room. In the corner, on a bench, were a basin and pitcher and a tall stack of towels. Beside the bench was the strange club-like staff, leaning against the wall. Byron sagged back into the pillows and closed his eyes.

"Forgive me," Hixima said. "I won't pester you with questions now. I'll bring your supper and then, after a rest, you may come and watch the sunset from the garden. Tomorrow, if you're well enough, you may join your friends for breakfast."

Byron sighed. He lay still and slept.

◈　◈　◈

In the morning, Hixima removed Byron's bandage. He leaned over the basin while she bathed his head with tingly soap. It soothed and strengthened the tender skin where his horn had been. Byron probed the spot with his finger. There was a hollow pit closed over with a fragile, leathery skin.

"You mustn't worry it," Hixima said. "It isn't fully healed. It needs fresh air and sunshine and so do you."

"What happened to winter?" Byron said, bowing his head to Hixima as she toweled his hair dry.

"It's there, all around us. But not inside Bilérica."

"Why not?" Byron said from under the towel.

"This is the place of summer," Hixima said, kneading his head. "The last magic of Silverlance."

"Silverlance?"

"Yes, indeed. He wove the charm for this place before he went away. It will fade upon his return. Then the seasons will come again."

"Why?"

"It will no longer be necessary."

"Where did Silverlance go?"

"He went to give battle to the enemy, in a secret place, just they two."

"The enemy . . ."

"Yes, a terrible foe." Hixima smoothed Byron's hair back with the towel. "But that was long ago."

They stepped outside and Byron looked up behind him at the house where he was lodged. It was a tall place of stone with ivy-covered walls. Byron had his own entrance that stepped out into a garden. A little path led out along a wide brook where willow trees grew. Morning sunlight splashed down through the green wisps. A gentle breeze set them swaying. Birds were singing everywhere and the first warmth of the day was drying up the dew from the tall grass and hedgerows.

Westward, the mountains carved the horizon with their

gleaming, snowy peaks. The Old Mountain towered in the south, very tall, passing in and out of sight through the waving green leaves of the birches and poplars of Bilérica.

Byron saw the star, white and high in the east. He stopped to gaze at it until he heard voices and laughter coming from the house. He took Hixima's hand and continued.

On a flat lawn in front of the house was a long wooden table laden with a breakfast feast. Byron saw all his friends. Raefer and Shilo were pouring drinks from pitchers. Rufus was setting out baskets of buns. Dindra came from the back of the house carrying a tray covered with plates and bowls.

"He's here!" Raefer cried. "Byron!"

Raefer ran around the end of the table and raced to greet Byron. The others put down their burdens and hurried to do the same. They crowded around him and crouched down to him, hugging him and patting his back. He lurched and staggered with the movement of the crowd.

"Stand back and give him room," Shilo said.

"Sure, sure," Reafer said, stretching wide his arms to fence out the others.

"Oh, Byron," Dindra said. She folded her arms and unfolded them, wincing back a tear.

"You made it through, Byron," Rufus said. "We all did and here we are."

"I ..." Byron said. He fought with his own breath to get the words out. "I ..."

Byron started to cry. Everyone did. They all stood there, gathered together.

"We made it, Byron," Rufus said. "You made it."

"We're all here," Dindra said. "Everything's all right."

There was a rumbling whimper and two huge bears came

bounding around the corner of the house. A gang of smaller animals followed them.

"Manakar!" Byron called. "Lucia!"

All the animals collected around Byron, sniffing him and perking their ears. Lucia pressed him to the ground and started grooming him. She sniffed his wounded head and licked it.

Byron laughed. "It got bit off," he said. "Bit off by a troll or something."

"You've gotta tell us all about it, Byron," Raefer said. "You're the guest of honor."

Lucia looked around at Hixima and let Byron up.

Byron wiped his eyes on the back of his wrist. "I am?"

"Yep," Shilo said.

"That's what the chair's for," Rufus said.

"It's like a throne," Byron said, looking at the great wooden chair that stood at the head of the table. "Hey, Rufus, your vines are blooming. Yours too, Raef."

"Sure they are," Rufus said with a smile. "It's summer in Bilérica."

"Shilo," Dindra said, looking around. "Where's Nosh?"

"The kitchen!" Shilo cried and she ran off toward the house.

"Come sit, Byron," Dindra said and she led him toward the table.

A loud crash came from the house. "Nosh, you tunnel rat!" Shilo hollered. "Get back here!"

There was another loud crash, like a pot hitting stone. Out the door came a short, stout figure holding something to its face. As it ran, it chewed and stuffed more of whatever it had into its mouth. Shilo appeared behind the fellow, clutching a rolling pin. Her face was red and wrathful.

"He cut into Byron's cake!" Shilo yelled.

"Oh, Nosh!" Dindra said.

"There'f plemmy lefff," Nosh said covering his head as he ran.

Shilo lifted the rolling pin above her head and set off after the dwarf. Nosh ran out through an arched trellis in the hedgerow with Shilo close behind.

"Go get the rest of it, Raefer," Dindra said with her hands on her waist. "Save a piece for Byron."

"Who is he?" Byron said.

"The prince of the dwarves," Dindra said, still looking at the arch where Nosh had gone out. "Raefer and I met him under the mountain."

"Hello, Byron," said a voice. Byron turned to see Nosh grinning at him over the low hedge. "I'm Nosh. I'm pleased to meet you." Nosh held out his hand and Byron took it. Nosh's grip was strong and warm. Byron smiled.

"Are you following the star, too?" Byron said.

"I sure am." Nosh looked left and right and then climbed through the hedge onto the lawn. "Only took one piece. Couldn't keep my hands off it, just sitting there. Don't know why she doesn't take it as a compliment."

Shilo came in through the same arch where she'd gone out after Nosh. She glared at him as she passed and went back into the house. Raefer came out carrying what was left of the cake. The group gathered around the table.

"Come, Byron," Hixima said. "Take your seat."

Byron looked around at everyone. They all smiled. He looked from the big chair to Hixima and she nodded.

"We all had to do it, Byron," Shilo said, approaching the table. She set down a platter of steaming eggs and swatted Nosh's hand away from the muffin tops.

Hixima gave Byron another long, slow blink. "You must tell what became of you under the mountain. Each one here has done so, sitting in this chair. And so will you."

"Don't worry Byron," Raefer said. "You can eat first."

"When will I hear about all of you?" Byron said.

"There's plenty of time for that," Rufus said.

"Na muffa fell," Nosh said through a mouthful of muffin top.

"Nosh, can't you wait a second?" Shilo said. She shook her head and snapped her napkin into shape for placing on her lap. She looked at Byron. "We'll tell you our stories while we eat."

Byron was quiet during the meal. His appetite was enormous. The others laughed and talked as they ate, telling their stories and remembering things they had forgotten of the time in the tunnels. Rufus and Shilo told of Thrym and the Balefire, of the old dwarf king who had vanished in the mines. Dindra and Raefer told of the vast, beautiful forests of mushrooms, of the gnomes and trumpet fungus.

"So," Raefer said, "when we heard Rufus and Shilo's version of what the centaurs had said at that three-way fork in the tunnel, Dindra and I realized we'd all heard the very same thing. We were only a few feet away from each other and didn't even know it!"

"We must've just missed you, Byron," Dindra said. "Oh! That reminds me! We found these."

Dindra reached into a bag under the table and took out Byron's knife and monocle.

"Dindra!" Byron said. "I never thought I'd see these again! Oh, Gradda's monocle ..." The cut leather strand was replaced with a silver chain. Byron held it up, then looked at Dindra with a sidelong frown. "Did you ... try it?"

"Sure I did," Dindra said with a shrug.

"Me, too," Raefer said.

Byron frowned. "In the daylight?"

"Well sure," Dindra said. "When else? In the dark?"

"And it didn't hurt or anything?" Byron said.

"Hurt?" Raefer said with a laugh. "No. It didn't even magnify as far as I could tell. Just clear glass."

Byron looked at the smoke swirling in the lens of the monocle. He shrugged and hung it around his neck.

"But if we hadn't gone down to the Mushroom Forest," Dindra continued, "we'd never have met Nosh."

"You'd've met me here," Nosh said.

Raefer shrugged. "But how would we have found it?"

When everyone had eaten and drunk their fill, they all sat back and pushed their plates away. A happy silence fell and everyone was smiling.

There was a whistling of wings.

"Look out!" cried a voice from somewhere far away.

Byron looked up and saw a large, dark form in the sky. It twisted and contorted into all different positions, reaching and stretching. When it was near enough to see it turned out to be a small griffin, flying totally out of control and heading straight for the chair where Byron was seated.

"Quill!" Hixima shouted. "Veer off, Quill!"

"Look out!" the griffin cried. "I can't stop!"

Byron tried too late to evacuate the chair. The whole thing went over in a mash of feathers and hair and hooves and flapping wings. Byron's napkin shot up into the air. When he opened his eyes he was flat on his back several feet from the chair, staring up at a pair of shining dark eyes that looked at him over a jagged, bronze-colored beak. Byron blinked. The griffin didn't. There was merriment in her eyes.

"Hello," she said. "I'm Quill. I'm the one who found you."

Byron said nothing. He lay stiff and still looking up at the great, shining eyes.

"Quill!" Hixima cried. "What have you done? Byron, are you hurt?"

"No," Quill said. "He isn't hurt."

"No," Byron said. "I'm not hurt."

Then he smiled and Quill's eyes sparkled, still looking at him. She hopped away to let him up. Hixima knelt before him and helped him to his hooves.

"You're sure you're not hurt?" she said.

"Yes," Byron said as she brushed him off and examined the wound on his head.

"I'm still working on the landings," Quill said. "I've got takeoffs nearly down."

"Yes," Byron said. "I'm sure."

"I didn't miss anything, did I?" Quill said to Raefer. "He hasn't told his story yet, has he?"

"Nope," Raefer said. "We were waiting for you."

"Good!" Quill said and she walked around in a circle, stretching her wings. "I'm the one who found you, you know. I showed Miroaster the way. You'd be dead if not for me."

"Thank you," Byron said. Hixima was pulling down his lower eyelid and peering into his eye.

"And he's no better off now, because of you Quill," Hixima said. "How many times do you need to hear that you must land on the hillside and walk down?"

"Sorry, Hixima," Quill said, drooping her head. "I was afraid of being late. Mother kept me so long at the scrolls this morning. I didn't want to miss it."

"Are you hungry?" Nosh said.

"No thanks," Quill said, "I've eaten."

"Hey, that reminds me!" Raefer said. "Byron, the horses are here! Cryolar and his friends brought them after they dropped us at the tunnel. Still don't see why he couldn't just bring us here, too."

"I told you," Quill said. "Mother had already denied you passage. It would have been treason."

"Very well, very well," Hixima said. "Let Byron tell his tale. Quill, find a place to sit, please. Everyone hush now and listen."

Quill sat beside Dindra and settled in. Nosh got up and made a dash for the sticky buns. He and Raefer had a silent fight over the last one. Shilo and Rufus stood the chair up and moved it in place. Byron climbed up and put his hands on the arms. Everyone sat looking at him, resting chins on fists. Byron took a breath and began.

"Well," he said, "everyone was already in the tunnel and I was afraid Baruwan would open the gate. So, I went back for the keys . . ."

"I *knew* it!" Dindra said. "Didn't I say so, Raef?"

"Yes, you said so," Raefer said, rolling his eyes. "Forty times."

"I threw my knife at Baruwan," Byron continued. "I ran as fast as I could in all that darkness. It was a long time before I remembered the torches . . ."

When he finished, Byron stared into the near distance for a while and relaxed into the chair with a sigh. The others looked around at each other with their mouths open. No one spoke. A long time passed before Hixima stood and broke the spell.

"And now, Byron," she said, "you are with your friends again."

"Yes," he said. He looked around at each one. "Yes."

"The Balefire," Nosh said. "You saw the Balefire in your dream."

"And you never saw the knight who led you out?" Shilo said.

"What makes you think it was a knight?" Rufus said.

"Who else but a knight would ride a horse into a tunnel to rescue someone?"

"I never saw any horse," Byron said.

"Maybe it was a ghost," Raefer said.

"Or an echo," Hixima said.

"An echo?" everyone said together.

"Yes," Hixima said. "Perhaps of some forgotten hero, lost doing a forgotten deed. The world is full of such places. In such places, help comes to those who need it."

Byron blinked and sat forward. "Maybe that's what happened at the ruined tower! The night the wolves came."

Dindra shook her head. "No, Byron, that isn't what happened."

Byron frowned. "But you said yourself it was probably a ghost."

"An echo is not a ghost, Byron," Hixima said. "No indeed, but a leftover, a bit of goodness that lingers on in the aftermath of a mighty deed. But Dindra is right. What happened at the tower was neither ghost nor echo."

"What was it then?" Byron said.

Hixima smiled. "I will show you, if you would like to come and see."

She helped Byron down from his chair and they set off, hand in hand, toward the house. The rest of the group followed along with Manakar and his troop. Byron looked back at them and saw them whispering to each other.

"What are we going to see?" he said.

"A friend," Hixima said.

"Who?"

"I will introduce you. We're going to the back of the house. The view of the star is better there."

To the east, beyond Bilérica, all was white, locked in the grip of winter. Inside the magic borders, summery hills rolled along, filled between with tall leafy trees. A stream wound through, peeking out in silver glimpses that twinkled with sunlight. In the gentle slopes where three of the lower hills met, an orchard grew in neat rows filled with the pink and white blossoms of dogwood and cherry. Byron stopped to gaze out at the colorful trees.

"The orchard is ever in bloom," Hixima said.

"I think I smell it from here," Byron said.

"Then breathe. The fragrance will do you good."

Byron walked his fingers along the low, flat railing of the terrace, gazing out. As they went around to the east side of the house, the star came into view, brighter and nearer than ever. Byron gasped and clutched Hixima's hand.

Sitting on a raised portion of the terrace, looking out on the eastern world, was a huge, shaggy form. It turned as Byron and Hixima approached. Byron stopped, frozen to his spot on the bricks, trembling. His heart pounded in his ears. He looked unblinking into the eyes of an enormous wolf and as he stared, Byron saw that one of its eyes was blue.

chapter 12

Lukos

t had a bandage on its forepaw and a large spot on its shoulder where the fur had been shaved. It looked fatter and cleaner, but still fierce and watchful. It sniffed the air in Byron's direction, then turned to resume its watch.

"There is nothing to fear," Hixima whispered.

"But it's . . . it's . . ."

"His name is Lukos. He is a friend. Steady now. I'll call him over. All right?"

"Y . . . yes . . ." Byron said, clutching Hixima's skirt and stepping behind her.

"Lukos?" Hixima called.

The wolf turned and labored down the stair from the raised level. It limped along, keeping the bandaged forepaw in the air. It stopped a few feet away and sat down again.

"This is the ghost of the ruined tower," Hixima said. "You found only wolf tracks the next morning, for it was a wolf who saved you."

Byron's mouth fell open.

"And Lukos looked in on you throughout your journey.

More than once he stood down the other wolves when you and your companions slept."

"And the wolves in the tunnel," Byron said. "The ones I found, the ones that chased me . . . and the lizard thing that was there when I woke?"

"The wolves who chased you slew the salamander. It wanted you for itself. But Lukos fell upon them even as they finished the creature off."

"Then why did he growl at me when I lit the torch?"

"Lukos was wounded and bleeding. And he knew you were afraid of him. He feared what you might do with a firebranch to wield."

"Firebranch?"

"What Lukos calls a torch."

"And the creature who bit off my horn?"

"Lukos saved you from that, also."

"I thought he meant to come back for me," Byron said.

"He did but not to hurt you. When he returned he found you were gone. The night you first saw him, Byron, the night the star first appeared, Lukos was pursued, even as you were. The wolves that were with him were seeking his life."

"But . . . but why?" Byron said.

"For the same reason they sought yours, once they knew you were abroad. Byron, Lukos is following the star."

Byron caught his breath. All his flesh went bumpy and he stepped out a bit from behind Hixima. Lukos looked at Byron and sniffed the air. His one blue eye caught the sun. Then his ears perked and he looked at something behind Byron. Byron turned. His friends were gathered at the corner of the house, watching.

SILVERLANCE

Hixima placed a hand on Byron's head. "Come out now," she said, "and I will introduce you. Lukos, this is Byron Thorn, whose life you saved. Byron Thorn, this is Lukos, king of the western wolves."

❖ ❖ ❖

Lukos approached. He could have rested his chin, without lifting it, on Byron's head. Byron flinched a little as the wolf drew near, but held still while Lukos sniffed the wound where the creature had ripped the horn from its place. The Wolfen King sniffed Byron from head to hoof, then returned to the horn wound. When he was done he stepped back and looked at Hixima.

Hixima looked into the wolf's eyes. "Lukos is sorry he could not prevent your wound," she said. "The creature that did it is strong and wounded Lukos also."

Byron looked back and forth between Lukos and Hixima.

"She speaks with animals," Shilo whispered in Byron's ear. Byron looked back to see that the others had drawn near. "Only she doesn't have to talk or hear them."

Byron shrugged. "It's all right," he said. "Tell him it's all right . . . and thank him for saving me."

A moment later Hixima nodded. "You've already told him, Byron. Lukos understands. He has more to say to you, if you will hear him."

Byron nodded.

"Byron Thorn," Hixima said. "I am Lukos, king of the wolves. It was my grandfather who waged war on the Woodland Throne and my father who agreed to peace after the years of bloodshed between your people and mine.

"I remember your name. You are the satyrling who survived

the rogue wolf attack nine years ago, the attack that nearly brought war to the woods again after a generation of peace. It was your family who was taken that day, all around you. It was I, Lukos, who hunted out the rogues one by one.

"Some believe I did so to secure peace and to prevent the wrath of your young king. That is true, but I ran also for you and the debt my people owe you. I have thought of you often since that time. I have hoped to help you if I could. When the star arose I, like you, was summoned. When I saw you at the bridge and took your scent, I knew you and thanked the Wandering Wolf that my chance had come."

Byron stared at the Wolfen King. He felt Hixima put her hand on his head. He heard the voices whispering behind him.

"His whole family?" Raefer said.

"His mother and father, sister and brother," Dindra said. "He was only three when it happened."

"How did he get away?" Rufus said.

"No one ever knew," Dindra said. "My father found him hiding in a stone wall. He came to live with us until his grandfather could be sent for. My mother says, judging by the nightmares he had, Byron saw everything that happened that day."

"Poor Byron," Shilo said with a crack in her voice.

Byron heard them, but they were far away. He looked deep and unblinking into the eyes of the wolf. Lukos leaned toward Byron and sniffed the air. Then everyone caught their breath at once, even Hixima, whose hand swept from Byron's head to her throat. Lukos crouched to the ground in front of Byron and rolled over on his back, showing the coarse white hair of his belly. He looked at Byron upside down, twisting his body and whimpering.

Byron didn't move. His mouth hung open and his chest

heaved. Lukos rolled over and came to all fours. He stepped forward and sat down before Byron, taller than the satyr. He leaned down and poked Byron in the armpit with his snout. Byron wiggled a little and a smile pulled at his lips. Then Lukos poked Byron in the neck and nuzzled him. Byron tucked his chin into his shoulder and laughed. He threw his arms around the wide neck of the huge wolf and buried his face in the fur. Lukos lay his chin down on the back of Byron's neck and gave a shuddering sigh through his long, gray snout.

"Hello, Lukos," Raefer said, stepping forward. He put out his hand to pat Lukos on the head. "Hello, boy," he said.

A growl rumbled deep in the throat of the wolf. Raefer pulled back his hand and straightened. "That's a fella," he said, putting his hands behind his back.

"Nice going," Rufus said, nudging Raefer as he stepped back beside him. "Gonna give the king of the wolves a little scratch behind the ears?"

"Shut up, Rufus," Reafer said, folding his arms.

"Lukos!" Hixima said in a loud whisper. "It was you!"

Lukos lifted his head and looked at her.

"What?" she said. "Forgive me . . . I didn't mean to hear . . . your thoughts were exposed . . . your mind was on the satyr, I understand, but Lukos, he must know! Yes, he must. Who can hear me? I'm speaking aloud . . . oh! Forgive me . . ."

Hixima glanced at the others and fell silent. She and Lukos looked at each other for several moments.

"Byron," Hixima said. "I have seen the day your family died. It's there, in Lukos's memory. In his warmth and sadness for you he was remembering it all, unguarded. Byron, it was Lukos who saved you. He was too late to save your family. He arrived leading a group of the Unseen Pack and drove the rogues away.

He sent his companions after the rogues and stayed with you, watching from a distance until the Son of Thunder came and found you."

Dindra gasped and covered her mouth.

"Who's the Son of Thunder?" Rufus said.

Dindra lowered her hand. "My father."

The others looked on in wonderment. Hixima set her hand on Byron's head. Byron was dazed.

Lukos sniffed the air in the satyr's direction. Then he turned and loped away to his post on the upper porch. He turned his back on the company and sat looking east at the star burning bright and high in the clear morning sky.

Chapter 13

The Clarion Fades

 any days passed. One morning Hixima gathered the group together for a day abroad in the hills and woods of Bilérica. They carried bags of food and water and set off at daybreak. Manakar and the other animals went with them, walking along single file on the forest path.

"Keep an eye out for Quill," Hixima said. "She may be able to join us today."

"Where has she been?" Shilo said.

"Queen Gulthenna is more watchful than ever," Hixima said. "It's hard for Quill to get out unnoticed."

They walked in the sun-dappled woods. Hixima paused to greet every animal she saw as well as many who came at her call. Shilo watched and listened to everything Hixima did in those moments as deer and chipmunk, skunk and squirrel, snake and frog and turtle came out of hiding, eager to have a moment with the Warra priestess.

"I can talk to them," Shilo said. "But it always seems faint."

"Faint?" Hixima said.

"It's as if they're very far away, down a hole or something."

"That is how it begins. There must be one or two who you hear more clearly."

"The cardinal," Shilo said. "Most times."

"And how long have you known him?"

"Four years. He was the first one I ever heard talking."

"Ah, it was he who woke you."

"Woke me?"

"Yes. He knew you would hear if he persisted, so he did. Then one day you heard a word or two in his song."

Shilo stopped in her tracks. "That's exactly what happened."

"The word you heard was your own name."

"Yes!" Shilo said. "How did you know?"

"It happened to me too, Shilo," Hixima said. "Long ago."

"Look at this, Rufus!" Raefer shouted from further ahead. He was crouching down among the tall ferns that grew along the side of the shady path. As Rufus approached, Raefer opened his pouch and started gathering the small yellow flowers that grew beneath the ferns.

"Moratene is useful for more than just sleep potions," Hixima said. "Byron, you should gather some too. I'll show you how to make a balm for your wound."

"We'll have more than we can carry!" Raefer said. "I'm gonna make a new dart."

"Sleeping potion?" Nosh said. "What are you talking about?"

"We're dryads," Rufus said. "That's the sort of thing we do."

"You put your enemies to sleep?" Nosh said. "That's a little bit sissy, isn't it?"

"We'll see how sissy it is when you've got a two-headed giant on your hands," Raefer said.

At lunchtime Quill joined them on a high hilltop. They spread their blankets near a tall standing stone, in view of the orchard on the southern slope of a neighboring hill. The fragrance of the apple blossoms reached them as they ate in near silence, gazing about from their vantage. The mountains towered close in the west. The sun shone in a blue sky, sparkling in the snow and ice of the woods and hills and valleys. Yet on the hilltop, a warm breeze was blowing and the air was full of butterflies.

Evening was warm and starlit. Byron took his supper by lamplight outside his door. Tree frogs sang all through the woods. Fireflies blinked and the shout of the barred owl cracked the night. There Byron sat, chewing and thinking, when Lukos strode forward out of the black.

He sniffed at Byron's meal. Byron offered the wolf his pick of the plate, but Lukos only sat down, looking into the darkness. His ears were forward. Lukos sniffed and perked his head at the sounds and smells of the night.

Byron frowned. "Anything wrong?"

Lukos looked at him, sniffed, then resumed his watch on the darkness. Byron raised an eyebrow, then went back to his meal. He scraped the last of the gravy off his plate with his spoon, put it in his mouth and pulled it out upside down. Then he heard the faint sound of a gate creaking. Lukos perked his ears. Both of them listened.

"Who's that?" Byron said.

Lukos looked at him and whined.

"Somebody's going out."

Lukos growled a low, throaty growl as Byron slid off his chair.

Byron looked back at him over his shoulder. "I'm just gonna see who it is."

Lukos whined.

"I'll be right back," Byron said. "Come with me if you want to."

Lukos stood and loped past Byron into the darkness. Byron frowned as the wolf went by. "What's eating you, anyway?" he said. Lukos blended with the night and slipped away up the path without a sound.

⬚ ⬚ ⬚

There was a lamp glowing in the woods, already far off. The moon had not yet risen and the woods were dark and dense. Lukos came loping back along the forest path to see what was keeping Byron.

"I can't see as well as you do," Byron said.

Lukos sidled up to him and crouched down, waiting.

"What ... you want me to ride you?"

Lukos whined and looked at Byron. Byron stood back from the wolf and eyed him from tail to snout.

"What'll I hold on to?"

Lukos gave a low growl. Byron looked into the woods. There was no sign of the lamp. He took a deep breath, stepped forward and slung one leg over Lukos.

Lukos lurched forward.

"Whoa!" Byron said. "I'm not on yet!" Byron clutched a fistful of fur. "There, okay, I think that'll ... whoa!" he said as Lukos sprang forward. They were off at a run and Byron ducked low against the wolf's back to avoid the branches and weeds that stuck out into the path.

Lukos moved with astonishing speed. To the left and right of the path the woods were black as ink. Lukos strode along as if bounding in an open field at midday. On the path ahead, the lamp appeared and vanished again in the trees. Lukos crept in, stalking as if to make a kill and peered out from behind the trunk of an enormous tree. A stream ran near with a wooden bridge arching across it. The figure hung the lamp on a post at the foot of the bridge and threw back her hood.

"Hixima," Byron whispered.

She left the lamp and went across the stream. As Lukos padded up, Byron slid down off his back and crept onto the bridge. He stood there, peering into the trees on the other side. Lukos gave a low, menacing growl.

Byron turned. The wolf was looking into the darkness of the woods. Byron started back and Lukos took a step toward the trees, growling.

"What is it?" Byron said.

Lukos bolted. He disappeared into the woods without a sound. Byron stared after him. "Lukos!" he said in a loud whisper. "Lukos!" The wolf did not return.

Byron sighed and looked at the lamp. He headed across the bridge. A delightful smell filled the air. He pressed on until he came to a clearing and a long, low slope rose up and away from him, covered with blossoming trees. Fireflies were everywhere, blinking and swirling.

He set off up the hill through the orchard, breathing deep the fine, sweet smell. It took a long time to reach the top of the hill. As he stepped out onto the open crest, he saw the star burning, bright and clear in the east. The first edge of the full moon rimmed the far end of the hilltop. Fireflies swarmed in the air, living stars, red and green and yellow. Across the hill, someone was laughing.

It was like a bell, clear and inviting, speaking words that Byron could not make out. Another voice answered, deep and rich. The two voices laughed together and then fell silent as the moonrise progressed.

Slow and steady it came, climbing from the darkness beyond the world. Two shapes appeared, black against the bright white glow. One was a woman, her hair and cape lifted by the breeze.

The other was a horse, tall and broad with a vast mane and great shags of hair on his hooves. The woman's hand rested on the horse's neck and together they watched the moonrise.

Byron blinked. The moon was enormous and the star burned near. All around fireflies danced. The woman broke away from the horse, stepping and twirling like a young girl, chasing the flickering lights, catching them and letting them go. The horse nickered and stepped toward her, lifting a hoof and shaking his mane. Byron crept forward, crouching low, until he could hear the words they were saying.

"Now may I?" Hixima said.

"Yes, now. The moon is up."

"Thúmose has seen his moonrise."

"On to lesser things."

"Is it very bad today?" Hixima said, stepping toward the horse. The rich, spicy smell of moratene wafted toward Byron on the nighttime breeze. Hixima reached up and caressed the horse's forehead. The horse nickered and lowered his head to her, resting his chin on her shoulder.

"Thúmose, you bear your pain so patiently."

"It is mine to bear."

"You mustn't worry it."

"I'm trying. It is very itchy lately."

Hixima caressed the horse's brow for a long time. They did not speak again. The moon climbed above them and their silhouettes disappeared. Byron went back down the hill, into the fragrance of the orchard now filled with moonlight. Across the bridge he stopped and peered into the deep dark of the wood.

"Lukos!" he whispered. "Lukos! Oh, why didn't I bring the monocle? Hixima will be along soon; she'll want to know what I'm up to."

Byron stepped off the bridge and headed for the house. An owl cried, answered by another. The trees and night echoed with the sound. Moonlight crept across the forest floor. The sound of the stream died away. Bryon stopped. The hair on his arms prickled.

He whirled around. "Lukos?"

Nothing stirred.

Byron took a step back the way he'd come. He stopped to listen again. "Lukos?"

Off to the left, deep in the trees, there was a crash of undergrowth and broken twigs. Byron froze where he stood. "Lukos?" he croaked.

The owl called. Another crash sounded, near at hand. Byron turned and ran.

At once there were footfalls on the path behind. Byron's blood went cold and rushed to his eyes. The world went purple. He strayed from the path. Twigs and branches lashed him. The footfalls drew near and Byron was lifted from his hooves.

Strong, rough hands gripped him. Byron was hoisted and held over the shoulder of something a bit bigger than Nosh. It turned and headed off into the woods, crashing with heavy feet through the undergrowth, glancing off trees as it went. Then, darker than the darkness, came another shape, silent and fast. Lukos was upon them, growling low and lunging at Byron's captor.

It shrieked and growled. Lukos darted around, snapping at its legs from behind. Byron squirmed and kicked. He pounded the tough, bumpy hide with his fists. Lukos whined as the creature landed a kick on his side but the wolf returned, more wild, more savage. The brute released its grip and Byron flew spinning to the ground.

He landed against a tree with a grunt and gasped to recover his breath. Wriggling on the ground he choked and gulped for air. Lukos snapped and snarled and the creature made a kind of froggish growling sound with its throat. Then a pale blue light appeared.

It hurtled through the forest like a ball, as big as a pumpkin, caroming off trees, leaving sparks and smoke and a trail of bluish white light. It struck Byron's attacker and exploded in a flash. The creature shrieked again and staggered back, lumbering into a tree.

In the utter darkness that followed, Byron stared about, blinking. His heart pounded in his ears and his mouth was dry. Footfalls crashed away into the night. Silence followed. Then a wet nose poked Byron in the neck and a large tongue licked him.

"Byron?" called a voice.

Another light appeared in the air about ten feet away. Hixima emerged from the darkness beneath it. She held the light up and it dripped from her hand to the ground where it pooled at her feet and soaked into the forest floor. Then she scooped more of it from the air with her other hand and threw both fistfuls into the darkness above. The woods lit up like early twilight. Byron and Lukos both gazed at the priestess. Her face was twisted with concern.

"Are you hurt?" Hixima said. "Either of you?"

"No," Byron said. Lukos sat down beside him.

Hixima approached them, peering at the wolf. "The same?" she said. "Are you sure? No ... yes ... yes, of course I trust your sense of smell."

"What's he saying?" Byron demanded.

"That it was the same creature," Hixima said, "that attacked you under the mountain."

"But it was so much bigger!" Byron said.

Hixima peered into the woods where the creature had gone. "Yes," she said. "Lukos agrees."

Her light faded. "Very well," she said and another appeared. She held it between her hands and it grew to the size of a pumpkin. Then she let go of it and it floated into the air. "The orb will guide you in. Get back to the house and lock up."

"What about you?" Byron said.

"I must purge this creature from Bilérica. Then I must weave a hedge around us so it cannot return. Do not expect me before morning. I'll be all night about it. I'll have to go to a high place." Hixima stopped for a moment in thought. "Off with you," she said. "Lukos is your guardian and that is reason enough for calm."

She turned and headed for the path. Her footsteps died away. Lukos sniffed the ground where the creature had trod. Then he crouched to the ground beside Byron. Without thinking, Byron climbed onto the wolf's back and together they set off for the house.

All the companions were gathered on the terrace, looking east. Byron saw the huge shapes of Manakar and Lucia, surrounded by the rest, staring in total silence toward the horizon. The star was gone from the sky. Byron ran forward and slapped his hands on the low terrace wall.

"Shilo saw it go," Dindra whispered to him. "She called the rest of us to come. She was the only one of us watching."

"What could we have done to stop it?" Nosh said. "What difference does it make who saw?"

Byron sat down on the step leading to Lukos's platform. He

put his chin on his fist and sighed. Lukos sat next to him, facing east, sniffing the wind that began to rise. No one spoke again. One by one they slipped away to bed and burrow, heads bowed, shoulders drooping. Byron went to his room. He lay on the bed staring up into the darkness and Lukos, Wolfen King, took up his post by the door.

Chapter 14

Mr. Thumose

lue light flickered all night. The wind came in surges, howling and dying. Byron stood for a while by his window, watching. Each time he ventured out into the strange spell-weather to see if the star had returned, he could only stand and let his shoulders sag with disappointment.

Hixima stopped her conjuring sometime in the dark before dawn. Byron lay awake all night, listening to the wind, until the first birds began to sing and morning white grew in his window from the black and dark blue of nighttime.

"Guess I'll go see what's for breakfast," he said when the sun was fully risen and a mote-filled sunbeam fell through his window. Byron splashed his face with water from the basin, took the strange staff from beside the door and went out.

The world was very green and still wet with dew in the shady places. Lukos was not waiting on the stoop. Byron frowned a little and shrugged.

"Guess he figures Hixima's spell is enough," Byron said as he stepped out the gate and headed off to join his friends.

He found them gathered on the terrace. Lukos stood on his lookout, watching the east. He turned and sniffed the air as Byron stepped around the corner of the house. The wolf put his ears back a little, but no one else noticed Byron. A moment later, Nosh and Rufus came out carrying pitchers and cups. Nosh was shaking his head and frowning.

"No, no," Rufus said. "If you put the toothpick in and it comes out dry you've overdone 'em. The trick to fine sticky buns is to undercook 'em just a bit, so they're nice and stretchy."

"It's a fine line between stretchy and raw," Nosh said. "I say get the cake part baked and let the sticky part cover your mistakes."

Rufus smiled and shook his head as they approached the group. He and Nosh started filling cups with juice from the pitchers.

"The same creature?" Dindra said. "Thanks, Nosh." She sipped her juice but never took her eyes from Shilo.

"That's what Lucia told me," Shilo said. "Only it was bigger."

"Bigger?" Raefer said.

"That's right," Shilo said. "It tried to carry him off but Lukos stopped it."

"What are you talking about?" Nosh said.

"Byron was attacked last night in the woods," Shilo said. Nosh almost dropped his pitcher. "What?"

"Shilo got it from Lucia," Dindra said. "Lucia got it from a raccoon that lives by the fruit cellar. The woods are buzzing with it. Lukos isn't talking, of course."

"The raccoon got it from a skunk that heard it from an owl who saw the whole thing," Shilo said. "The owl heard Lukos tell Hixima that it was the very same creature Byron met in the tunnels, the one that pulled off his horn."

"But it was bigger?" Nosh said.

Shilo nodded. "That's what Lucia told me."

"Is it following him?" Dindra said.

"Sure seems that way," Shilo said. "Lucia said Hixima finally ran it off with a blast of light. She went up to the hilltop to cast a spell that would drive the thing away. Then she made a hedge to keep it out of Bilérica."

"Where's Byron now?" Rufus said.

"Still sleeping," Shilo said. "I checked a little while ago."

"So that's what all the blue light was about last night," Rufus said. "And that wind!"

"I've seen Hixima's magic before," Quill said. "But not like that. Even my mother was amazed. We watched all night from the aeries."

Nosh put his hands behind his back and shifted his weight from one foot to the other. "Uh ..." he said, "what blue light?"

Everyone snapped their heads around. Even Lukos took his gaze off the east and looked at Nosh. He sniffed the air in the dwarf's direction, then turned to face the sky again.

"You didn't see?" Shilo said. "It went on all night, how could you not see? The whole hilltop was covered with dancing light and the wind was howling."

"It looked to me like it was coming from Standing Stone Hill," Raefer said.

"It was," Quill said. "Wasn't it beautiful? Hixima's light is such a happy shade of blue."

"Nuts," Nosh said. "I slept right through it."

"I know," Dindra said. "I could hear you snoring."

"A dwarf needs his sleep," Nosh said, tipping the pitcher over Raefer's cup.

"Thanks Nosh," Raefer said. "And don't feel bad. You'll get your chance."

"Oh, right," Rufus said with a laugh. "Things like that happen every week around here."

"Where's Hixima now?" Raefer said.

"Still in her chamber," Shilo said. "I heard her moving around as I went by."

"She must be exhausted," Dindra said.

"It must've been some spell she was weaving," Raefer said. "There's still a little breeze from it."

"I wonder if it'll keep us in as well as keeping things out," Rufus said.

"Don't suppose it matters, now that the star is gone," Nosh said.

Rufus shrugged. "We have to get home don't we?"

"Well, there's no hurry is there?" Dindra said.

"Maybe not for you," Rufus said. "But if I get back soon I won't have so much scout training to catch up on."

"Couldn't we wait for spring?" Shilo said. "We'll have to get permission from the griffins."

"My father's gonna brain me when I get home," Nosh said. "And Uncle Dornthelf ... I don't think I can ever go back."

"I wonder how things are in Woody Deep," Dindra said.

"I don't get it," Raefer said. "It can't just be over, just like that. I don't get it."

"Who's gonna tell Dyion?" Nosh said.

"I think we all should," Quill said. "As soon as we see him."

"He's not gonna like it," Dindra said.

"What else can we do?" Rufus said.

"I don't know ..." Dindra said. "Nothing I guess."

"I just don't get it," Raefer insisted. "How can Silverlance expect us to find him if he takes away our guide? I just don't get it."

"Well, I hate to say it Raef," Rufus said. "But maybe there is no Silverlance. It's only a story after all."

Raefer shook his head. "So, why did the star appear in the first place?"

"Just a weird thing that happened," Nosh said, shaking his head.

"No way," Raefer said. "It all adds up. Midwinter, full moon, new star, findrels out of the western wood. I say it all adds up."

"Well we did the best we could, Raef," Rufus said. "Just let it go at that."

Byron stood with his fists clenched tight on the staff. He grit his teeth and snarled. His face was red and his nostrils flared. He took a deep breath and set off at a run for the front of the house. He stopped for a moment at the sound of laughter coming from the terrace. He stomped a hoof, turned and kept on, running as fast as he could down the path into the woods.

He ran and ran until the tears stopped falling and his face was taut with their dried streaks. He wandered through the woods, crossed the stream three times and climbed a very steep hill. Near the top he stepped out from under the trees and set off across the grassy crest. Byron turned from east to west as he topped the hill. There, in the middle, was the standing stone.

It was dark against the blue sky. The surface was cold and rough beneath Byron's hand. Pink clover dotted the grass all around, shimmering in the strong wind that rushed across the hill. He put his back against the stone and lowered himself to the grass.

"All this way for nothing," he said. The wind whistled in his ears. "Now what? Rufus is a fungus-brain. No Silverlance."

Byron sniffled.

"Oh, what's the use? It was crazy enough when there was a star to follow. I can't just go off without my friends, can I?"

"Certainly not," said a deep voice. "Unless they've abandoned the quest, in which case you *must* leave them."

Byron sprang to his hooves and turned. He staggered back

several paces holding the staff before him. Beside the stone stood a great big farm horse, gray as the rock. It was wide through the shoulders, had a long, dingy tail and a mane that fell over its eyes and forehead. Huge shocks of the same dingy hair covered its fetlocks and hooves. The horse blew through its nostrils and lowered its head.

"Don't be afraid," it said.

"You spoke!"

"Forgive me. I thought you wouldn't mind."

"No . . . no, I mean . . . I understood you . . ."

"Of course you did, I spoke in a language that you know. What did you plan to do with that?"

Byron looked at the staff in his fists. "Oh," he said. "Sorry. I . . . you startled me." He set the staff against the stone.

The horse leaned down and smelled the strange, glazed object. He nibbled at it with his lips and nickered as it slid against the rock and fell into the grass. "Where did you get it?"

"Under the mountain," Byron said. "I found it in the ashes . . . before the creature came."

"A prize then," the horse said. "No adventure is complete without a prize to show for it." He stepped away a few paces and lowered his nose to the clover. He didn't eat but breathed the fragrance through his gaping nostrils. "Again, I ask your pardon for startling you." He lifted his head and looked at Byron. "My name is Thúmose. And you, I believe, are Byron Thorn."

Byron blinked. "That's right."

"Hixima has told me about you. She told me of the wound you suffered. Does it still trouble you?"

"Not really . . . well . . . a little."

"Yes. Such things are slow to heal. I took a bit of a wound myself once, long ago."

Byron peered at Thúmose. Under the shags of hair that fell between the horse's eyes, he could see the edge of a scar. The flesh was pink and swollen and glistened a little in the sunlight.

"And she told me why you have come," the horse continued. "You must be very disappointed at the setting of the star."

Byron slouched. "Yes."

"Yes, a long way to come for nothing. But you are not alone. You've made friends along the way."

"Yes."

"Yes. Tell me why you left your home."

Byron shrugged. "I wanted to follow the star."

"And so you have."

"Yes ... but ..."

"There is more?"

"I wanted to find out where it led."

"And you haven't."

"No."

"How do you know?"

"I don't feel ... I don't feel finished yet."

"I see. Then, you are right."

"I am?"

"Certainly. You feel there is further to go."

Byron nodded. "Mm-hm."

"And there is, Byron. There is always further to go."

Byron frowned and looked at the clover. He poked at it with his hoof. "But my friends won't come with me, not without the star."

"Why do they need the star?"

"It was our guide."

"You remember what it looked like, don't you?"

"Yes."

"And near enough where it was in the sky."

"It was always right in the path of the sun."

"There you are. You know where to go. Go that way until it feels right to stop. If it never does, then keep going."

"Forever?"

"Why not? You've already begun."

"They'll never go for that. They're already talking about home. All except for Raefer."

"Bosh!" the horse said. "That silly star was only a beginning. One sign takes up where another leaves off. And they will not always be so clear. That is the way of things, Byron. Why, you might follow that star for the rest of your life and never see it again."

"Really?"

"Really. You will only know each sign for having followed the one before it. Did you honestly think you'd only get the one to go on in all the years of life ahead of you? Who could manage that?"

"I don't know. I'd say you could, Mr. Thúmose."

"I've had a star or two of my own to follow. At any rate your friends must choose for themselves and so must you."

"Well . . ."

"You set off alone once before."

Byron looked at the horse.

"Where was the star when you were wandering in the belly of the mountain?"

Byron said nothing.

"Was it the star that carried you in its talons to the mouth of the tunnel?"

Byron folded his arms and looked at the mountains.

"Was it the star that carried you on its back through the snowfield woods?"

Byron sighed.

"Remember the rope bridge?" Thúmose said. "Remember the wolves? Remember the villagers and the hunters who tried to take you? Remember that hideous two-headed brute who tried to eat you? Remember the salamanders who would have burned you like straw in the ember groves, for believe me Byron, that is what they intended. Remember that wicked little beast that took your horn?"

Still Byron said nothing.

"Where was the star in all of that?" the horse continued.

Byron looked at the ground.

"If Silverlance wants you to find him, the path itself will guide you."

"Silverlance ..." Byron said, looking east.

"Byron, what would Gradda tell you to do?"

Byron looked at the horse, then beyond him to the Crestfalls. The tall peaks gathered around the Old Mountain like spears. Byron lifted his chin. "Gradda ... He'd tell me to follow my heart and not my head."

"And what is your heart telling you?"

"My heart says continue, Mr. Thúmose, my heart says keep on."

"And what do you say to that?"

"Yes, Mr. Thúmose, I say yes."

"Good! In that case, you must seek the place called Tri-lithon."

"Trilithon?" Byron said.

"Yes. You will know what to do when you get there. A pity Miroaster isn't here. A better guide you could not ask for but his business is urgent, dire even. No, he can't help you, but there is someone who can. His name is Peter Oatencake."

Byron smiled. "Peter Oatencake? What sort of name is that?"

"Does that matter? He's a stout fellow and clever. He will help you, if you can find him. Perhaps Hixima can send him word of your coming. Now, Byron, run and tell your friends all I have told you. Say to them that you are going on with or without them and that you are leaving tonight in darkness."

"Tonight!" Byron cried. He jumped up and down and slapped his thighs.

"Yes, Byron, tonight. There are times when it is wise to wait. This is not one of those times. Off you go, now. Find your friends at once. You have much to do to prepare."

Byron set off toward the hillside. "To Trilithon!" he shouted and he leaped into the air. "Trilithon, Mr. Thúmose!"

"And beyond, " Thúmose called back, "to where morning is born! Byron!"

"Yes, sir?" Byron said, turning and smiling wide.

"Don't forget your staff."

"Oh! Right!" Byron said. He ran back to the standing stone, snatched up his staff from the grass and dashed away across the hillcrest. "Goodbye, Mr. Thúmose!" he called over his shoulder. He kept on running until he reached the house, short of breath, smiling as wide as he could.

It was lunchtime. The companions were sitting at the table on the lawn, laughing and talking together. "Trilithon!" Byron shouted. "Trilithon, everybody!"

Dindra looked up and smiled. "There you are. Lunch is ready."

"Where ya been, Byron?" Quill said.

"Pass the bread, Raefer," Nosh said. "Hello, Byron."

"Trilithon!" Byron cried. "We've got to go to Trilithon! Mr. Thúmose told me!"

"What's Trilithon?" Raefer said, standing up.

"Come and eat your lunch, Byron," Rufus said. "We've got something to tell you."

Byron shook his head. "I know what you're gonna say. Forget it. I'm not going back, I'm heading for Trilithon."

"What's Trilithon?" Raefer said.

"Byron, the star has gone away," Rufus said. "What more do you want?"

"We don't need the star anymore," Byron said. "At least I don't. I'm going on. I'm heading for Trilithon."

"Byron, what's Trilithon?" Raefer shouted.

"I don't know, Raef," Byron said. "but Mr. Thúmose told me to go there."

"Thúmose?" said a voice. Hixima came toward them wearing a long robe. Her hair was loose about her shoulders. Her face was pale and drawn and there were shadows under her eyes.

"Oh, Hixima," Shilo said. "Are you all right?"

"Yes, Shilo," Hixima said with a weak smile. "I'll be fine with a bit more rest. The spell-weaving last night was more than I bargained for. What's this about Thúmose, Byron? Have you been talking to him?"

"Yes," Byron said. "I saw him on top of Standing Stone Hill."

"He came to you there?" Hixima said. She looked at Byron with wonder in her eyes.

"That's right," Byron said. "He told me to find a place called Trilithon. He told me to go by myself if I had to, but to leave tonight, in the dark. I'm going. I'm going to Trilithon."

"I'm going with you!" Raefer shouted. He ran to Byron's side and the two embraced and locked hands.

"Raefer you can't be serious," Rufus said. "This whole thing was bad enough when we knew where we were going. Now you don't even have a star to go on!"

A whimpering growl turned everyone's head. Lukos came around the side of the house and trotted up to Byron and Raefer. The wolf sat beside Byron and poked him in the neck with his nose. Lukos lifted his tail and slapped it to the ground one time.

Byron looked at Rufus. "I guess that makes three so far."

"One wolf and two buffoons," Rufus said. "That ought to be enough."

"If Silverlance wants us to find him, then the path itself will guide us," Byron said with a firm nod.

"That's the spirit, Byron," Raefer said.

Hixima smiled. "Did Thúmose tell you that?"

"Mm-hm," Byron said.

"Did Thúmose tell you how to find this Trilithon place?" Rufus said.

"No," Byron answered, "but he told me who could. A man named Oatencake."

"Oatencake?" Hixima said.

"You know him?" Byron said.

"Yes, I know him. He's an able man and trustworthy. He has a special magic about him."

"Well, I'm not turning back," Dindra said. "Byron wanted to run off the moment he saw that star. If he's not finished that means it isn't over. I'm coming too, Byron."

"So am I," said Shilo. "Calling it quits when we still have a lead to follow just doesn't feel right."

"Well, count me in," Nosh said. "I can't go home anyway."

"I'd like to come, too," Quill said. "I know my mother will shriek about it, but I knew I wanted to join you all when I met you in the high chamber. What do you say? May I?"

"Of course you may," Dindra said. "You've already joined us, didn't you know?"

"Come on, Rufus," Raefer said.

Rufus folded his arms.

"Hixima trusts Thúmose," Raefer said. "Don't you, Hixima?"

Hixima raised her eyebrows and nodded. She did not speak, but her face was very serious.

Raefer shrugged. "And you trust Hixima, right, Ruf?"

"Well ... yes ..." Rufus said, looking sidelong at Hixima.

"Please, Ruf?" Byron said. "We can't turn back now, we just can't."

Rufus dropped his arms to his sides and looked at Byron.

"Yeah, Rufus," Dindra said, "please come."

"You some kinda sissy, Rufus?" Nosh said.

Rufus frowned. He looked at the mountains and sighed. "All right, I'll come," he said. "The sky is full of stars. That big one can't be the only one that knows the way."

"That's the stuff, Rufus Nimbletwig!" Raefer said, tousling his brother's hair. "We'll make a dryad out of you yet."

"But if we ever meet this Silverlance I'll want to ask him a question or two," Rufus said.

The companions gathered together in a mass of clasped hands, slapped shoulders and ruffled heads. They started to sit down at their places when Lukos gave a low growl and barked.

"Lukos is right," Hixima said. "You have only enough time to prepare yourselves. Remember it is still winter in the world outside Bilérica."

"Well, Byron has to eat," Dindra said. "He never even had breakfast."

"Right you are, Dindra," Hixima said. "Byron, you sit and eat your fill. Rufus and Nosh clear away the dishes he's not using.

The rest of you follow me. You'll need food and full water skins and fresh torches and tinder for all."

Rufus and Nosh set off for the kitchen with armloads of dishes. The others followed Hixima toward the gate. Byron sat down to the table and began helping himself to the food. A wide smile stretched across his face. As he sat chewing his first mouthful, Raefer stepped up beside him.

"Thanks, Byron," he said.

"For what?" Byron said.

"For seeing it through. You're the only one who could've done it."

Byron shrugged and took another bite.

Raefer smiled. He clapped his hands and ground his palms together. "Trilithon!" he said and he ran off to catch up with the others.

CHAPTER 15

A WIZARDS' DUEL

hey waited in torchlight, six hooded forms all silent. The garden was a glade of dancing shadows. Hixima appeared. Her face was worn and tired.

"The hedge takes strength to maintain," she said when she saw their shared glances of alarm. "Don't worry about me, I have carried greater weight than this before. Come, there is no knowing how much time you have. Let this be goodbye, for you must be silent as you leave Bilérica."

"Where are Manakar and Lucia?" Shilo said.

"With Thúmose, in the orchard," Hixima said. "Manakar was not happy about it, but Thúmose convinced him. The animals have come to their journeys' end."

"I wanted to say goodbye to them," Shilo said.

"I will say it for you," Hixima said.

One by one they embraced Hixima and thanked her. She held Byron longer than the rest and kissed the wound on his head. When they had said goodbye Hixima turned and set off toward the gate. A great light appeared in the sky to the north.

It was ball of purple flame with a shadowy tail, soaring high into the night. All of Bilérica lit up beneath it and it exploded with a crack like thunder. Streaks of purple spread out in all directions in the sky. Fields and fields of sparks shot everywhere, but nothing of the flame reached the ground. Instead, the fire had struck some huge invisible dome. Sparks and trailers spread out across its width.

"That's over Standing Stone Hill!" Quill said.

"Of course," Hixima said. "I anchored the spell to the stone itself! How could he have known?"

"Who?" Byron said.

Hixima's face went grave. "Ravinath."

"Ravinath?" Byron, Dindra and Shilo all cried out together. "Ravinath is out there?"

"Who's Ravinath?" Nosh said.

"No time," Hixima said. "I must go to the hilltop to defend the hedge. I'll hold him out as long as I can. Get far away and quickly. Oatencake may have heard of your coming already."

As she spoke, Hixima scooped a fistful of light from the air and shaped it into a ball. "Follow the lamp. Be quick and quiet. Good luck to you all and may you come before Silverlance at last!"

Hixima set off running for the hilltop. Another long arch of purple light appeared in the sky, exploding as before. A spider web of blue light streaked out in all directions, giving shape to the invisible dome. The ground shook and a fire broke out in the forest to the west.

"It's cracking!" Quill said. "The hedge is weakening!"

"Come on!" Rufus said. "No time to lose!"

Hixima's blue lamp led them into a hollow with tree limbs entwined above it. Another stroke of purple light filled the shadows. There was a terrific explosion. The blue maze appeared again as the dome of the hedge shuddered beneath Ravinath's magic fire. Hixima's answer flashed blue and bright, high off Standing Stone Hill. Seconds later there was a terrible crack as it struck its mark somewhere to the north.

"Come on," Rufus said and they pushed forward.

Further in, the hollow narrowed down into a gully with steep sides. The blue lamp stopped and hovered for a moment. The light dripped to the ground and disappeared into the soil. Rufus lit a torch and held it before him, peering into the darkness.

"How do we find an invisible gate?" Byron said.

Purple light filled the sky, followed by a loud crack that shivered the magic hedge. Blue lines appeared before the group, reaching to the ground at the mouth of the gully. A dark space, shaped like a door, appeared in the blue lines. The companions passed through the hedge, leaving the place of summer behind. Seen from outside the hedge, Bilérica looked hidden beneath the snow. No footprints marked the ground in the gully through which the group had come. There was no sign of their passing.

Hixima's blue light shot into the sky. The concussion was slow, mounting like distant thunder. The ground trembled and shook snow from the trees. Lukos sniffed the air and growled.

"Where is that flying rat?" said an angry voice. "Led us on a blind hunt in the dark."

Another voice answered. "No flying squirrel was ever mind enough for five minutes alone with Ravinath. It wouldn't dare lead us wrong."

"Both of you shut your yaps!" hissed a third voice. "Do you want to blow a horn while you're at it?"

Rufus jabbed his torch into the snow. The companions crouched in the darkness behind the rocks at the mouth of the narrow. The night was clear and starry through the trees. Moonlight slashed the winter wood with crisscrossing shadows. Somewhere in the forest ahead there were muffled hoofbeats moving to and fro.

"How far off are they?" Raefer whispered.

"I can't tell," Rufus said. "It sounds like they're all over. We could walk right into them."

"Well, we can't stay here," Nosh said. "Or they'll walk right into *us*."

"Everyone hush!" Dindra hissed. "They'll hear you!"

"Listen!" Shilo said.

An owl called from somewhere deep in the woods. Another answered it and then a third. Close by a fourth owl hooted, low and throaty.

"They're speaking!" Shilo said. "This one close by says to stay low and wait."

One of the owls further off gave several loud hoots.

"There are eleven of them," Shilo said.

"Owls?" Byron said.

"No, not owls!" Shilo said. "Centaurs." Another owl sounded in the distance. "It says 'The one with the net is very near.' "

"Baruwan," Dindra said.

"How near?" Rufus said.

The closest owl hooted again, low and deep and drawn out.

"Near enough to hear," Shilo whispered.

Everyone ducked low. Dindra crouched to her haunches with Byron huddled close on her back. Lukos sidled up to them and settled into a stalking stance, ready to spring.

Another stroke of purple light opened in the sky. It lit the wood like day. Shadows fell thick for a moment, then the light faded. Everyone ducked and covered their ears from the crack that followed. The ground shook. Then all was quiet.

Again the owls called. The woods echoed with the sound. They were moving among the treetops, sometimes calling from the wing.

"They're tracking the centaurs," Shilo whispered. "They're keeping each other posted."

The trees blinked into clear view in the light of Hixima's blue fire. A strong wind followed the rumbling explosion and came sweeping through the forest. Snow billowed and hissed. Byron covered his face until it was over and he looked up just in time to see a huge dark shape appear from the trees on the left side of the riverbed.

In the moonlight the markings on Baruwan's face and chest and arms were like thick, black scars. He held a long spear in his fist and the chain of his net glinted under the moon. He stood with his side to the group as he crossed the riverbed and stopped in the middle. He switched his tail. One great hoof rose from the snow and fell again with a muffled thud.

When Baruwan turned his head, Byron could see the markings on his face. They moved and distorted the centaur's expression, twisting it and bending it. Byron watched in horror as the face of the centaur shifted and changed. The owls called. Baruwan looked for them in the trees. Purple light flashed above the forest. Baruwan did not flinch in the crash that followed. The centaur looked around once more, then set off at a walk up the right bank of the riverbed.

Long minutes passed. The owls continued to call, each time from farther away. The cries echoed in the forest until at last they faded into the distance and all was quiet. The owl in the nearby tree hooted louder than before. Shilo stood and looked up at him on his perch as she brushed the snow from her cape.

"They're gone," she said. "They've moved off to the south. All of them."

The owl swooped down and landed on the upturned branch of a fallen tree. It looked at Shilo and blinked.

Shilo gasped. "The flying squirrel? Are you sure?"

The owl blinked again.

"But you caught him?" Shilo said. "What will you do with him?"

The owl continued to look at Shilo.

She wrinkled her nose. "Well, I suppose that's what owls do with squirrels."

She turned to the others and found them all looking at her with blank stares.

"He says the flying squirrel told Ravinath everything!" she said.

"Uh ... Shilo," Byron said. "The owl hasn't made a sound."

"Not a peep," Nosh said.

Shilo frowned. "Of course he has. He's been telling me all sorts of things. The flying squirrel told Ravinath where we were and he was leading them to the hedge gate. Ravinath even figured out that Hixima's spell was anchored to the standing stone because of something the squirrel said."

"Shilo," Dindra said. "You can hear his thoughts ... just like Hixima!"

Shilo blinked at Dindra. "I can ..."

The owl hooted and flapped into a tree. It stared down at Shilo.

"You will?" Shilo said. "That's wonderful! He says he'll guide us to Peter Oatencake's winter camp."

"How far is it?" Rufus said.

"We may reach him tonight if we move fast," Shilo said, still focused on the owl. "The animals are keeping watch."

"Ask him his name," Quill said.

Shilo frowned, concentrating on the owl. "His name is impossible to pronounce. He says call him Jyro. He's one of the exiled owls of Faerwood."

"Where's that?" Raefer said.

"A bit north of here," Quill said.

"For a griffin, maybe," Nosh said. "It's four or five days on foot."

"They live in the forest here now," Shilo said, staring at the owl. "If Silverlance returns, there may be hope of their going home someday. That's why he's helping us."

"What drove them out?" Byron said.

Shilo squinted at the owl. "He says a wicked mage came to the wood in the years after Silverlance. Those who survived and were able to flee have never returned, for the evil remains. He says there are many places on this side of the mountains where evil is strong.

"No … all right … I won't," Shilo continued. "He says I should just keep answering with my voice. Eventually, I'll stop needing to speak. Is everyone ready? All right, Jyro, let's go."

A blue flash overpowered the moonlight. Jyro set off, spreading his wings wide and floated away into the shadows. The companions gathered up their things and followed.

All night the magic flames raged. Thunder shook the hills without pause. Jyro led the companions by hidden ways, winding and narrow, deep into the densest places of the wood. The moon went west beyond the mountains and the stars shone brighter in the darkness. From a snowy hilltop the companions looked back.

To the left was Standing Stone Hill. Another hill, not as tall, stood to the right. Bolts of purple and blue flared and crackled between the hills as the duel of Ravinath and Hixima continued. The companions huddled close together to watch the volley of fire. Hixima's blue flame leaped up. For a moment the stone itself could be seen, a tiny white splinter on the hillcrest which, from the world outside Bilérica, seemed covered with snow.

From the other hill, a dark purple light flickered and ran in great cracks down the hillside. It gathered again on the hilltop and shot across to the other hill in a long arch. High in the sky the two flames clashed and lit the world. Both lights flared and vanished.

So it went.

Purple light followed blue in flash after flash of towering flame. In a great, sudden surge Hixima's light erupted more powerful than ever. Fire broke out on the hill where Ravinath stood. A creeping darkness spread out from the middle of his hill, engulfing the blue flames. The woods went dark for a time.

There was no sound. A strange wind arose. The ground trembled. The group looked on as the snow billowed around them. Then the wind died to utter calm. There was a heavy silence and the purple light returned.

It spread out as before, running in cracks down the hillside, but it roamed out much farther into the valley. It set the woods aflame where it passed, then gathered back into itself on the hilltop. A second later it blazed out again, spinning, hurtling through the air toward Standing Stone Hill.

The valley shook. The wind howled, slashing the companions with razor snow. The flash was blinding, the crack enormous and terrifying. Byron covered his eyes and the shock hammered his chest. Everyone cried out in alarm. When it was over, Standing Stone Hill was burning. Fire raged in the woods below. Hixima's blue flame was still.

As daylight grew the companions stared across the valley. Shilo wept. Byron sat shaking on Dindra's back, his face stricken. The others gaped with blank, witless stares. The woods all around the foot of Standing Stone Hill were black and burning. The slopes were charred free of all growth and the crest, where the standing stone had been, was simply broken off like a tree stump, smoking and smoldering with little fires dancing here and there. Jyro sat in a tree hooting at them. It was a long time before anyone noticed.

"What's he saying, Shi?" Dindra said. "He sounds anxious."

Shilo's voice cracked. "He wants us to get off the hill . . . before the sun gets any higher."

Dindra looked east. "He's right, everyone. Baruwan might see us here."

"Or Ravinath," Byron said and he sniffled.

"Poor Hixima," Quill said.

"Maybe . . . maybe she's all right . . ." Nosh said.

No one answered.

Jyro hooted and flapped his wings. He swooped in to lead the way and the companions followed. Byron looked back until the charred neck of Standing Stone Hill was out of sight. For a while longer he kept looking back, watching the haze of smoke that gathered against the mountains.

ϲhαpt℈ℜ 16

Eα℈twαℜd

 ours passed. The group marched on, silent, following Jyro through the woods. The snow was deep. The companions wept or simply stared ahead of them as they marched. In the midafternoon as Byron sat gazing into the woods, he felt the sting of fresh tears returning at the memory of the hilltop. Dindra looked back at him and stopped.

"Shouldn't we eat?" she said.

Everyone halted.

"Yes," Rufus said. Jyro came back and perched in a tree.

"Just the thing," Raefer said with a firm nod. "Come on everyone. Let's make a real lunch with a fire and hot drinks."

"Great idea, Raef," Dindra said. She looked back at Byron. "Come on, off you get. Start clearing a place for the fire."

"Do you really think a fire is a good idea?" Rufus said.

"I think a fire is exactly what we need," Dindra said. "It won't show in broad daylight, and we'll keep it hot so it won't smoke. Come on Ruf, you and Raefer get some wood together."

Soon Nosh was coaxing a small flame up from the sticks. Raefer peered over his shoulder. Nosh saw his shadow and looked up.

"Quit lookin' will ya?" Nosh said and hunched his shoulder over his work.

"Just show me how you do it," Raefer said. He stood back and put his hands on his hips.

"Raefer, leave him be," Shilo said.

"But he doesn't use a flint, or tinder or anything," Raefer insisted.

"Help Byron with the drinks," Dindra said. "Hixima gave us four jugs of cider. Get it warming, will you?"

At last they were seated with cups of steaming cider in their hands and plates of dried meat and fruit before them. They ate in silence for a long time. The sun pressed on deep into the afternoon and the shadows changed direction on the snow-clad forest floor.

"Who is this Ravinath, anyway?" Rufus said.

"He's a centaur," Byron said. "A sorcerer."

"He's very old," Dindra added. "He was a hero in the Wolfen War. Lukos probably remembers him."

Shilo snapped her head around to look at the wolf. "Did you say something?" she said. Lukos looked at her and she squinted a little. "He says he remembers Ravinath well. All the pups were afraid of him. He was wild and fierce and carried a power that the older wolves feared. He was terrible to see and few wolves stood their ground in his presence."

"So he was a hero?" Nosh said.

Dindra nodded. "A great one. But something happened. After the war was over he went off by himself and started his society. That's the painted centaurs, like Baruwan."

"So why is he chasing you?" Rufus said.

Shilo turned her head to Lukos. "He's chasing all of us, Lukos says."

"Why?" Nosh said.

"To stop us from reaching Silverlance," Shilo said, still looking at Lukos.

"Silverlance," Rufus muttered. "What of 'im?"

Lukos uttered a low growl that rumbled deep in his chest. "Can you save yourself from the likes of Ravinath?" Shilo said, speaking for the wolf. "The owl was right, there are places in this land where evil lives and is strong. Dark days are coming. Dark things emerging. Ravinath has already shown himself."

"But is Silverlance even real?" Rufus said.

"If he isn't," Shilo said for Lukos, "then we are doomed."

"Doomed indeed," said a voice.

Everyone turned to see a strange man leaning against the tree where Jyro was perched. His arms were folded and he gazed into the fire. He had one eyebrow raised and he did not blink.

"Lucky for us he is real," the man said. "Real as that fire there burning." Then he looked up and noticed the others gaping at him. Even Lukos was surprised and came to all fours. Jyro flapped his wings in mild alarm. "Ah, forgive me!" the man said. "I've forgotten my manners. Comes of days alone out here with the wind in my ears. Allow me to introduce myself. My name is Peter Oatencake."

He was tall and broad-shouldered. He wore a tattered brown cape with the hood up. Pressed down on top of the hood he wore a straw hat with a wide, flat brim and a cone-shaped crown with a hole in it. Beneath the cape he wore a battered shirt of rings, grey wool leggings and thick fur boots cross-gartered to his calves. On his hands he wore woven mittens and through the crook of his arm he bore a terrible-looking weapon. The haft was wooden, a bit longer than that of an axe and fixed to the end was a hooked blade about a foot long and very, very sharp. Everyone stood and faced the man, but nobody, not even Lukos, moved a step toward him. All eyes were fixed on the strange weapon he was holding.

Oatencake looked around at the faces. "Now, now," he said, shouldering the blade. "Have no fear of the slash hook, unless you mean some harm to Oatencake."

"No, sir," Byron said. "We don't mean you any harm."

"As I hoped, little findrel," Oatencake said. "You're a bit far from home, aren't you?"

"Yes, sir," Byron said.

Oatencake smiled. "Now winter is a slow season. Oatencake hasn't so much to do: a bit of trappin', a bit of trekkin', a bit of checkin' on this neighbor or that. But that doesn't mean he's naught on his mind. What is it you want out here in the wild so far from home?"

"You don't know?" Rufus said.

"The animals have a way of mixing their messages," Oatecake said. "Chitterin' and chatterin' seldom gets the point across and I've never been able to hear them clearly. All I could gather was that you were abroad. And after the firestorm last night I guessed you'd brought trouble."

"We didn't mean to," Raefer said.

"Well, maybe not," Oatencake said. "Still, it's come. But don't you worry. I've seen the centaurs you're runnin' from and I'd be of a mind to help anyone with those fellas at their back. The word I got came from Hixima; that's enough for me to lend a hand."

"Mr. Thúmose told us to find you," Byron said. "He said you could show us the way."

"Thúmose?" Oatencake said. He stared at Byron for a moment. "You've been to see Thúmose? And just where is it he wants me to take you?"

"Trilithon," Byron said. "He said you could lead us to Trilithon."

Oatencake recoiled as if he'd been struck. "Tril ... What in the name of piracy are you goin' there for?"

"We were following the star," Byron said.

Oatencake blinked and shook his head. "The star!" He looked around him, then sat down on a large rock and planted the slash hook butt first in the snow.

"Yes, sir," Byron said. "Until it went down ... and Mr. Thúmose said we shouldn't stop, not ever and ..."

Oatencake laughed and put up his hand. "All I wanted this winter was to smoke enough trout for the spring time."

The companions glanced around at each other.

"You do know the way," Shilo said. "Don't you?"

Oatencake looked up at her. "Well, of course I know the way. I just don't relish the journey, as you might imagine."

The group looked at him with blank stares.

Oatencake returned the look. "Did Thúmose mention the Valley of the Nine Spires?" he said with a squint.

"No," Byron said.

Oatencake leaned forward. "Or Shadowmaw Gap?"

Byron looked sidelong from left to right. "No ..."

"Why?" Rufus said, looking hard at Byron.

Oatencake nodded. "And I don't suppose he said aught of Qualnáchnabard?"

"No," Byron said. "He didn't mention any of those ..." he glanced at Rufus, "places ..."

"And why would he?" Oatencake said. "You'd only turn

back if you knew what lay ahead. Well, I know why he sent you to me. I know the way, sure enough. I've wandered among the spires many times hunting this or stalking that. But I've come in sight of the temple on just three occasions and never did I venture far inside. I suppose it had to be Oatencake to do the job? Miroaster nowhere to be found?"

"No," Byron said, shaking his head.

"No, indeed," said Oatencake. "Off on some errand of urgency, I doubt not."

"Mr. Oatencake," Raefer said. "Did you say we're going through this place you mentioned? Qualna ... Qual ..."

"Qualnáchnabard," Oatencake said. "The Temple of Borántu. No I didn't say it. But we are, straight through. To reach Trilithon we must pass through Shadowmaw Gap. Qualnáchnabard is built clear across the gap from one cliff wall to the other and for who knows how deep beneath the ground.

"Just reaching the temple will be a hardship, the least of our worries but the first of them. And marching through it is unknown danger plain and simple."

"Why ..." Nosh said. "What's inside?"

"Echoes," Oatencake said. "Echoes of an ancient foe. Ah, well. Oatencake will do. Let's be at it, then, the sooner we're gone the sooner it's behind us."

Jyro left them with a hoot and a flapping of wings. The companions set off behind Peter Oatencake and marched until long after sunset. That night they cut pine branches for lean-to's to keep off the snow that fell. The shelters were warm with the companions all snuggled down. Oatencake kept watch. In the morning they woke to his whistling as he fixed them a breakfast of food he'd taken from the woods while they slept.

"I never feel the need to pack my victuals," he said as he turned the strips of browning meat. "There's everything I need all around me."

By seven o'clock they were fed and marching with their guide before them, whistling as he went with his slash hook over his shoulder.

"Well that's enough for me," Nosh said as they walked along. "If he was gonna do us dirty he'd've done it while we slept. I say we can trust 'im."

"I trusted him before," Raefer said. Then he peered at the back of Oatencake's head. "You know, I think he sleeps as he walks along."

"I'm sure of it," Shilo said, stepping up beside them. "And have you noticed how light your feet are? I think he's resting for all of us."

"How can that be?" Nosh said with a frown.

"How should I know?" Shilo said. "I just know I feel a little bit like a leaf on a stream when I'm walking behind him."

So it went. They kept a brisk, steady pace. Oatencake went along as if he were walking down the lane to his own cottage, nodding to the creatures he saw without breaking his stride or the tune he was whistling. The forest and hills and lakes went by, day after day. In time, the trees began to thin and the hills emerged from cover. Soon the forest was behind them and a wall of mountains emerged on the horizon. As they crested a tall hill Oatencake stopped to take in their whereabouts.

Westward, behind the group, the snowy tips of the Crestfall Mountains could be seen above the edge of the forest. Tall Rathrágodrak stood among them like a tooth. Eastward, the other chain of mountains lumbered along from north to south like a row of giant trolls marching to war, hulking and slouching with huge weapons thrown over their shoulders.

"The Dragon Mountains," Oatencake said. "The eastern frontier of Everándon. Said to be impassable, except for Shadow-maw Gap."

"How far is it?" Quill said.

"Closer than where you came from," Oatencake said. "Without the trees to slow us, we'll make the valley's edge in two days or three."

"I can still see the Old Mountain," Shilo said.

Oatencake nodded. "Of course you can."

"Are we all Everándons?" Byron said. "Is Silverlance really our king?"

"We are and he is," Oatencake said. "You need never have doubt of it."

"But how can he return after so long?" Rufus said. "He's just a story after all."

Oatencake gazed into the distance. "Well, Rufus," he said. "I figure a story doesn't last this long unless it has some truth to it."

As the valley drew near. Oatencake quickened his pace. Even riding on Dindra's back, Byron noticed the mysterious vigor Shilo had mentioned in following behind their guide. It was as if they were being towed. Between each step they took was a moment of effortless movement forward.

They came to a ledge overlooking the vale. It stretched for miles to the north and south. The sun was setting and the

Dragon range turned red and orange. The Nine Spires looked like pillars of flame with their shadows reaching east across the flat valley floor.

"Another day, maybe less," Oatencake said, setting the slash hook down. "Here we'll camp until morning."

Dark mist covered the valley, like shadow. It swirled and billowed waist deep on Byron. He sat on Dindra's back all morning until they came to the first of the spires. It was hundreds of feet high. Oatencake stopped and rested the companions, ordering them to eat and drink.

"Of old it was the place where the Judges came to meet," he said. "Until the enemy came."

"The Shadowbreather," Rufus said.

"Yes," Oatencake said. "The Shadowbreather. He made war on the Judges for a long, terrible time. One by one he threw them down and the Years of Fire came."

"What happened to him after that?" Byron said.

Oatencake lifted an eyebrow. "Silverlance," he said. "He brought war to the enemy. When the last days were upon the people of Everándon, Silverlance went out to meet the foe in single combat. A greater contest could never have been held, for two greater warlords did never live."

"What happened?" Rufus said in a whisper.

Oatencake shook his head. "Neither of them returned. It's said one of the Firedrakes followed Silverlance to the place where the struggle happened. But if she saw what took place and lived to tell it, it's a tale I've not heard."

"Who were they . . ." Byron said. "The Firedrakes?"

"Well, it's not altogether clear," Oatencake said. "It was a time of secret societies and orders. The Firedrakes served the

Silverlance in their own way and carried out tasks he'd give to nobody else. And the Shadowbreather had his covens and his minions serving him also."

"But the war came to an end," Nosh said. "What happened? Did we win?"

"In a way, yes, we did. The Wegs, that's the strongest of the Shadowbreather's underlings, his marshals, they were put down and sent running. But Everándon suffered with no one to rule. The Thanes, they were the marshals of Silverlance, they fought amongst themselves. There was word of betrayal and the land was slowly divided.

"After that came the long darkness. Years and more passed with lost memory and petty wars until we all settled down in our little groups and stayed well apart from one another. It's been a long, long time since Everándon saw all her people one. But if I'm not mistaken, it's a time from which we may well be emerging."

In the midafternoon they came to a place where the ground rose above the mist in a long, gentle slope. A huge skeleton lay stretched across the crest of the slope, with the remains of a vast wing stretching out from the side of it. The other wing lay in bits, smashed beneath the weight of the creature's flesh, which had long since turned to dust.

"Mirador," Oatencake said. "The Great One, chief of the Judges, the last to fall to Borántu."

"Father of Mirabell," Quill said.

"That's right," Oatencake said. "You griffins are great ones for the lore. Will you tell the story?"

"Mirabell was the fairest dragon ever born," Quill began. "Her father was Mirador and her mother was Isporeth. She was the first creature ever killed by the enemy."

"The Shadowbreather killed Mirabell?" Byron said.

"That's right," Quill said. "When she emerged from her molting place. You see, a baby dragon can't be harmed by anything, fire, swords, nothing. But after fifty or sixty years, they go inside a cave and molt. When they come out, they're grown up dragons with a softer belly. It's still pretty much impossible to kill one, but it can be done.

"Well, Mirabell was the most beautiful young dragon that ever lived. She had such a shimmering coat of scales that no one ever knew what color she was, red or silver or green. Everyone loved her and came from all over to see her and hear her fabulous call. It was decided that Mirabell would succeed her father as High Judge when he died.

"When she came out of her molting place, she was silver with green and red and yellow all through. But no sooner did she emerge than the Shadowbreather fell upon her and killed her, wounding her in the underbelly, where all dragons are weakest."

"And this skeleton was her father?" Shilo said.

"I guess so," Quill said. "I never knew about it."

"It must be a hundred feet long," Rufus said.

"Seems to have fallen from a great height," Oatencake said, "by the way that wing is smashed. He must have fought Borántu in the sky."

"But the bones should've gone away by now," Raefer said. "Back to the ground."

"Not dragon bones," Oatencake said. "No, indeed."

As they approached the mouth of Shadowmaw Gap, they passed beneath the north turret of Qualnáchnabard. A maze of stairs wandered around among the rocks beneath a complex of towers and turrets built into the mountain. Across the mouth of the gap stood another mountain with another complex carved into it. Shadowmaw Gap opened between the two fortified peaks and wound away into the heart of the Dragon Mountains.

As the group began the long, slow descent into the gap, Byron looked back to see the Valley of the Nine Spires disappear. Sheer cliffs surrounded the company, casting thick, cold shadow into the crag. After a long, silent march, they came before the main portal into the Temple of Borántu.

Chapter 17

Qualnáchnabard

An enormous wall of stone barricaded the gap. It was hundreds of feet high and hundreds more wide, covered with strange, letter-like characters carved deep into the rock. The marks were scattered about everywhere; no lines or columns set them apart from each other and it was impossible to tell if the marks even had a right side up.

A long, wide stair led up to a deep alcove that furrowed back into the wall. The roof of the alcove was supported by a forest of pillars and filled with thick shadow. The company stood and stared at the fortress, unable to speak.

Oatencake nodded. "Qualnáchnabard, the Temple of Borántu. If we're lucky, we'll get no deeper down than the maze."

"Maze?" Raeter said.

"A maze indeed, like no other," Oatencake said.

"Who built this place?" Nosh said.

Oatencake shrugged. "Some say the dwarves, some say the gnomes, some say the giants. No one knows. It was long ago. But these cliffs are shot through with shafts and vents and lesser gateways. When the unmagic was strong this place carried a hex of confusion."

"Unmagic?" Shilo said.

Oatencake nodded. "The power of Borántu. It's said there

were many paths through Qualnáchnabard. The walls of the maze would shift without warning and if you didn't know the logic of the hex . . . well, once those halls were filled with the screams and madness of the lost."

"How are we gonna get through?" Rufus said.

"Not to worry, not to worry," Oatencake said. "When Borántu went away the magic faded. The walls stopped moving and one path became fixed. Miroaster has ventured here on occasion and lucky for us he made a map. Even luckier, the last time I saw him he left that map with me for safekeeping."

"What'd they do here?" Quill said.

"Who can say what all?" Oatencake said, shaking his head. "The priests of Borántu were a gruesome company. This is his temple where they came to worship him and bring him tribute."

"Who would worship him?" Raefer said.

"Most everyone by the end of his reign," Oatencake said. "Then Silverlance came and gathered back what remained of those true to Everándon. Some who'd gone over came back all right, for Silverlance is a forgiving sort, but many more stayed beneath the shadow and fought for the dragon. This was his stronghold, here at the edge of the land."

"That's when the war happened," Byron said. "The war that covered the world."

"Is this where they fought . . ." Rufus said. "Silverlance and Borántu?"

Oatencake looked west. "The only mention I've ever heard of it says the duel took place under Rathrágodrak, beneath the mountain of the Balefire. It was about that time that the Balefire was stolen, or went out, or whatever became of it."

"It never went out," Nosh said. "Not if my cousin Thrym is right."

"And I hope he is, youngster," Oatencake said. "I hope he is and I hope you live to see it burning again."

◈ ◈ ◈

Hundreds of enormous pillars were set at random in the long, wide alcove leading up to the entrance. As the company pressed on, the roof sloped downward, the pillars got shorter and fewer and the walls drew closer together until all that remained was a small, square opening. The darkness inside defied the light of the torches. Lukos looked back and sniffed the air. He perked his ears and gave his tail a wag.

"What is it, Lukos?" Byron said.

Lukos turned and nipped Shilo on the leg.

"Ah!" she gasped, stifling her cry. "I'm sorry!"

Lukos looked at her.

"What was that for?" Rufus said.

"I tried to see his thoughts," Shilo said, rubbing her leg. "I won't do it again, sir."

"All right, all right," Oatencake said. "Quick and quiet all the way through. Don't tarry and don't talk. I daresay some of the ancient madness still clings to these walls."

"Have you been through before?" Byron said.

"Not all the way, no," Oatencake said. "Hush now."

"How long will it take?" Dindra said.

Oatencake shrugged. "A whole day maybe, maybe less. All right then, let's go."

A stair awaited them. They climbed in a tight bunch with Oatencake a few steps ahead. Hooves and feet met stone, metal jingled and leather creaked. The echoes of their passing filled the hall with a low, laughing sound. Rufus reached up to quiet

Nosh's cooking gear. Raefer fastened the lamp-hat Nosh had given him to his head and Byron lit it with his torch.

"This darkness," Byron whispered. "It's like . . . like water all around me."

Raefer nodded. "Only you can't swim to the surface."

Byron nodded too. Then something caught his eye. A small mark was scratched in the wall. It was an open angle with another line sticking off the top. Very soon it passed beyond his torchlight.

A foul smell filled the place. At the top of the stair they came to a three-way passage. Oatencake stopped and held up the map. The others crowded in behind him, covering their mouths and noses. Thick, endless dark surrounded the torchlight. Their shadows danced and stretched away into the enveloping gloom. Every sound echoed and stirred the strange, whispering laughter. A faint breeze blew from inside the maze. Oatencake held his torch high and frowned as he peered into the tunnel.

"What's wrong?" Shilo said. "Doesn't it say which way to go?"

"The map is plain enough," Oatencake said. "We go left and then left again the first chance we get. But something's different. There was no wind before and this stench . . . it wasn't so strong. Something isn't the same. Everybody stay wakeful."

Stairs led up and down. Through turn after turn, passage after passage, room after empty room, they marched for hours. In the torchlight Byron watched the maze go by. The floor was all black stone set with carvings, strange mosaics and symbols in dark, fiery colors. Intricate painted scenes survived the ages in the darkness of the place. Giants and dwarves fought each other, as did centaurs and griffins, satyrs and wolves. Flames and engines of war were depicted, burning towns and fleeing people of every tribe in Everándon.

Time after time, on the walls or on the floor, Byron saw the strange, crude mark scratched into the stone amid the crafted images of warfare and pillage and suffering. It was a simple image of a few lines, always pointing forward. Each time he saw it he tried to see it better, building on the memory of the last, until it was clear in his mind. He was tracing the mark in the air before him with his finger when Oatencake stopped and turned around.

"Special quiet, now," the man said. "We've reached the New Moon Chamber."

They stepped out into a huge room open to the sky. The moon was high and filled the hall with pale light. The floor was covered with windblown snow and sand. Beneath it, in large patches, could be seen a huge mosaic of the same patternless mix of symbols carved into the face of the temple. Balconies looked down on the floor of the place. The company entered through one of the many passages that opened from the dark confusion of Qualnáchnabard.

"What is this place?" Raefer said

"The center of the maze," Oatencake said. "Borántu came here to bask in the new moon. He hated the moon most of the time, especially when it was full."

"Why?" Dindra said.

"Because," Oatencake said, "it carries the light of the sun into the nighttime. Borántu was strongest when the moon was new. It's said that Silverlance agreed to meet him on such a night. It's lucky we've the gibbous moon above us now. I wouldn't want to venture the heart of Qualnáchnabard on a night when the moon was new."

Oatencake held his torch low to the dirt-covered floor. "Well, now," he said and everyone looked. There in the dirty snow was an enormous hoofprint.

"Ravinath?" Raefer said.

"No," Byron said.

"How can you be so sure?" Nosh said.

"Ravinath is a centaur," Dindra said. "Centaurs don't have cloven hooves."

"Satyrs do," Byron said. "But nothing so big as that."

Byron set his own hoof beside the print. It was tiny by comparison. Oatencake lifted the torch and held it out into the moonlit chamber.

"What's that?" he said, peering ahead. There was a dark shape on the floor. As the group drew near, Dindra caught her breath. Sprawled in front of them was a lifeless centaur.

◇   ◇   ◇

Everyone spread out to count the bloodied, broken bodies. There were nine of them in all. The centaurs were cast about the floor of the chamber as if by some terrific wind. They were twisted and bent into impossible positions, lying in heaps, contorted and mangled. They were cast aside, hurled about and remained where they fell, some all alone in remote shadows, some jumbled and tangled together.

"Who could have done this?" Shilo whispered.

"Hush, girl," Oatencake said. He lifted the map. "That's the door we want, beneath that low balcony."

The ground rumbled. It was very faint but everyone felt it. It came again, stronger, and stopped. Then came the bellowing. It was like the kettle horns of Woody Deep, but it had a growl in it. It came from somewhere behind the walls or under the floor.

The rumbling started again, growing louder and steadier. It didn't stop and the bellow sounded above it.

"Where's it coming from?" Dindra cried.

"Which door did you say?" Quill cried.

"Steady now," Oatencake said. "Don't go rushing off into the maze!"

"But it's getting closer!" Rufus said.

"And it could be coming from our door," Oatencake said.

Everyone turned full around, looking at all the entrances into the chamber. The sound was unmistakable. Hooves were thundering up from somewhere in the darkness. The bellow came again. It was loud and violent and Byron's stomach nearly failed him. He clutched his staff tight in his little fists and forced his legs to hold him up. All the torches flared up high and went out. The map in Oatencake's hands burst into a billowy flame and burned away to ash in a moment.

It was true. The hoofbeats emerged from the echoes of the maze and a huge form stopped in the shadows of the very doorway Oatencake had pointed to. It bellowed again, louder and more terrible. Shilo screamed. Lukos padded up to Byron and stood in front of him. The hoofbeats began again as the dark shape charged forward. Into the moonlight galloped the most terrible thing any of the companions had ever seen.

"Minotaur!" Oatencake cried, stepping up with his slash hook. "Get away, all of you, on! Get to the door if you can!"

It was enormous. From the waist down it had the body of the biggest, wildest bull that ever was. Its arms and torso were those of a man, with great broad shoulders, long thick arms and enormous hands. Its huge head was that of a bull, with long, fiercely pointed horns.

And it was utterly berserk.

Everyone scattered to get away as it leaped among them, snorting and grunting and slobbering, wagging its massive head with awesome force. It stomped with its hooves and jabbed with its horns, all the while reaching and grabbing and swinging with its terrible fists. It coughed and let out a savage bellow as it dashed around trying to trample and gore and destroy. It never slowed. The companions scrambled in every direction, screaming and crying out.

Lukos charged up to the minotaur and attacked it at the heels, trying to cripple it. The monster turned and reached back with a great hand. Lukos darted out from under a stomping hoof and bit the hand as it came into reach. The minotaur threw back its head and bellowed, wheeling with alarming agility to face the wolf.

Oatencake strode in behind, swinging the slash hook. The blade landed square on the minotaur's lower back and glanced away, leaving the monster uncut. It whirled again as Oatencake ducked and rolled out of the way. The monster looked back and forth between the man and the wolf, snorting and coughing. It lifted its head to bellow again and lunged at Oatencake with both enormous hands.

It caught him by the cape and pulled him toward its grasp. Lukos ran straight under the monster and landed a strong bite on the minotaur's belly. The wolf's great fangs did not pierce the skin, but the monster jumped and bellowed and set about stomping with all four hooves. It let go of Oatencake and looked down and around, trying to crush Lukos any way it could.

Byron, Raefer and Rufus stood together in a tight bunch.

"They're only making it angrier," Raefer said.

"It gets stronger the madder it becomes," Rufus said.

Byron stomped a hoof. "We have to help them."

"Raefer," Rufus said, "give me your new dart."

The brothers set to work. Raefer held the sharpened twig while Rufus opened the flask of sleep juice.

"How much?" Raefer said.

"All of it," Rufus said.

Raefer blinked. "But what if we run into trouble?"

Rufus and Byron looked at each other and then at Raefer, with their eyebrows up.

"Oh, right," Raefer said.

"That should do it," Rufus said, taking the dart. He stuffed moss into the groove that held the sleep juice. All three stood up and set off together toward the raging minotaur.

Rufus broke into a run, telling Byron and Raefer to stop. They stayed on his heels, running with Rufus right past the monster as the older dryad hurled the dart. It spun fast through the air, struck the minotaur on the back of the neck and fell to the floor. One great hoof came down on the dart and crushed it to splinters. The monster raged on and never even knew Raefer's best dart had been thrown.

"It's no use!" Oatencake shouted. "Run for it, all of you! I'll hold it as long as I can!"

Everyone gaped at Oatencake in complete horror. No one moved. The man strode in to deal another useless blow, gaining only the brute's angry attention.

"I haven't got long!" he shouted. "Go now! Lukos, you must protect them! Go!"

Lukos didn't move. He stood sniffing the air in the direction of the door by which they had entered the chamber. Then a tremendous roar filled the darkness of the maze. It shook Byron's chest. Everyone snapped their heads around and even the minotaur stopped in its tracks.

chapter 18

Beyond Eugrándon

haking its enormous head, the minotaur bellowed in reply. The roar came again and silence fell. Then there was a sound like distant drums, a quiet thunder. It was the sound of great padded feet slapping against the floor of the maze, drawing near. The clacking sound that accompanied each footfall spoke of great claws and the shaking ground told of the enormous size of the creature that strode upon those feet. The roar came again and into the moonlight bounded a huge grizzleback bear, roaring and slashing with its claws.

"Manakar!" Byron cried.

The whole company shouted the name.

Standing to full height, Manakar bared his horrible teeth and swiped the air with his tremendous arms. The minotaur swished its tail and scraped the mosaic floor with its hoof. The bear and the minotaur faced each other. Battle hung between them like a storm brewing.

Dropping to all fours, Manakar bounded forward and smote the minotaur across the face. The minotaur's head snapped to the side and four red lines appeared on its snout, dripping blood. The monster bellowed and shook its head, then burst forward, flailing with its fists and hooves, lowering its head to gore with its horns.

Manakar fell over backwards and the minotaur trampled across him. The bear rolled to his feet and charged forward, taking the minotaur from behind. Manakar threw his weight onto the minotaur and bit down hard on its huge shoulder. The minotaur wagged its head and struck Manakar between the eyes with a horn. Manakar staggered off to one side, swatting at the air. Both creatures stepped apart, growling and watching each other. The minotaur bled from the wounds on his face and shoulder. Manakar shook his head, clearing away the pain that the minotaur's horn had given him.

Again came the minotaur; it struck Manakar on the side. The bear lifted an arm to fend away the horns. The minotaur ducked beneath the slashing claw and buried its head in Manakar's side. It hauled upward with a sweep of its mighty neck. One horn furrowed a gash into the flesh on Manakar's chest, the other slashed through his back. The bear was lifted from his feet and pitched full length to the floor.

Throwing itself forward, the minotaur reared and came down on the bear, pounding with its hooves and pummeling with its fists. For a moment Manakar was trapped under the weight and ferocity of the minotaur, but he rolled onto his back and lashed out with his rear paws. The great, sharp claws raced along the minotaur's underbelly and the monster jerked away, limping off to one side, leaving Manakar to lumber to his feet. The two beasts stood apart, panting, bleeding, circling, watching.

Snorting and coughing the minotaur flew at Manakar. The bear charged in to meet the monster and the two collided in a terrible embrace. The minotaur butted with its great head while its arms encircled the bear and its front hooves gored at Manakar's belly. The bear took blow after blow with his own great arms pinioned to his sides by the vast strength of the minotaur.

"Manakar!" Byron shouted.

Then the minotaur began to falter. It coughed and wagged its horrible tongue. Its eyes opened wide and great blasts of hot breath shot from its steaming nostrils. The two beasts turned and everyone could see what was happening. Manakar had his enormous jaws locked on the minotaur's throat. With every breath the monster took, Manakar tightened his bite. The mino-taur's head leaned back and it released its great hug on the bear. Manakar reached around with his own massive arms and clutched the choking brute. The creature flexed its bulk against the bear's grip, but it was weakened from the loss of blood and the stranglehold of the bear's great jaws.

Manakar squeezed until some large bone in the minotaur's torso cracked with a loud, terrible sound. Then the bear jerked its head about and there was another loud pop as the minotaur's neck gave way and its head lolled to one side. Manakar released the monster and the mighty brute fell in a heap at the bear's feet. Manakar dropped to all fours, sniffed the minotaur, then lum-bered off and began licking his own wounds.

"Manakar!" Byron cried and he ran across to the bear.

"Careful, Byron!" Oatencake shouted. "Give 'im room, he's badly hurt."

Manakar bled from many deep wounds. The two long scrapes in his back and chest were the worst and the bear could not reach them. He bowed his head low and shot out his long tongue at the chest wound, then turned his head and tried to reach the wound on his back. In the end he gave a great, deep whimper and his whole body sagged. He sat there with his chin resting on his mighty chest and his two great arms relaxed at his sides. Lukos crept in and sniffed Manakar, whining and crouching low.

Nosh knelt down and set about lighting his torch. Shilo was

weeping. "Oh, Manakar," she said, "you saved us! Please be all right!"

"We've got to help him!" Dindra said.

Rufus shrugged. "How?"

"It's no use," Nosh said. "I can't get it lit."

"You can't?" Raefer said, astonished.

"No, I should think not," Oatencake said.

"Whaddaya mean by that?" Nosh said with a glance at Raefer.

"It's the mind of the maze," Oatencake said. "It'll abide no torch fire. That minotaur came up through some hole into the deep places. I'd say the old madness is leaking back into Qual náchnabard."

Raefer gaped at Oatencake and blinked. "Hixima can help him!"

"I could fly!" Quill said. "I could fly back and tell her!"

"She'd never get back in time," Rufus said.

"There must be something we can do!" Byron shouted. His own eyes filled with tears and he stomped his hoof.

Oatencake nodded. "The healing clover would help him, if we could reach it."

"The what?" Dindra said.

"It's said to grow all around at Trilithon. It's said that if you can get it fresh and apply it at once, there's no wound it can't mend. That's our only hope, the healing clover."

"We've got to hurry," Shilo said. "He'll die!"

"We can't help the bear until we get clear of the maze ourselves," Oatencake said. "I can see little hope of that without the map."

Everyone stopped. They all looked around at each other. For a moment no one spoke.

"We don't need a map," Byron said. "We can follow the unicorn!"

"The unicorn?" Oatecake said, lifting his eyebrows.

"Byron," Dindra said, "what unicorn?"

"The one scratched in the wall," Byron said.

"In the wall ..." Oatencake said. "Show me, Byron, where did you see it?"

"I've seen it all along the way. It's like a trail. There must be one down the passage where the minotaur came from."

Byron ran across the floor with Oatencake fast behind him. The others looked around at each other and then followed. They stopped at the door as Byron and Oatencake stepped over a fallen centaur and into the shadows.

"How're we gonna see it without torches?" Nosh said.

"I don't need a torch," Byron said. "Just a minute."

No moonlight fell inside the door. The company stood in utter darkness. Byron set the monocle to his eye and looked around.

Figures and colors came alive. Hideous shapes and figures crowded around him. Byron searched the wall for the mark, wandering ahead several paces.

"Byron, where have you gone?" Oatencake called in a loud whisper.

"Don't worry," Byron said. "I can see fine. Here!"

It was scratched on the wall just above the level of Byron's eye. He touched it with his finger. "I found it!" he said. "This'll lead us out!"

"How can he see it?" Rufus said. "I can't see my own hand."

"Never mind," Oatencake said. "If we're going to help the bear we've got to trust Byron. It's the only hope for any of us. Agreed?"

"Agreed," said the others in turn.

"That is if Manakar will come with us at all," Nosh said. "Just look at 'im."

The bear sat very still, panting. Moonlight washed over him. Beyond his large form, the huge shape of the vanquished minotaur lay where it had fallen.

"Shilo," Oatencake said, "speak to the bear. Tell 'im there's hope, if he can make it the rest of the way."

Shilo tiptoed up to Manakar, cooing his name. She sat with him a while, speaking with her thoughts. Soon she came back to the group, shaking her head.

"He says to go on without him. He says he didn't come all this way and fight as hard as he did just to slow us up now."

"He won't slow us up!" Byron said. "We can't just go off and leave him there."

"We have to help him!" Dindra said. "We'll go and get the clover and bring it back!"

"No good," Oatencake said. "Its power would wear off long before we got back with it. No, the bear has to go on or there's no saving 'im. Tell 'im it isn't far; we're nearly through!"

"I told him that already," Shilo said with a shrug.

"Hmm," Oatencake said, gripping his chin. "Very well ..." He leaned down to whisper in Shilo's ear.

Shilo nodded. "All right," she said. "I'll tell him."

She went back to Manakar's side and spoke to him in hushed tones. The bear lurched and grunted and rolled onto his paws. With a great groan he hoisted himself up and started toward them. The others looked around at each other and then at last, every eye was on Shilo.

"What'd you tell him?" Nosh said, putting his hands on his hips.

Shilo shrugged. "I just said what Peter told me to say."

"I mentioned that a bear could find sweeter clover growing nowhere in Everándon," Oatencake said. "Not even in his own imagination."

"That's it?" Rufus said. "That's all you told him?"

"Seems it was enough," Oatencake said, looking into the darkness where Manakar had gone. "One thing I've learned about grizzlebacks, they're very serious about their clover."

Each companion walked with a hand on the shoulder of the one ahead. Manakar stayed at the rear of the group, loping along, leaning to one side with his weight on his right foreleg. Turns came and went in the hundreds. Flights of stairs climbed and descended in the total darkness. Mark after mark told Byron the way. Once he looked at the floor to see a symbol that made his stomach churn. He gave a little cry of alarm but didn't stop moving. He looked back at it as it disappeared beneath the marching feet of his companions.

"What's wrong?" Shilo said.

"The mark!" Byron said.

"What mark?" Nosh said.

"There was a symbol in the floor," Byron said. "It's Ravinath's symbol. I saw it the night of Midwinter!"

"And we saw it again at the Ghostwood fence!" Shilo said.

"Here's another turn," Byron said. "Yes, there's the unicorn. Wait, ow!"

Moonlight smote Byron's eye, shining down through a shaft in the roof. He let the monocle drop and jammed his palm into his eye.

"What's wrong, Byron?" Shilo said. She and Nosh were both shading their eyes from the brightness of the moon. "Stars!" she cried. "Stars and fresh air!"

Through the shaft, the light fell on a wide stair leading up and out. The companions filed past Byron, who waved them on, still pressing his palm into his eye.

"I looked right at it," Byron said, rubbing his eye. "I turned and looked right at it."

"What?" Rufus said as he went by.

"Nothing, I'm fine," Byron said. Oatencake stopped, letting wolf and bear go by. He looked at Byron with one eyebrow up and smiled.

"Now it's my turn to lead the blind," he said. "Take my hand, youngster. I'll see you the rest of the way."

Byron looked up at the stars and moonlight. The whole company was already out, standing black against the deep blue of the night sky. At the top of the stair he joined them in the cold clear air. Manakar was panting as he lapped the snow from an old stone rain basin. The others were looking east down a long, steep slope into a moonlit vale. Above them, across the vale, the Dragon Range cut the stars with a jagged line. A wide flat place, low between the two peaks, let in a great swath of the sky beyond Everándon.

CHAPTER 19

HEALING CLOVER

nowy hardwood trees covered the vale. The leafless branches strayed above the companions in every direction, forming a dark cage against the sky. Manakar moved slowly, but his pace was steady. Lukos went ahead often, scouting out the unseen places, running back to sniff and fret over the bear.

Soon the way became steeper, sloping ever upward. They came to a stone platform where began a stair, switching back and forth across the face of the slope, up to the flat place between the peaks. The sky turned a milky blue and the stars faded.

It was a wide, smooth area lined with great paving stones. An enormous dark shape stood in the middle of the platform, silhouetted against the stars. Manakar reached the platform and collapsed. The bear lay there gulping the air, with his tongue dangling on the stone.

"Manakar may not make it," Shilo said. "But he intends to try. He has one last march left in him. We'll wait here until he's ready."

Manakar stayed apart, lying on his side. The companions sat huddled together, snuggling against Dindra at the base of the huge, dark shape that stood in the middle of the saddle. Oatencake sat among them, clutching his slash hook with both hands. Byron looked up at the shadowy figure that towered above them.

"What is it?" he said to Oatencake.

"I haven't a clue," Oatencake said. "A statue of some sort." He was quiet for a time as he gazed up at it. Then he sighed. "That's a strange little staff you've got," he said to Byron.

Byron handed it to Oatencake. "I found it in the caves."

Oatencake nodded. "Light as a feather," he said, weighing it with one hand.

"Strong, too," Byron said. "I whacked it on a rock."

"I'll wager that old minotaur couldn't do it harm," Oaten-cake said. Then he frowned. "It has a very curious shape." He handed the staff back to Byron. "You've kept it well. And the monocle? Where'd you come by that little treasure?"

"My gradda gave it to me," Byron said. "I wonder what he's doing now."

"Your gradda," said Oatencake. "Well, you're a wonder, Byron, a wonder through and through."

In the west, the black shape of the temple emerged from the gray. Portals and turrets and platforms appeared in the cliffs high up, placed with clear vantage on the vale.

"That's odd," Nosh said with a frown. "Those turrets look made for war engines. It's as if they expected attack from this side."

Byron yawned and tried to sleep. His eyes would not stay shut, so he let his gaze climb to the top of the sky. There above him was an enormous hoof poised to fall on him. Above that, a pair of huge, fierce eyes looked down on him from the shadows that still clung there. Byron froze for a moment, then jumped to his hooves, screaming at the top of his voice.

Everyone sprang to their feet and scattered. They caught

their breath and stared up as the sun revealed the gigantic statue of a unicorn. Its tail and mane were cropped and bound for battle. Its fetlocks were fitted with terrible blades and it was armored: breast, head and flank. Through a hole in its helm stuck the long, spiraling horn. It stood with one hoof raised, as if taking the first step into war.

"Sorry, everybody," Byron said.

They all stared at the rough stone carving. A shaft of golden light flooded up from below it, streaming out into rays all around it, casting it in silhouette. The yellow light of dawn was breaking over the edge of the world. Byron ran to the eastern side of the platform and looked out.

A thousand pieces glittered with a blinding gleam. All the world below was golden and glowing as morning broke upon the calm flat of the sea. Byron stood at the edge of Everándon, smelling for the first time the fragrant salt air, hearing for the first time the cry of the ocean birds and feeling for the first time in his chest the pounding of the waves upon the shore.

His companions gathered around him and looked out. The sun climbed out of the east and cast its likeness onto the endless sea. Then Manakar went lumbering past them, grunting with his thunderous whimper and set off along the steep trail that led down from the far side of the platform.

Little caps of white appeared on the water and the hiss of the surf grew louder. The slope leveled off to a sandy path that led down still further to the beach. Sea birds cried. The companions traveled south with the vast, calm ocean on their left and the rocky eastern slopes of the Dragon Range on their right.

Manakar struggled with the soft footing. His wounds were staunched by his clotted, matted fur, but his pain was greater than ever and his strength was failing.

"He won't stop again," Shilo told the group, "until he reaches Trilithon or dies."

In the late morning Manakar turned away from the sea and headed toward the mountains again, following a path into the dunes.

"Where's he going?" Rufus said.

Oatencake shook his head. "Best to wait and see."

At the top of the first dune Manakar stopped to sniff the air, then toppled over and fell to the bottom of other side. Everyone cried out and ran to him, but he growled them away and struggled to his feet.

He stood motionless for a long time before setting out again. When he did, he fell forward with his arms stuck beneath him. The wound on his chest began to bleed. It dripped in large spots on the sand. Manakar struggled to stand and fell forward again with his neck and chin outstretched. The company gathered around the ailing bear. Twice, Manakar growled and gave his rumbling whimper.

Lukos sniffed the air toward the mountains and ran off into the dunes. Byron watched him go. A low hill covered with golden, slumbering grass stood close by. Lukos ran toward the top and disappeared over the crest. He reappeared, running back down the slope with all his great speed. Behind Byron, Manakar whimpered again.

"Nothing for it," Oatencake said. "Here the old boy stays. You can't hope to move 'im if he doesn't want to move."

"But he'll die," Shilo said.

Manakar was still. He was breathing in small gasps. His eyes were tight shut. Lukos ran in, leaped behind the bear and bit Manakar hard on the rump.

Manakar roared. Everyone stepped back.

"Leave him be!" Shilo shouted.

"Lukos!" Byron cried.

Again, the Wolfen King lunged in and bit Manakar on the leg. The bear growled and turned his great head around, pushing himself up with one paw. Lukos darted behind the bear, biting and snapping. Manakar turned his bulk to face the wolf. Great drops of blood spilled from his newly opened wound. He faltered and settled to his belly again, growling and panting.

Lukos ran around behind Manakar and began his assault again.

"Lukos, no!" Dindra cried.

"He's driving him forward," Rufus shouted. "You can do it, Manakar!"

Byron looked up at the golden hillside. "Trilithon . . . We're nearly there!" he shouted. "Come on, Manakar, you can do it!"

"Come on, Manakar!" Nosh shouted. "Come on old boy!"

Shilo made two fists and shook them. "You can do it, Manakar! You beat that minotaur didn't you?"

"Manakar! Manakar!" Raefer shouted.

Lukos kept it up. Manakar growled and lumbered to his feet. Lukos backed away and barked at the bear. The bear stopped, listing to one side, and turned. He looked up and sniffed the air. Then he gave a wail that pierced Byron's heart.

"Yes, you can!" Shilo shouted. She stomped her foot and great tears sprang to her eyes. Her voice was shrill and loud. "Yes, you can Manakar, please!"

Manakar took a step forward. Blood splashed onto the sand. The companions walked along beside the bear, shouting and cheering him on. At last Manakar faltered and dropped to his haunches. He stopped in his tracks and sat down. Lukos approached the bear, sniffing, but did not growl or nip.

Manakar let his head hang deep to his chest. His vast girth twitched with small gasps for air. He trembled all over and his tongue, swollen and dry, hung from his mouth. His eyes were closed and the blood ran freely from his wounds, down onto the golden sand.

Byron turned to look at the hilltop, then he set off with all his speed, weaving in and out, up and down among the sandy grassy dunes with nimble little strides. Up the slope he went until he came to the center of the hilltop and there he found the Trilithon.

Two huge, flat slabs of gray stone stood on their edges. Another slab lay across the top of them. The whole thing stood dark against the blue of the sky. The ground all around was covered with succulent pink and white clover.

"Manakar," Byron whispered.

He crouched down and gathered up two fistfuls of the clover. As he stood, he peered at the Trilithon with narrow eyes. He started toward it, clutching the clover before him.

A thin, glistening stream of water whispered along the ground. It pooled in a low spot where the clover was submerged up to its tips. As he came near, Byron saw the sky between the slabs of stone and there, burning white and clear against the brilliant blue, was the Midwinter star.

It pulsed and glimmered with a tail like a sword.

Byron looked down at the clover he was holding. "Manakar," he said.

He turned and headed off toward the sea. He looked up to find the star but it wasn't there in the eastern sky. Byron stopped. He looked at the stone structure, then at the horizon again. He ran back to the Trilithon and there was the star, shining as he had seen it a moment before.

"It's inside," he said. "It's inside Trilithon! Mr. Thúmose was right!"

Down the hill and into the dunes he ran. His companions were still gathered around Manakar, who sat very still with his head hanging limp.

"Manakar!" Byron called and he ran straight up to the bear, holding out his fists.

"Here you go, Manakar," Byron panted. "Here's clover from Trilithon."

"Byron ..." Dindra whispered, fetching her hand to her throat.

Byron held the clover under Manakar's nose. The bear twitched. His nostrils flared and sniffed the fragrance of the pink and white flowers.

"Maybe they're too old," Byron said. "It took a moment to get back."

But Manakar let out a rumbling whimper and lifted his head. He leaned forward onto his front paws and pushed off with his hind legs, sniffing around for the clover. Byron smiled and held up the flowers to the enormous bear. The bear snuffled his nose into Byron's hands, smashing the flowers and scattering them on the ground. Byron laughed and began leading the mighty Manakar toward Trilithon.

"The star is back!" Byron said as they navigated the dunes.

Nosh frowned. "Where?"

"Inside Trilithon," Byron said.

"Inside?" Nosh said.

"Just wait!" Byron said with a laugh.

Manakar struggled through the dunes and up the gentle hillside. The others watched as he staggered forward and collapsed into the pool where the clover grew beneath the water. He lay there in the little ocean of pink and white and didn't move. His eyes were closed. His body rose and fell with the motion of his breathing but with every gulp of air, Manakar's breath faded until he lay motionless.

"Manakar?" Shilo said.

"Is he ... dead?" Nosh said.

Peter Oatencake stepped up and drew his knife. He held the polished metal in front of Manakar's nose. "He isn't breathing," he said.

Lukos splashed into the paw deep water and sniffed the bear from head to foot, then backed away whining and growling. Everyone was silent. They watched and waited for their friend to move, but he didn't.

"Manakar?" Byron said. He crouched down beside the bear and put his hands in the deep, thick fur. "Manakar?" Byron's eyes filled up with tears and he cried.

Everyone did. They stood or sat or lay upon the ground, weeping for their fallen friend. His great body was peaceful and still. For a long time, no one spoke. Then Raefer looked up toward the Trilithon.

"Byron, you were right!" he said, wiping the tears from his eyes.

"What about?" Byron said, still crying.

Raefer pointed. "The star!"

Everyone turned. The star was there. They could see it between the uprights of the dolmen.

"Oh, Manakar ..." Shilo said and another wave of tears took her.

"Wait a second," Rufus said.

He got up from the ground and ran to the dolmen. First he looked through it, then went around behind it. Then he came back and looked through it again. He scratched his head and looked back at his friends.

"It's shining inside the dolmen!" he called.

"What?" Raefer shouted back.

"That's what I told you," Byron said.

"What does that mean?" Quill said.

"I mean it's not in the sky," Rufus called. "It's in the dolmen."

They brushed themselves off and went to join Rufus, each one of them making the same tour of the stone structure. First they looked between the slabs. The star was burning clear and white in the sky. Then they stepped around behind the dolmen to find nothing but the empty eastern horizon. At the front once more, they found the star, burning bright between the uprights of the Trilithon.

Byron stepped inside the dolmen.

Everything went dark. The star shone before him. The stone of the slabs stretched on like a tunnel. Water trickled past his hooves. Byron heard the others calling him and he looked back. There they were, standing in the sunlight, peering into the dolmen. They seemed to be at the end of a long hallway and they looked afraid. Their voices were shrill and fearful as they called his name. Byron went back and had not taken three steps before he was among them again.

"It's a tunnel!" he said. "We have to go through!"

No one spoke.

"Well?" Byron said, looking around.

"Through to where?" Quill said.

"Wherever it leads," Byron said with a shrug.

Oatencake stood with his hands on his hips, shaking his head with wonder. "The edge of the world and beyond," he said.

"Byron's right," Raefer said. "We can't stop now. Wherever we're going, the star is back to show us the way."

"What about Manakar?" Shilo said.

"We did all we possibly could for Manakar, little one," Oatencake said. "His wounds were just too much for us."

"He saved us," Shilo said.

"He did," Oatencake said with a nod. "I'll bury him proper, right there beneath his clover."

"You're coming with us," Dindra said. "Aren't you?"

"No, Dindra," Oatencake said. "My job is done. It was never for me to follow the star. I'll stay here and bury our friend."

"We'll come back, Mr. Oatencake," Byron said. "I know we will."

"I believe you, Byron," Oatencake said. "Now, if any of you would like to say goodbye to Manakar, go right ahead. But I think you should be on your way."

Each of them touched the great, silent bear and whispered goodbye. They moved away from him in silence and gathered at the dolmen. Byron stepped forward and set off down the strange, dark tunnel of Trilithon.

Chapter 20

Trilithon

yron stepped through and turned full around as he came to a wide-eyed stop. Trilithon stood in a great circle with others of its make, tall and dark against the clear, dim glow that lit the horizon on every side. Stars filled the sky above. The air was damp and fragrant and warm. Waves crashed in the darkness. A low breeze was blowing. One by one the others followed until they all stood together, gaping.

"The end of the world," Quill said.

"Or the beginning," Dindra said.

Nosh put his hands on his hips. "Where's the star?"

They all looked around, every which way into the sky. The star was nowhere to be seen.

"What's that in the middle?" Rufus said.

It was a circular stone wall about as tall as Byron. A rivulet leaked out near the top and flowed past the companions into the Trilithon.

"A pool of water," Dindra said as they approached the wall. She looked up to the sky. "Full of stars."

"Stars?" Byron said.

He climbed up onto the wall and looked over the side. There, on the surface of the pool, mingled with the stars of the sky, was the Midwinter star, white and clean. Byron looked up. There was no sign of the star in the sky above him. He looked down into the pool again and laughed.

"It's in the water!" he said. He stepped up to the edge of the wall and prepared to dive in.

"Byron, wait!" Rufus called. He held up his hand and looked at the ground. "Look at this, Raef!"

Byron stopped.

"Hoofprints!" Raefer said.

"And look at the ground where I'm standing," Rufus said.

"It's all wet," Raefer said. "There's been a splash here recently."

"A big one," Rufus said.

"Baruwan?" Nosh said.

"Or Ravinath," Dindra said.

Byron looked into the pool. "Or both."

Lukos put his paws up on the wall and waited next to Byron. His ears were perked forward and he was panting, looking down into the pool. The others stood around the stone circle so that each could see everyone else. The light of the star shone up, shimmering through the water.

"Uh ..." Quill said. "Who first?"

Byron did not speak. He stepped forward, clutched the strange staff in both hands and dived in.

Beneath the water the star kept shining. Byron toiled downward, pulling himself toward it. He heard another splash above him, then another as his companions hit the water. Then, instead of fighting to pull himself down, he was being drawn forward, as if floating to the surface. The star was still before him, but now he was swimming up. He splashed out at the top with a cry and a gasp for air. He was in a pool of water near a sandy bank. The

stars were emerging into the evening twilight and the Midwinter
star was bright among them.

Byron crawled up the bank as others began to surface. Lukos
came up and strode out. He shook hard several times and started
grooming himself. Dindra appeared next, then Nosh, Rufus,
Shilo, and Raefer.

"Is she coming?" Dindra said.

"No," Raefer said. "She couldn't do it."

"Quill?" Byron said.

"She stayed behind," Dindra said.

They all stood looking at the pool.

"Maybe she'll change her mind," Raefer said.

"We'll give her some time," Dindra said.

A hot, dry wind was blowing. Ripples of sand spread out to
the edges of the world in every direction. It was a vast, silent
desert. The star was low on the horizon and trembled with the
heat that rose from the waving sand.

"How long should we give her?" Nosh said.

No one answered. They were all looking around. The sun
was going low. It was larger and redder than the Everándon sun.
Night was coming and a strange constellation emerged in the
highest part of the sky.

"What's that?" Byron said, pointing toward the star.

A small black dot appeared in the sky. It seemed to emerge
from inside the star. It moved fast and straight toward them,
growing larger as it came.

"It's a bird," Rufus said.

"A big one," Raefer agreed.

A few moments later the bird was circling above them. It
came lower and lower with every turn until it landed on the sand
before the group. It was as tall as Byron and stood a few feet

from the satyr with its wings open, shifting its weight from one foot to the other. It turned its head from side to side, looking at Byron first with one eye, then with the other.

"Oh, the poor thing," Shilo said. "It's hurt."

It had long tail feathers and wide wings. The plumage had once been bright with red and gold and orange feathers. Three long feathers, one of each color, stood out from the back of its head like a faded crown.

"It's smoking," Nosh said.

Small glowing embers lit the tips of the bird's wings and nestled among the feathers on its body and pinions. Wisps of smoke rose from the smoldering plumage. The bird moved about in distress. It stepped a bit closer to Byron with every move, craning its neck and recoiling it in caution. Byron stood very still looking sidelong at his companions. The bird stopped and stood near, peering at Byron with alternating eyes.

Then it sprang.

Byron cried out.

Smoking, smoldering wings beat him about the head as the bird shrieked and thrust at him with its claws. No one had time to respond. The bird snatched the strange staff from Byron's hands and flew away.

"Hey!" Byron shouted. His face turned from shock and fear to wild anger in a moment. "Hey! No!"

The bird headed off the way it had come and disappeared again into the star. Byron set off running. The others shouted at him to wait, then hurried after.

Long shadows went before them, cast by the low sun. The star hung before Byron; he ran as fast as he could. His little hooves poked deep into the sand, making the way hard and slow.

He came at last to a tall cluster of fiery red rock that stood alone in the ocean of sand. It glowed bright against the twilight sky, a tongue of flame lit by the lowering sun. Near the top was a black shadow where a hole opened into the rock. The bird flapped in from beyond the rock and landed on the edge of the hole. Its wings were smoking more than ever. In its beak it held a large, gnarled stick. With a great stretch and tuck of its wings, the bird waddled into the hole and disappeared.

"Did it have the staff?" Dindra said, stepping up beside Byron.

Byron shook his head. "No."

"Where's Nosh?" Raefer said.

"He's back there," Rufus said. "He's a little slow, that's all."

Byron looked at the opening in the rock with a frown. He looked up at the star. It pulsed in the sky above the rock.

"That's the biggest it's ever been," he said.

Nosh came jogging up. "Sorry," he said. "I can go and go, just not very fast. What is this place?"

"Yeah, Byron," Raefer said. "Where are we?"

"We're there," Byron said without taking his eyes off the hole in the rock.

"Where?" Dindra said.

Byron shrugged. "Wherever there is. I'm going up."

Huge boulders littered the base of the pillar. Nothing grew anywhere in sight. Sandy paths wandered among the stones. The companions spread out to explore. Byron was standing with his palms on the face of the pillar, looking up in frustration, when Raefer and Lukos came running around the side.

"I found an entrance," he said. Lukos perked his ears and looked at Raefer. "Well, Lukos found it. This way."

They followed Raefer and Lukos to the dark side of the rock. The shadow of the pillar stretched far out onto the sand. It was cool in the shade and the rock was a deeper, darker red. At the top of a narrow path there was a passage cut from the sandy stone. Inside was a steep stair that climbed up into the pillar. Byron looked back to see that everyone was gathered. Dindra gave him a firm nod. Byron looked up the stair, took a deep breath and stepped inside.

It led up through a carved passage. A rich, sweet fragrance filled the stair. Byron put in his monocle and led the way. After a long, careful march his eye began to itch. He let the monocle drop. "It's getting light ahead," he said.

A large chamber opened at the top of the stair. Many holes were cut into the rock, letting in the fiery red glow of the setting sun. On a stone block in the middle of the chamber was a huge nest of sticks and branches, woven through with fragrant, colorful fronds. Byron's staff was built into the front of the nest, wedged against a branch of twisted wood.

Smoke seeped out through the crannies and gaps of the branches. The strange bird was there, fidgeting around inside the nest, bobbing its head, rocking back and forth. Wisps of smoke rose from its outstretched wings and from the top of its head. Byron took a step toward the nest.

"Not too close, now," said a voice.

Everyone turned. A large form stood looking out through an opening in the rock, black against the deep red of the setting sun.

Dindra gasped.

Lukos growled.

Byron stepped back. "Ravinath."

"Yes," said the centaur, taking a step forward. He was covered with terrible symbols. Every inch of his body was marked with chalky white paint and dark outlines. On the front of his massive shoulder was the one mark, large among the rest. His long gray hair hung down his face. He stared through it at the companions one by one; one by one they shrank from his gaze. Ravinath looked at them and a faint smile puckered the corner of his eye.

"A pity your griffin friend isn't here," he said, approaching the nest. "She could have told you the story of this remarkable bird. It's a favorite among her kind."

The bird squawked and bobbed its head. Ravinath broke off a branch from the nest and held it up to his nose.

"Leave it be," Shilo said.

Ravinath turned and raised an eyebrow at her. "It has nothing to fear from me, little one." He tossed the twig to the floor of the chamber. "Quite the contrary, it is you and I who must be concerned. The molting phoenix is unimaginably dangerous."

"Don't be silly," Shilo said. "Can't you see that bird is sick?"

"Not sick," Ravinath said. "Molting. You see this bird is very old. It's about to die and live again. This is the way of the phoenix. In a short time now, when the sun has set, the phoenix will burst into flames and be consumed. Then from the ashes of the pyre a new bird will be born.

"You are lucky to have come when you did. It means you'll be here to witness it. Of course it also means you'll be consumed in the hottest fire there is. You see, when it comes, the fire of the phoenix will overflow this chamber by hundreds of feet. Billowing flame. I'll be watching of course, from a safe distance. Then when you're dead and the fledgling is here alone, I'll return to kill it. I've come all this way, after all."

"How could you have smelled him with all this incense?" Shilo said to Lukos. "Don't blame yourself."

Lukos lowered his head and growled as Ravinath approached the group. The centaur snapped his wrist as if to throw something. Lukos yelped and collapsed to the ground. Ravinath looked hard at Byron.

"You see where this satyrish madness has led you?" Ravinath said. He clutched Dindra's hair and pulled her head back. Dindra gave a sharp cry and looked up at Ravinath through brimming tears. "To your deaths," Ravinath growled. He stared into Dindra's eyes. She began to shake and cough. Ravinath let her go and stepped away. He turned his back to them. "Yes," he said, "you have followed the star to the end." He turned to face them. "Well done."

The companions stood still as stone.

"Don't worry about the wolf," Ravinath said. "A stout creature like that shouldn't stay asleep very long, though long enough I daresay. He'd have tried to fight and I can't be bothered with that now."

Ravinath looked at the entrance to the stair and appraised it. Then he held up his hand. In the center of his palm there was a purple glow. It grew brighter and larger until he was holding it in his tremendous grip. He looked at it for a moment. Tipping his head, Ravinath glanced at the bird. It was fretting and dancing and flapping its wings, smoking more than ever. The first glow of flames appeared deep in the bottom of the nest. The sun in the window behind Ravinath had reached the horizon and was beginning to set. Ravinath looked at the light in his hand again.

"There," he said. He looked at the entrance to the stair. "Just enough." Then he looked at the companions. "Just enough to block the stair behind me and seal you all inside."

"Quick!" Rufus yelled. "Everybody out!"

Ravinath lifted his other hand. Byron felt a grip wrap around him like a tight blanket. His arms were pinned to his sides and his legs were clamped together. From the corner of his eye he saw Raefer freeze also, held fast by the binding hex.

"Please," Ravinath said. "You'd only crowd the exit and make it impossible for me to get out. The sun will set in a moment and it won't be long before my little orb explodes. All of you step away from the entrance please ... at once ..."

Byron's legs began to walk sideways. The whole company faced Ravinath, sidestepping their way across the chamber between him and the smoking phoenix. Over Ravinath's massive shoulder Byron could see the sunset. It was a third of the way down. The flat horizon was rippling with heat and in the red glow was a small black dot.

Ravinath stood with both hands up. The glow, bright in his fist, began to smoke. The dot in the sunset got bigger. It shifted in the air and soon Byron could make out the flapping of wings. There was a faint cry of alarm. Byron looked at Ravinath. In his concentration on the double hex, the centaur had not heard. Ravinath glanced at the smoking orb and clenched his other fist. The grip on Byron's body grew tight and painful. It was hard to breathe. The black dot filled the window behind Ravinath.

"Look out!" Quill cried as she slammed into Ravinath's back at top speed.

Grunting and growling, the centaur toppled forward in a flurry of feathers. The glowing orb flew from his grasp and landed on the sandy stone floor. It rolled across the chamber with a hollow grinding sound.

Byron followed the orb with his eyes. The grip on his body was released as Quill and Ravinath both tumbled onto him. As he fell beneath them, Byron saw the orb drop into the stairwell.

"Run!" he cried, grabbing Ravinath's hair in both hands. "And don't crowd the stair!"

Nosh scooped Lukos from the floor and labored into the stairwell with the wolf across his shoulders. Dindra followed with Shilo behind her. As Byron wrestled with the flapping wings and flailing arms, he heard Dindra cry out. A loud crash and a wild clopping of hooves echoed on the stair.

"Help her up!" Rufus cried as he followed Raefer down. "Where's the orb?"

Byron and Quill kicked and clawed and snapped at Ravinath's head. The centaur growled and flailed as he struggled to get his hooves beneath him. Byron slipped free of the pile and stepped back.

Quill cried out, flapping and slashing with her wings and talons as Ravinath grabbed her leg. Byron's face went dark and he snarled. He leaped on Ravinath and bit down hard on the centaur's ear.

Ravinath hollered and let go of Quill. A loud explosion shook the floor. All three of them stopped. A billowing of purple smoke and stone dust shot up out of the stair.

Flames took the enormous nest. The bird was a dark shape in the smoke and fire. Its great wings were spread wide and it stood still with its head turned aside. Byron looked at the sun. Only a small portion of it remained. The sky was aflame with rippling red and orange.

"Byron, what's happening?" Quill cried as she clambered to all fours.

"The phoenix is molting!" Byron shouted. He kicked Ravinath in the eye. "And the exit is sealed!"

Ravinath recoiled with a shout and covered his face with one hand. Byron leaped to his hooves.

"The phoenix ..." Quill said, looking with wonder at the bird. Then she blinked and her eyes went wide. "Molting?"

"The window!" Byron shouted. He kicked Ravinath right in the throat. Ravinath gagged and coughed and swung his open hand at Byron.

"Byron, I can't!" Quill moaned as Byron grabbed her by the head and tried to drag her across the chamber.

"There's no other way!" Byron shouted. He let go of Quill and ran to the window. Ravinath dragged himself to his hooves. Quill looked back at the centaur as he strode toward her. His face was red. He held his throat and his eye bulged from the socket, dripping with bloody tears. He charged toward Quill with his free hand outstretched.

Quill bolted for the window. "Ooooh!" she said as she approached. "Aaaaaaah!" she cried with all her voice and she leaped forward into the air. The sun was only an edge of shimmering gold, like a curved sword on the horizon. Ravinath stretched out both arms, reaching for Quill as she spread her wings and crossed the threshold of the window. Byron flung himself out behind her, brushing Ravinath's fingertips with his hoof as he spanned the sickening drop and landed full on Quill's back between her wings.

Quill was shrieking. Ravinath was wailing. The rock was shaking and rumbling. Above it all, Byron heard a sound. It was bells and flutes and jingling crystal, a shimmering, beautiful sound, wet and mournful and new. Byron tried to look back but couldn't. The sound smote his heart and filled his throat.

Then Quill began to fall.

She cried out and flapped with wild, frenzied strokes. Still she kept falling. As the desert sand passed beneath them, it drew nearer. A great wind came up and drove them into the ground. They landed hard and Byron flew through the air. He rolled onto his back, spitting sand from his mouth. Then he turned and saw the fire of the phoenix blazing brilliant against the dark of the distant, starry horizon.

Byron stood and watched. His shadow leaped out and

danced behind him. He could feel the warmth from the flames as they shot out from the windows of the chamber in long, thick streams, casting orange light on the desert all around. It lasted for several moments at full strength, then faded until nothing remained but the dark shape of the rock spire blocking out the stars beyond it. High above, the Midwinter star burned on a field of stars so thick and near that the sky seemed almost white. Byron turned to Quill. The griffling was standing, watching the rocks, unblinking.

The world was silent.

"Did you hear it?" Quill whispered. "Did you hear the song of the phoenix?"

"I heard it," Byron whispered back.

"Wait'll I tell mama," Quill said. "There's no lovelier sound in the world."

"I hope the others got out in time," Byron said. "C'mon. Let's go see."

Chapter 21

Hoofbeats in the Darkness

tars appeared where the sun had set. Darkness deepened. Byron and Quill approached the rock spire, making their way around to the passage. They peered into the shadowy rocks.

"Dindra?" Byron called. "Raef?"

"Byron?" said a voice. "Byron is that you?"

"Yeah," Byron said. "Quill's here too ..."

Nosh appeared from the shadows and threw his arms around him. "We thought you were dead!" Nosh cried. "You little scrub bucket, we thought you were all burned up!"

Byron winced and gasped for air inside Nosh's powerful hug. Quill backed away from the dwarf as he set Byron down and turned his tear-filled eyes on her.

"I'm fine, Nosh," she said with a nervous laugh. "Good to see you, too."

The rest of the group came bounding out of the rocks. "Byron!" they called. "Quill! How did you get out?"

They all had tears on their faces and in their eyes. Lukos bounded around, wagging his tail, sniffing Quill and Byron as they told of all that had happened.

"So, Ravinath got stuck in his own trap," Rufus said. "Sure a good thing you came along, Quill."

"Even better you stayed behind," Raefer said. "You'd've been stuck up there with the rest of us and nobody to help."

"The baby phoenix!" Quill said. "Let's go see!"

◈   ◈   ◈

"The phoenix fire must've cleared the entrance," Rufus said as they reached the opening. "This was completely sealed."

"It must've restored the stair, too," Raefer agreed. "It's like Ravinath's explosion never happened."

"Mmm," Dindra said, taking a deep breath. "Smell that."

A gorgeous fragrance filled the stair and a clear light penetrated the darkness. The companions gathered in the chamber. All the portals looking out were filled with starry night. The walls and ceiling and floor sparkled with tiny points of a thousand colors. Strange, beautiful runes and hundreds of birds, large and small, were carved all over the room.

A solid slab of gold and silver stood in place of the stone block where the nest had been. It was covered with inlaid shapes of wonderful creatures and symbols. The nest was gone and on top of the golden slab was the fledgling phoenix, moving about with awkward, unsteady jerks, stretching its white, downy wings.

"Morning," Byron said. "Mr. Thúmose ... this is where morning is born!"

"He's so bright," Shilo said, gazing at the phoenix. "He sheds light."

"Does he speak?" Dindra said.

Shilo looked at the bird, concentrating. "Oh ..." she said. She pressed her hand to her heart. Her voice trembled and tears brimmed in her eyes. "Beauty ... his mind is all beauty ..."

The bird chirped and it was musical. The whole company caught their breath at the sound.

"Byron," Nosh said. "Is that your staff?"

On the floor beside the golden block was a silver rod. It had a broad flat butt and narrowed to a terrible point. In between it twisted gently in a spiral with gleaming edges. Byron reached down to take it in his hand.

"Ouch!" he said.

"Is it hot?" Raefer said.

Byron shook his head. "It's sharp."

"Here," Raefer said, taking off his cape. "We'll make a sheath."

When they were done, Byron slung the rod, wrapped tight in Raefer's cape, over his shoulder with Nosh's suspenders. He looked at the bird.

"I think he wants us to go," he said.

"We can't just leave 'im here, can we?" Nosh said.

"I'd say he'll be all right," Shilo said. "He's the phoenix, after all."

"Yeah," Rufus said, looking around at the chamber. "This has been happening forever. I think the little fella knows what to do."

"All right, then," Dindra said.

The company withdrew in silence. The phoenix light guided them down the stair and into the desert night. Above, the stars were close and clear and the companions stood looking up for a long time.

Byron frowned. "The star is gone."

Everyone searched the sky.

"You're right, Byron," Nosh said, turning full around.

"It won't be back," Dindra said. "Will it?"

"No," Rufus said. "We don't need it anymore."

"Who knows?" said Raefer. "It came back once before."

"Now what'll we do?" Quill said.

"Go home," Rufus said with a shrug.

"But we never found him," Raefer said. "We never found Silverlance."

Lukos growled and looked up.

Everyone turned.

A black shape moved toward them in the sky, blocking out the stars. It flew on huge wings and a wind came before it. Lukos growled and barked and sidled up to Byron.

"He wants you to get on, Byron!" Shilo cried as the wind picked up and billowed the sand.

"What?" Byron said.

Lukos barked and whined, crouching low.

"Byron, it's your creature!" Shilo cried. "Run!"

A blast of wind lifted Byron's hair. The black shape was above them. It was the size of a man and had two huge outstretched wings, beating to keep it aloft. Byron froze. The wound on his head began to throb. Lukos was growling and barking at the creature. Byron's legs were trembling. He turned and ran with all his speed onto the desert sand.

The creature followed.

Byron could hear it. He could feel it. The sand billowed around him beneath the great beating of the terrible wings. Byron's mind raced. He remembered the little stump of a creature that had taken his horn. He remembered the strength of the brute that had attacked him in the woods of Bilérica. Now it was above him, enormous, winged. Byron fought back a great wave of tears and ran on.

His companions called to him. He couldn't make out the words. The wings beat low above him, pounding the sand with powerful wind and a great hand seized his shoulder. Byron felt his hooves leave the ground.

There was a savage growl and Lukos was with him. The Wolfen King leaped high and attacked the creature's arm with a terrible bite. It released Byron and he fell to the ground, crashing in a heap, tangled with Lukos in a mix of struggling limbs.

The creature wheeled and flew off.

Byron could see it, flapping away on its great wings. It flew in a long, curving line, coursed around and headed toward them again. Lukos jammed his nose into Byron's armpit. He crouched down. Byron righted the strange rod on his back and climbed onto the wolf. Lukos turned and dashed away with all his great speed in flight from the strange menace above, making for the gateway pool back to Trilithon.

But the creature was fast upon them.

Lukos bolted left and right, darting quick and random. The creature was clever, keeping high enough to respond to the moves of the wolf, yet low enough to pounce when the time was right.

A hundred yards from the pool, Lukos began to tire. He made two sharp turns, slower than before. His tongue dangled from the side of his mouth and he whined a little. Byron clung tight to the wolf's fur. The great wings above them beat one terrible time, hoisting the brute into the air.

Byron looked up as the creature turned into a dive, beat its wings one time again and hurtled toward them, plummeting head first with two long arms outstretched. Byron saw a pale light in its eyes. When it was just a few feet above them, Lukos exploded into a run.

Byron nearly fell off the back of the wolf. The creature slammed into the ground and lay motionless for a moment on the sand. Byron looked back to see it stand and spread its wings.

He was still looking back when he heard the splash and felt the water.

He let go of Lukos and began to swim down. He pulled with all his strength until, as before, the other surface began to draw him. He gasped for air as he splashed up within the pool inside the circle of dolmens.

Lukos was already out, shaking himself dry. Byron pulled himself over the wall and fell to the ground. He sat there for a moment, coughing and holding his head. Lukos growled and trotted over to one of the dolmens, sniffing the air, peering into the darkness beyond the ring.

Dindra splashed up with a cry. Raefer followed, then Shilo, Quill and Rufus. A moment later Nosh pulled himself over the wall, waving off Raefer's offered hand.

Lukos growled again, deep and fierce. There were hoofbeats in the darkness out beyond the dolmens. The Wolfen King turned and barked at the companions. Everyone stood looking with wide eyes in the direction of the hoofbeats.

"Where's the creature?" Byron said.

"It flew off," Dindra said, still sputtering with wet.

Then there was a deep, rumbling sound like thunder under the ground. The stone wall around the pool trembled and the water rippled and lapped. A huge roiling bubble burst on the surface of the pool. The companions all turned. For a moment there was silence.

And then it came.

It exploded upward in a torrential blast. The creature shot out with staggering power, pulling the water with it in a vast, unhindered splash. It lifted itself high with a mighty thrust of its wings and hung there, above the ring of dolmens, as all the water fell back again in sheets, soaking the ground for dozens of feet in every direction. Byron gasped and choked for air, covering his face with his hands until the water stopped falling. When it was over he looked up and saw the creature in the dim, mysterious twilight.

It had huge, leathery wings with barbs along the edges. Its head was covered with a nest of long, straight horns like a crown. Its back and the backs of its wings were covered with dense black feathers. Its arms and legs were long and lean and sinewy, its hands and feet were large and clawed and its face, deep in shadow, had a great, curved nose, thin lips drawn back in a snarl, and eyes of white fire. It hung there in the air above Byron and when it fell upon him even Lukos could not stop it.

But there were hoofbeats in the darkness.

Byron heard a deep whistling sound above the screams of his friends. He looked up to see the net, spinning wide on a masterful throw. It covered the diving creature even as it reached for Byron with an enormous claw. The heavy weights pulled it away and wrapped the net around it in a single motion. The creature lay there, its wings bound to its back, struggling and shrieking in the tight wrap of Baruwan's net. Then Baruwan himself came charging up and took hold of the net before the creature could escape.

"These children are mine, demon!" Baruwan shouted. Every inch of him was covered with the awful markings.

Baruwan crouched and wrestled with the creature, trying to gain control of the net. It fought hard, kicking and raging against the chain links and howling in a sharp, shrill voice. Baruwan lifted a hoof and set it down on the creature's chest, but a single, taloned hand reached through a gap in the net and slashed the centaur's fetlock. Baruwan growled and pulled back.

Lukos ran forward, weaving among the scattered companions, and positioned himself between Byron and Baruwan. His gray hackles bristled and he growled from deep inside his chest as he watched the struggle between the centaur and the strange winged creature from beneath the mountain. The companions stayed where they were, looking on in horror.

"Everyone out!" Rufus cried.

Raefer helped Byron to his hooves. They joined hands and followed the others into the dolmen. Lukos followed and loped along beside Byron through the dark passage. Byron saw each of his friends appear in silhouette against the blue and step out into the day. As he reached the opening he could still hear the creature howling and the rattling of the chain net. He had to put up his hand to shield his eyes against the sunny sky that greeted him.

Oatencake was there, walking toward the great, motionless figure of Manakar who lay as they had left him.

"Peter!" Shilo cried.

Oatencake turned. "Go on, now, if you're going," he said. "There's no telling how much time you have!"

"What?" Raefer said.

Oatencake let his shoulders drop. "You've decided not to go, then?"

"No," Rufus said. "We went."

Oatencake blinked. "But I just left you. Or, you only just left me."

"Whataya mean?" Nosh said. "We've been gone for hours."

Oatencake shook his head. "Not three whole minutes ago. And I spent one of them in a bit of silence for you, hoping."

Everyone turned to look at the Trilithon.

"Ah, well," Oatencake said. "There's no point questioning. Magic is magic."

"Someone's coming!" Rufus said.

Everyone turned. A group of walkers appeared over the slope of the hill.

Chapter 22

Byron Silverthorn

ixima!" Shilo cried as she set off running.

"Mr. Thúmose!" Byron called.

"Rifkin!" Rufus and Raefer called together. "Resh!"

Thúmose and Hixima walked side by side up the hill of Trilithon. With them was a small band of dryads all armed with bows, quivers of arrows and long, slender swords.

"We found it, Mr. Thúmose!" Byron called as he ran. "We found where morning is born!"

"Yes, Byron," the horse called back. "Well done!"

Shilo ran into the arms of the Warra priestess as the rest of the companions came up.

"Hello, child," Hixima said with a laugh. "Hello, all of you."

Rufus and Raefer threw themselves on their brother. All three toppled to the ground and rolled in a heap over the clover. Rifkin twisted and moved and in a moment he was on top of them, pinning them each to the ground with a single hand to the chest. They squirmed and laughed. Raefer threw clover in Rifkin's face.

"At last we've found you!" Rifkin said. "And if joy were not my master I'd kick you down the hillside! Stand up and let me look at you!"

"We're all right," Raefer said. "Honest."

"You look well enough, little cousins," Resh said. He shook his head and took them both in his arms. "Whose mittens did we find in the woods? Never tracked so clever a quarry!"

The other dryads stood smiling, leaning on their bows.

"How'd you escape the centaurs in the cave?" Rufus said with a shrug as Resh released them.

"Barely!" Resh said. "Never seen so tough a bunch."

"Which one of you had enough sleep juice to bring down the ettin?" Rifkin said.

"We used all we had between us," Rufus said.

"We were so worried, Hixima!" Quill said. "We saw the hilltop where you were standing!"

"Yes, the standing stone is gone," Hixima said, shaking her head. "A symbol of ancient goodness. But I'm perfectly all right. Miroaster came to my aid, once again."

"Miroaster," said Oatencake. "And where is he now?"

"Gone again," said Thúmose. "Gone away on an errand only he can perform."

"We reached Hixima's house a few days after you left," Rifkin said. "We all set out together to find you, knowing the old centaur was afoot. Manakar couldn't wait for us. He set off running and I'd say he never slowed till he reached you."

"Oh, Manakar!" Shilo said. "Please, Hixima, can you help him?"

"He saved us in the maze," Nosh said. "We'd never have beat that minotaur on our own."

Oatencake nodded and looked at the bear.

"We saw the brute for ourselves," Thúmose said. "Manakar is mighty indeed."

"Please, sir," Byron said. "We can't leave him there, can we?"

"There is time for everything," Thúmose said. "But first things must come first. Byron Thorn, you have something that belongs to me."

"I . . . what, Mr. Thúmose?" Byron said.

"The staff you've been carrying," Thúmose said. "I thank you for keeping it safe."

"The staff?" Raefer said.

Byron looked at Raefer and shrugged. He unshouldered the scabbard they had made and set it on the ground. The two of them unwrapped it. The cape was shredded to ribbons on the inside. Raefer held it up and laughed.

"Much longer and it would have cut you, Byron," Nosh said.

Byron laughed and nodded. The rod lay glittering in the sun.

"You were wise to keep it wrapped," Hixima said, crouching to look at the sharp, twisting rod. She reached into her robe and took out a pair of mittens made of tiny links of woven chain. They glittered almost as brightly as the spiraling blade. She put them on her hands and lifted the object from its wrapping.

"Are you ready, Sire?"

"I am," Thúmose said.

"Sire?" Rufus said, exchanging a glance with Nosh and Byron. Thúmose lowered his head.

"Shilo," Hixima said. "Come and help. Clear the mane away from his forehead."

Shilo stepped forward and did as Hixima commanded. She smoothed back the faded gray mane from Thúmose's forehead, exposing a great, red wound. It was inflamed and glistened with moisture. A long, deep shudder went through the horse as he stood there, waiting.

Hixima stepped forward and set the broad end of the spiraling point into the wound. She shifted it a little and turned it. Then there was a great flash of light. Thúmose neighed and staggered backward, lifting his head. As he did he was transformed before their eyes.

His coat became gleaming white, like snow in the sunshine. His long mane and the great tufts of hair at his fetlocks burned with golden light that left them brilliant yellow. Thúmose neighed a great, trumpeting neigh that shook the ground and he reared high, goring the air with his massive, black hooves. The strange spiraling blade stood out from his forehead like a sword. It caught the sun and flashed with silver light.

Everyone covered their eyes. When they opened them again, Thúmose was bounding around the hilltop, leaping and bucking and bobbing his head. He charged around them in a circle, kicking his hind legs. They stared at him in fear and wonder as his pounding hooves tore the grass and trampled through the clover.

"The unicorn!" Shilo cried.

"Mr. Thúmose!" Byron called.

"Silverlance!" Raefer shouted and clutched Byron's arm.

"Yes!" Hixima said, clasping her hands on her breast. "Yes!"

"Can it be?" Rifkin said.

Lukos leaped into the air. He ran out and bounded around on the clover with the unicorn. Thúmose turned to play with the wolf and the two frolicked about until the wolf cowered down and rolled over on his back, tucking his tail between his legs. Thúmose leaned down to sniff Lukos and pull at the wolf's neck with his lips.

Byron and Raefer looked at each other with enormous smiles. "Silverlance!" they shouted together.

The unicorn came charging up and stopped hard before

them. "Yes!" he said. Thúmose took a step toward them and lowered his muzzle to Byron's head. "Or so I am remembered. Your wound has not fully healed, Byron Thorn."

"No, sir," Byron said.

"He keeps picking it," Dindra said.

"I do not," Byron insisted.

"Yes, you do," Shilo said.

"Sometimes it itches," Byron said with a shrug.

Thúmose nickered. "I know. But it's time you had relief."

Thúmose stepped back and lowered the point of his horn into the wound on Byron's head. There was a crackling sound and a flash of light filled Byron's nose and eyes and mouth. Byron laughed out loud and when Thúmose stepped away there was a small silver horn on Byron's head where the old one had been.

"Byron!" Quill said.

"Ah, Byron!" said Peter Oatencake.

Byron reached up and touched the new horn. It was smooth and the point was very sharp. He rubbed it with his thumb.

"And now to wake the sleeping bear," Thúmose said.

"Oh, Thúmose," Shilo said. "He isn't sleeping, if you could have seen his wounds . . ."

"No, child," Thúmose said. "The sleep of the clover is deep."

Thúmose lowered his head and thrust his horn into the soil. The clover lit up with dancing sparks and all the flowers shimmered. The whole area came alight for a moment and then the flash was gone.

"Come, Manakar," Thúmose said. "Enough of sleep!"

Everyone watched in silence. Manakar didn't move. Then he began to stir. He rolled onto his back and turned the side of his face into the water. He rubbed his snout into the clover beneath the water, blowing bubbles with his nose and lapping with his tongue. Manakar made deep grunting sounds that rumbled inside him. Then he sloshed to his feet, shook his vast body free of pool water, licked his nose and bumbled out onto the grass.

"Manakar!" everyone called at once and they ran to him.

Manakar fell to the grass and rolled onto his side. Shilo and Byron both threw themselves on his huge belly and tumbled over him. Lukos barked and whined and pranced around the bear as Manakar pawed at him and sneezed. Then Manakar rolled over and came to his feet, shaking the sundered clover from his fur.

He bounded up to Thúmose and crouched low. Thúmose nibbled at Manakar's neck and withers and the bear gave a deep, thunderous whimper. Then he came to all fours again, strode in among the companions and sat down.

Lukos growled and pranced a few paces toward the Trilithon. Everyone turned. Baruwan was standing in the entrance, peering out. All the dryads bent their bows. Baruwan didn't notice. He stared at the unicorn with wide eyes. When Thúmose looked, Baruwan ducked back inside the tunnel.

Thúmose nickered and it rumbled within him. "Baruwan," he said. "Come out."

Baruwan emerged into the daylight. His chest heaved and he stared at Thúmose. "Silverlance ..." he said.

"Yes," said the unicorn. "Come here. And bring your friend with you."

Baruwan stepped out, dragging the captured creature behind him. The net was cinched and bound so the creature could not move. It was curled up with its wings gathered in, staring at the company, jerking and twitching its head.

"Where did you get those silly marks?" Thúmose said.

Baruwan looked at Byron's horn and at Manakar who was lapping water from the pool. Then Baruwan looked at the silver horn of the unicorn and let his shoulders drop. He bowed his head and opened his hands. "I . . . I have served your enemy, great one."

"Then serve him no longer," Thúmose replied. "Wipe the marks from your body."

Baruwan shook his head. "They are cut beneath the skin."

"How did they get there?" Thúmose said.

"Ravinath," Baruwan said. "It is a hex mask, for protection and strength. First it was only on my face, but it spread."

"Does it hurt you?" Thúmose said.

"Sometimes, yes," Baruwan said. "Very much. But . . . they don't come out." Baruwan's voice cracked. Dindra's eyes filled with tears. She touched her throat with her hand.

"Nonsense," Thúmose said. "Come down to the sea and bring your catch with you. Follow me, everyone, to the water's edge!"

They made their way down the hillside and through the dunes. Baruwan labored along, dragging the weight of the struggling creature.

Thúmose waited for them up to his knees in the surf. The company assembled on the beach, then turned and waited for Baruwan. When the centaur reached them, he dropped the rope that bound the net and stood with his head down.

"Baruwan," Thúmose said. "Get in and wash."

Baruwan waded out into the water. Thúmose stepped up to him and scratched him on the neck with his horn. The cut was deep and bled at once. The centaur winced a bit but made no other sign that the wound had caused him pain.

"Now, Baruwan," the unicorn said. "Wash!"

Baruwan scooped the water and let it fall down his chest. He swished his tail a little.

"Not like that!" Thúmose said. "You have to stomp and splash!"

Baruwan looked back at the beach. The others were all staring at him. He looked down at the water and touched it with the flat of his hand.

"Here!" Thúmose said. "Let me show you!"

Then the unicorn charged into the water. He bucked and reared and shook his mane. Baruwan stepped back. The unicorn thrust his muzzle into the water and splashed Baruwan in the face. He did it again and again until Baruwan fought back. Soon they were bounding around, in the deeper water, bouncing and bucking in the sparkling waves. The silver horn flashed. Baruwan didn't notice when Thúmose ascended the beach and stood there, gleaming in the sun.

Dindra gaped at the painted centaur. "Is that Baruwan?"

"It is," Thúmose said. "More splash!" he called.

Baruwan threw more water into the air. The whole company looked on in wonder at the sight of the great and terrible Baruwan at play.

"Look at his neck!" Byron said.

A long dark trickle of black liquid flowed from the scratch on Baruwan's neck. The markings that covered his face and body receded up and out through the cut, until he was clean and even the hex mask bled away.

Baruwan looked at his hands and down at his body. He turned and gazed at Thúmose with wide eyes and he began to laugh. He threw back his head and howled. The mighty Baruwan stomped and bucked around in the water, laughing and shouting. He strode up onto the beach and shook his body from head to tail. He looked around at the others, nodding his head. "I have much to prove," he said. "I'm not afraid of that. To you, most of all, Byron and Dindra."

"Not to me," Byron said. "You saved me from the monster."

Dindra stood with her hand at her throat, gazing up at Baruwan.

"Monster?" Thúmose said. "What monster?"

"The one in the net," Byron said.

Thúmose swished his tail. "Monster, you say? Baruwan, turn it loose."

"No!" Byron cried. "It wants to kill me!"

"Baruwan," Thúmose said. "Will you do as I ask?"

"At once, great one," Baruwan said with a glance at Byron.

Inside the net, the creature had fallen still. It stared out through the chains with its huge eyes fixed on Thúmose. Baruwan trotted across the sand and took up the rope. He untied the heavy knot and stood back. The creature sprang to its feet and at once Thúmose was before it.

Two great, feather-backed wings opened and the creature stepped forward to fly. Thúmose leaped in front of the creature and it stopped. It turned to the left and took a step but the unicorn bounded across its path. It turned again. Again Thúmose was there. The creature gave a loud, shrill cry and Thúmose bobbed his head and neighed. The creature took a step backward and Thúmose advanced on it. At last the creature stood still.

"Now may I give you what you sought from the satyr?" Thúmose said.

Its wild eyes flickered. Thúmose stepped forward and thrust his horn into the thick hide between the creature's chest and shoulder.

It shrieked at the unicorn and clutched the shaft of the horn so tight that blood flowed out from between its fingers. Thúmose stepped back and reared high, neighing, then hammered his hooves to the ground. The creature staggered aside, pressing the wound with both hands. Then it opened its wings again.

It stepped forward and leaped into the air, pulling itself high. It exploded in a dazzling flash and then, in the sky above them where the horrid brute had been, was a beautiful creature of light.

It had yellow hair all spiked like flames and a gleaming silver breastplate. It wore a white tunic and its silver sandals and shin-guards were lashed to its legs and feet with golden cord. Its wings were white and vast, its forearms were braced with plates of silver and in its hand it bore a terrible spear. It had huge black eyes that glinted in the sun and it was silent. It flapped its wings so that it remained where it was in the air above the group and it looked down on them.

"No, Byron," Thúmose said, "no monster. Darakûn, Fire-warden, keeper of the Balefire. It was not you he wanted but that which you carried, the Lance of Silver, for he knew it could save him."

"But he was trying to hurt me," Byron said, looking up at the creature.

"Indeed," Thúmose said, "for he was bewitched and would have killed you in his madness. But he is restored now and only evil need fear him. Isn't that right, Darakûn?"

Darakûn clutched his spear before him and flew high into the air. He spun around and did a loop. When he returned his face was angry and wild. He swooped low over the company and then off to the west, flying up and away until he vanished from sight.

"Where did he go?" Byron said.

Thúmose lifted a hoof and let it drop. "Home, to Everándon, as should we all, but not without rest and food. Baruwan, you have much to prove, you say? I'll tell you how to begin. Cast that net of yours and catch us our supper. We will camp on the beach tonight and tell stories beneath the stars. In the morning, we will set off together for home."

Chapter 23

Hiding Wood

Thúmose guided them over the Dragon Range by an ancient path to the south. They saw nothing of the temple or the Valley of the Nine Spires. Instead, the company traveled without care, safe in their number. On the fourth day Oatencake turned aside from the group.

"Time for Oatencake to leave you," he said. "Time for Oatencake to go."

"Won't you come with us to Bilérica?" Hixima said. "You can rest there as long as you like."

"I've work unfinished at present, Madame Hixima," Oatencake said. "People waiting for me and me overdue."

"Come to us in the summertime," Thúmose said. "There will be healing work to do."

"The summertime, then," Oatencake said.

"Goodbye, Mr. Oatencake," the companions said together. "Thank you."

"Farewell," he said to each of them. "I can't imagine us not meeting again."

Then he nodded to the group, shouldered the slash hook and set off into the woods. His whistling died away and at last it was the sound of Thúmose's hooves that gathered the group back into the march.

Bilérica was deep in snow. Thúmose led the company to the broken top of Standing Stone Hill. He plunged his horn into the ground and there was a tremor. The snow sparkled for a moment and Thúmose lifted his head.

"The seasons rule again in Bilérica," he said, turning to Hixima. "But spring will be especially green this year."

Hixima stood beside him. Her arms were hidden beneath her cape and her hair moved on the gentle wind. The two were silent and stood with their heads bowed. The companions waited. Then Hixima smiled.

"Come along," she said. "The house will be cold. Nosh will make a fire and we shall prepare a special feast. Winter is welcome in Bilérica."

Manakar and Lucia greeted each other, wailing and rolling about on the snow. The other animals leaped about staying out of the way. Lucia stopped her play to sniff the places where Manakar had been wounded. Then she joined the other creatures in greeting Thúmose, who stood among them, meeting them nose to nose.

Days of rest came and went. The companions spent their time remembering their journey, sleeping and resting in the great room by the fire. Hixima spent long hours alone in her rooms with the door closed. Thúmose sent Lukos, Baruwan and the dryads off into the wild on secret errands and himself wandered Bilérica and beyond. Manakar, Lucia and the rest of the animal troop set off for home one morning without saying goodbye.

"I guess they miss the woods, too," Byron said.

He went often to Standing Stone Hill. One morning, just after sunrise, he was looking west at the Crestfall Mountains. Thúmose came and stood beside him.

"Here is where we met," the unicorn said.

Byron smiled.

"You want to leave Bilérica."

"I miss Gradda," Byron said. "I wonder how things are at home."

"I can tell you that all is well . . . for now."

Byron sighed.

"You have accomplished much, Byron," Thúmose said.

Byron touched his little silver horn. "Thank you for this," he said.

"Your prize," Thúmose said. "I had to take from you the one you found for yourself. For that I can never express my gratitude."

"Well, that's all right," Byron said with a shrug.

Thúmose nickered and nibbled Byron's hair. "You're a wonder, Byron Thorn. I believe I have chosen well."

"Chosen?" Byron said.

"What I have given you is a bud of the Silver Lance."

Byron rubbed the little silver horn with his thumb. "I like it," he said.

"I'm glad," Thúmose said. "Ah, the griffins have come."

Byron looked north. A group of dark shapes approached in the sky, moving fast.

"Onto me, Byron," Thúmose said. "We must get back to the house to greet them."

Byron blinked. "You mean . . . ride?"

"Yes, Byron," the unicorn said with a laugh. "That is what I mean."

Thúmose crouched down to the ground and nickered as Byron climbed onto his back. "Take hold of the mane!" Thúmose said.

Byron took a fistful of the long, yellow hair and pulled himself up. "Ya, haa!" he cried and laughed out loud as Thúmose stood up. The unicorn cut the air with his horn and a trail of sparks followed the point.

"Hold on tight, Byron," Thúmose called and he set off in snow-muffled thunder across the hilltop.

Thúmose moved as fast as sight itself. The snowy wood sped past Byron like a dream. It seemed he hadn't taken three breaths before they reached the feasting lawn. Thúmose came to a hard stop but turned himself in such a way that Byron hardly felt it.

A band of griffins stood there on the snowy lawn, preening and stretching their wings.

"Cryolar!" Byron said.

"Yes," Thúmose said. Cryolar and his companions all stood and folded their wings as the unicorn approached. "Thank you for coming, Cryolar."

"Of course, Sire," Cryolar said. "Hello, findrel. It's good to see you alive. It seems I was right to trust you!"

"Well, I don't know," Byron said. "Thank you for helping us."

"I hope to help you again," Cryolar said. "Is everyone ready?"

"Ready for what?" Byron said.

"Ready for home," Thúmose said. "Cryolar and his flight-mates will return you. The time has come."

"Wow, Byron!" Raefer said. He walked out of the house staring at Byron. "Did you get to ride 'im?"

Byron nodded. "He's so fast!"

"Wow . . ." Raefer said low. He eyed the unicorn from horn to tail.

The rest of the group was close behind Raefer. Hixima came last, wrapped in a blanket. Her hair was in her face and she shielded her eyes from the sun.

"Cryolar?" she said.

"Yes, madam," Cryolar said. "I've come to return our friends to their homes, those who have come far."

Nosh let his shoulders drop. He glanced around at everyone with a fretful look. "You're all leaving?" he said.

"Thúmose says the time has come," Cryolar said.

"But I can't go home," Nosh said. "I mean . . . I really can't."

"I'm sorry, Nosh," Byron said. "But I sure do miss my gradda."

"I know," Nosh said. He looked at the ground.

"How about coming with me?" Byron said. "Raefer's gonna come stay for a while. We're gonna build a fort in the parlor."

"Nosh will remain in Bilérica," Thúmose said. "I want him close."

"Oh, for rat's sake," Nosh said.

Byron laughed. "You come visit me sometime, okay Nosh? When Mr. Thúmose says?"

The dwarf nodded. "You bet I will, Byron."

"Good friends are never fully parted," said Hixima. "But there is one friend who will miss you dearly, Byron. He's waiting for you on the terrace."

"Lukos!" Byron said and he set off running.

He found the wolf on the upper porch, looking east. As Byron stepped up beside him, Lukos turned and sniffed and poked him with his nose. Byron put his arm around the wolf and stood for a moment.

"I'd ask you to come stay with me," Byron said, "but, well, you know how things are."

Lukos whined and slapped the snow with his tail.

"Goodbye, sir," Byron said. "Thank you. Thank you for it all."

The wolf whined and sniffed Byron's ear.

"The griffins are here now," Byron said. "I have to go."

Lukos looked east. Byron backed away and went off with great sadness in his chest, to join the others. He found Shilo and Hixima speaking together in hushed tones.

"Midsummer, then?" Hixima said.

"Yes, ma'am," Shilo said.

"Good," said Hixima. "I'll send Cryolar to collect you. Your parents will understand in time."

Shilo looked at the others who were all staring at her. "I'm coming back in the summer to begin my training."

"Training for what?" Byron said.

"To be a priestess of Warra?" Dindra said.

Shilo nodded.

"Shilo!" Dindra said. "Of course you have to come back! And now we all have even more reason to visit!"

"I look forward to that day," Hixima said. She embraced each of the companions and went to stand beside the unicorn.

"Goodbye, Mr. Thúmose," Byron said.

"Yes, Byron," Thúmose said. "Be well."

"I will," Byron said. "So long, Rufus. Maybe you can come get Raefer when the time comes."

"I'll see you then, Byron," Rufus said. "So long."

Rufus said goodbye to Dindra and Shilo and went to stand with the dryads.

Thúmose nickered. "So begins the journey's end."

A huge shadow covered Byron. Cryolar descended and took him in his talons. When Byron looked back Hixima, Thúmose and Nosh were already very small. Hixima was waving. Soon they were all too small to see. At last even the house was lost behind the trees and all was white with melting winter. Byron let the tears flow over in his eyes.

"So!" Cryolar said. "I have the privilege of carrying you a third time!"

"Yes," Byron said. His voice was faint.

"You have said farewell to good friends, Byron," Cryolar called. "A mighty deed. Be sad a while, but don't forget to be merry, for a warm hello awaits you!"

"Yes," Byron said. "Gradda."

"And you will find your people in celebration," Cryolar said. "Today is the first day of spring. The sunrise rites of Vernalfest are underway!"

"Vernalfest," Byron said. "They'll be on the Fiddling Green! Take me to the Fiddling Green, Cryolar!"

"To the Fiddling Green!" Cryolar said and he gave a mighty roaring shriek. Byron heard the other griffins respond and Cryolar banked away and up, gathering speed as he soared above the mountains.

❖ ❖ ❖

It was late in the morning when Cryolar gave Byron a gentle shake. "Time to wake up, Silverthorn!" he called.

Byron hung there in the solid grip of the griffin's talons as if it were his own little chair by the fire. He saw Woody Deep beneath him. Hiding Wood drew near and as Cryolar descended, Byron saw the white dots of the Hidden Hills peeking out of the trees. Soon he heard the sounds of music and laughter rising from the forest.

The Fiddling Green appeared below them and the woodren were gathered in great number. An enormous fire burned in the middle of the snow-clad lawn and the dancing was everywhere. As the wing-driven wind beat the fire and the griffins alighted, the music and dancing stopped and the woodren stood where they were, staring in a collective, stupefied gape.

Cryolar and his companions preened and combed their feathers with their beaks. Byron and Raefer stretched long and hard to work out the kinks and cramps of the journey. Dindra swished her tail. Shilo reached to get her cape on straight.

"Thank you, Cryolar," Byron said. "Thank you all, for everything."

Cryolar gazed beyond Byron at the gaping woodren. He had a smile in his eyes. "You're most welcome, findrel," he said. "You are all most welcome. I wish we could stay and join your festival, but Thúmose bid us return at once."

"You'll be back for Midsummer, Cryolar," Dindra said. "We'll be feasting then, too."

"Very good," Cryolar said. "Midsummer, then."

Murmuring and tripping over themselves, the woodren scrambled backward to clear a path as Cryolar and his flightmates trotted off across the green. The mighty wings fanned out and the majestic beasts lifted off.

Cryolar gave a roaring shriek that his flightmates answered. The companions watched them go, then turned to find all the woodren staring at them. Another commotion parted the crowd and a pair of huge bears came bumbling through the gap.

"Manakar!" Byron cried. "Lucia!"

Behind the bears, the whole troop of animals came waddling and bouncing along. As the companions greeted their friends, the woodren kept staring. A single voice rose above the whispers.

"All right, all right," it said. "Step aside there, step aside."

"Gradda?" Byron said.

Darius Thorn stepped forward, glaring up at a young centaur.

"Gradda!" Byron cried.

"Byron!" Darius said, opening his arms. "Byron Thorn, come here to me!"

Byron ran across to his gradda and nearly knocked the old satyr over.

"Mama!" Shilo cried as Milo, Filo and Fidelia Prinder emerged behind Darius Thorn. "Dadda!"

"Dindra?" called a deep, booming voice. Heavy hooves pounded in and a wide way was made for Palter Thundershod. "Dindra!"

"Father!" Dindra cried. At once she was in tears and she bolted forward into the enormous embrace as the great battle chief covered his daughter with his arms.

Gradda held Byron by the shoulders. "Byron, I can find no words ... let me look at you! How good ... how glad ... Byron, what's this?"

Darius smoothed the hair away from Byron's forehead. The sun caught the silver of Byron's horn. Darius gazed in wonder at his grandson.

"We found him, Gradda," Byron said. "We found Silver-lance."

"Silverlance ..." Darius whispered in wonder. "Byron ..."

"Father," Dindra said. "This is our friend, Raefer Nimble-twig."

Raefer stared up at the enormous centaur. "He's even bigger than Baruwan."

Palter reached down and touched the dried, leafy vine in Raefer's hair. "What wonder is this?"

"Raefer is a dryad," Byron said. "Can he stay a while, Gradda?"

"Can he ..." Darius said. "Well, of course he can, Byro, as

long as he likes. The two of you can make a fort in the parlor. Hello, Raefer. I'm Darius Thorn."

"Hello, Mr. Thorn," Raefer said. "Byron's told me about you, sir."

"Now, now," Darius said. "You call me Gradda. You'll be very welcome in our house, very welcome indeed."

"Well, Byron," said a voice. Byron turned as the Woodland King stepped out of the crowd. He wore a wreath of silver holly on his head and he was clad in rich green.

He fell to one knee and opened his arms. "Welcome home, Byron," he said.

Byron looked at Gradda. Gradda nodded and winked. Byron ran forward into the king's arms and disappeared for a moment in the fine, green cloth. Belden held Byron off and looked at him.

"Here's a tale to tell," he said, touching Byron' s horn. "Before you say anything, Byron, I ask your forgiveness."

"For what, Sire?" Byron said.

"Byron, I was a knight before ever I was king. I know the call of the quest. I should have helped you. Instead I called you a fool and ignored you. I'm sorry."

"You had wolves and Ravinath and . . . well, all right Sire, I forgive you."

"Thank you, Byron," the king said. He smiled and set his hand on Byron's shoulder. The he stood and went to Dindra. "I ask your forgiveness also, Dindra."

"Of course, Sire," Dindra said, drawing close to her father. "Of course I forgive you."

"Excellent," said the king.

Then there was a great popping sound. Two figures sprang from the trees dressed in black hoods. They were carrying torches, cavorting and contorting and howling. One of them threw a small packet onto the bonfire and it flashed up red and green. The crowd turned and looked at the masked newcomers who were standing in the open by themselves. The pair stopped their dance mid-stride and stood with their hips out and their arms still hoisted. They looked at the staring crowd and then at each other.

"Byron?" one of them said.

"Hey'ya Jolik," Byron laughed. "What, uh ... whatcha doin'?"

"Oh ..." Jolik said, "nothing much ... Welcome home."

"That you, Sheg?" Byron said, but they both turned and ran off into the woods.

"It's good you're back, Byron," the king said. "They're the best we've got when you're away."

❖   ❖   ❖

That night they ate supper with Arden, the king's poet. He made them remember all they could of the journey. The poet listened to every detail and when they left him, he was already at his harp, humming the melody for the long song through which he would convey the tale to the woodren.

A great feast was held the next day. Arden stood in the center of the Lore Pavilion. Byron, Shilo, Raefer and Dindra all sat in places of honor, listening to the tale of what had happened in Woody Deep in the days that followed their leaving. Arden sang of the heroics of Palter Thundershod, of the Woodland Knights and of King Belden himself, who strove with Ravinath in single combat and finally drove the centaur from the woods.

Arden finished his last ballad and paused. He begged the ear of the crowd for another song. Listen, he said, to a tale that took place beyond the mountains, beyond them and beneath, above them and between, a tale of bravery and friendship, of trust and fear and valor. He bid the audience hush and attend as he wove for them the tale of the Wanderers, the ones who followed the risen star to its end and carried back the crown of a king.

Byron saw again the unveiling of the star and the wolf with one blue eye. He recalled the crossing of Gladwater Ravine and the harrowing at the broken tower. He remembered anew the aid of the dryads, the stair of the griffins and the halls of their magnificent queen. He winced and curled his lip at the tale of the ettin and sat silent at the memory of his time beneath Rathrágodrak. He heard of Bilérica and Hixima and Thúmose. He remembered Quill and Nosh and Rufus, Lukos and Peter Oatencake. Arden told of the minotaur and the strange gate called Trilithon, the molting of the phoenix and the sundering of Ravinath.

Then the poet paused and called for special heed. He strummed his harp and sang on of the crowning of the unicorn, the bestowal of the silver thorn, the awakening of Manakar, the turning of the centaur Baruwan and the unmasking of Darakûn, the Firewarden. Arden moved about the hall as he sang, plucking his harp. As he finished he stood before the chairs of the companions and bowed. The hall erupted in a storm of clapping and stomping and cheering.

That night, Byron and Raefer lay awake in the fort they'd built in Gradda's parlor. They stared up at the bedspread roof recalling all they had seen and heard.

"Byron," Raefer said.

"Yeah."

"We really did it, didn't we?"

Byron touched his horn with his fingertips. "I'd say so, Raef."

"I knew we could."

"Me too."

The two were silent after that. Byron rolled onto his side and faced the embers of the fire. He stared into the orange heat for a long time until at last, in the deep hours of night, he fell asleep. As he slipped away into dreams Byron heard the embers fall and the song of the phoenix echoed in his mind.